Sever

ALLY WAGNER

Cover art by Matthew Weatherston

Edited by Christina Ramos

Layout by Eddy Espina

ISBN: 978-1-7367220-1-5 (paperback)

Library of Congress Control Number: 2023904237

Skin Series:

Skin

Shift

Sever

<u>*One*</u>

The repetitive *tap tap tap* against porcelain did nothing to ease the awkwardness that had settled in the air. Despite the clinking, clanking, and chattering going on around them, the tapping was all Cain could hear. His inner wolf's hackles rose with irritation.

"Would it kill you to at least try?" Cain huffed, pushing away his half-eaten blueberry muffin.

Kee stopped drumming her nails against the coffee mug and lifted a mocking brow at him. "It may."

He let out a heavy sigh. "You agreed to this, Kee."

She scoffed and raised the cup to her lips. "I agreed to ease the discomfort of this unwanted bond." She peered at him over the rim before taking a sip of the lukewarm coffee.

He dropped his hands to the table and winced when they slammed down harder than he anticipated. A month since he won the battle for alpha, and he was *still* trying to adjust to the new power. "You don't have to remind me of my fuck up every meeting, Kee."

She set down the coffee, pushed her dark blonde hair over her shoulder, and leaned back in the chair. Crossing her arms over her chest, she lifted a brow at him in challenge. "I'm sorry, am I not allowed to be angry at what happened to me?"

"I didn't say that," he grumbled. "But you're always mad at me."

She tilted her head at him with mock innocence. "Oh gee, Cain, why do you think that is? What could have possibly brought that on?"

His nostrils flared at the reminder of what his pack did to her. Tension rippled through his shoulders. "I'm sorry, Kee. I know I can never apologize enough for what they did to you or make it up to you, but it wasn't my doing. What matters is that you're alive. They're not."

She should have let it go. Should have accepted his apology and moved on, but a part of her would always be a bitter bitch. "But they're not all dead, are they? You spared the one who gave them the order to kill me."

The Alpha of the Los Angeles wolf pack balled his hands into tight fists at the reminder. "I was giving an unborn pup its best chance at survival." He said it slowly and in a low tone, as if trying to calm himself down. He didn't regret his choice to let the former alpha live. Warren's mate was pregnant, and to give the pup the best chance at making it to birth, Natalie would need both her mate and the pack alpha to coerce her to not shift during a full moon. "Please Kee, it's been a month. I don't want to fight about this again."

Had it only been a month since Cain marked her as his mate? That would make it almost three months since her attack. Almost three months with Lucas. A smile curved up her lips at the thought of her man. Boyfriend was too light to call what they had, lover not intimate enough. He was simply hers, and she was his.

Cain watched her face soften and felt a pang of jealousy hit him. It wasn't as visceral as when he first learned of her and Lucas, but his beast still snarled in response. "I take it you and the vampire are doing well."

She blinked out of her thoughts and looked at her ex-boyfriend. She had to applaud his attempt at keeping the contempt from his voice. It was almost believable. "We are. We have a date tonight after this. This is our time to spend together before the pack and I leave for Nana's for Christmas."

He nodded once and they fell into an uncomfortable silence once again. "Speaking of Christmas, I take it we're past the point of giving each other presents?"

Kee reached across the table and slid her hand into his rough, warm one. Almost instantly the searing heat that had been spreading along the back of her neck cooled. The mating bond seemed to purr in contentment at the contact, appeasing both their pain. "This is the only present I need."

He wrapped his fingers around hers and looked down at their hands. His wolf puffed up at the contact, a happy sigh blowing through his nostrils. "How's the pack?"

She perked up at the mention of her small pack, a smile curving her lips once again. "They're good. Samson is still settling into his new life, but I think he'll be okay. Conrad and Lucy are dating, and Mia transferred to the preternatural school here three weeks ago. The school is on winter break right now, so she hasn't had a whole lot of time to adjust to it, but I think she likes it. There are more wereanimals her age there."

He nodded. "LA has one of the biggest schools. Once we get more kids, they'll be split into smaller schools to accommodate their ages better. We already have the college for the older kids. A lot of students are preternaturals who didn't have the chance to further their education before the Monster Movement."

"Zach wants to go there after he graduates," Kee commented. "But as for the kids now, I think the fact they're still grouped in classes by age is good. The diverse classrooms are good for them. They get to learn about themselves and their fellow monsters while still getting an education," she said. "Plus, having the one class a day where they all divide up into their specific species is great. The kids can see how the older ones manage their shifting or magic."

Cain gave a rueful smile. "Yeah, I guess it's one of the only good things Liam and Warren did. It was their idea to start this school, and they took it to the other reigning rulers of LA County."

Grey eyes hardened to steel at the mention of the men. Warren had been the reason she almost died, but Liam was her father. If there was anyone she hated more than Warren in this world, it was her sperm donor. She had loved him, once upon a time, but she learned very early on that his love was conditional.

When she was seven, her family found out she wasn't a werewolf. Liam refused to allow her to ruin their lives. He tried to coax a wolf form out of her, trained her every minute he could, but to no avail. Even beating it out of her didn't work. When she couldn't shift into a wolf, instead changing into a cat, his alpha ordered Liam to kill Kee and her mom.

She barely escaped, but the mental scars of seeing her mom slaughtered in front of her remained.

"Yeah, one thing," she murmured.

He looked at her blank expression and felt his shoulders sag. "I know I said it, but I'm sorry I wasn't strong enough to fight the command," he began. "I tried, Kee. Really, I did. My wolf just wanted it so bad that it gave in to the alpha's order even when I fought against it."

She closed her eyes as she remembered Liam giving the order for Cain to mark her as his mate. Liam was the reigning werewolf alpha for LA County. So, despite Cain being the alpha of Los Angeles City pack, Liam outranked him.

"I know," she sighed after a tense minute. "I give you shit for it, but I know you tried. I've accepted it, but sometimes, especially when the mark starts burning, I get pissed about the situation all over again."

"I get angry about it too." He dropped his gaze to their hands. "I get mad about everything that happened to us, but we can't undo it. We'll never go back to what we were, and I've also accepted that, even if my wolf doesn't."

Kee was relieved to hear the honesty in his words. "Exactly," she started. "We're both different people now, Cain. A part of me will always care for you, but I love Lucas. He completes me in a way you didn't." She expected his beast to make an appearance and lash out at her, but he remained calm. *Good.*

He gave a single nod and ran his thumb over her knuckles. "I agree. I mean, you seem a lot happier now." He gave her a teasing grin. "You know, when you're not being a raging bitch."

"You're not wrong." She laughed and pulled her hand away. She was still smiling at him as she stood. "I have to get going, but I'll see you again in two weeks, alright?" She hesitated briefly before reaching out to stroke his cheek. "I want you to be happy, Cain. Truly."

He gave her a small smile at the contact. "I am, Kee. Katie and I," he pursed his lips together as he thought about the fellow wolf. "We're finding comfort in each other, I guess."

Her smile widened. "Good. You two make a good-looking couple," she replied. She gave him a feeble wave before walking away and out the door of the small cafe.

"All done?"

She looked at her weredragon in surprise, taking in his reclined form against the brick of the building. "I told you that you didn't have to wait for me."

Samson shrugged as he pushed away from the wall to join her. "You're my alpha, I wanted to make sure everything went okay."

Kee waited until he joined her side before walking back towards Byte. "You don't have to protect me from Cain."

He pushed his sunglasses further up his nose as they faced the sunset. "It's better not to take chances."

She followed the movement of his hand and blinked when she noticed a discoloration of skin popping out from beneath his sunglasses. She grabbed his arm, pulling him to a stop. When he turned to look down at her, she reached for his glasses but frowned when he ducked out of reach.

"Sam, what are you hiding?"

He turned from her. "Nothing."

"Then let me see your face," she said, worry trickling through her at the fact that he was concealing something from her.

"Kee—"

"Show me your face," she demanded, putting the alpha base to her voice.

His nostrils flared at the command, but he did as told. He turned his head back to her and let her remove his sunglasses. When she simply stared at him with a concerned expression, he dipped his chin. "It's nothing."

"Nothing?" Kee echoed as she took in the dark purple bruise around his eye socket, the hues of yellow and green telling her it was recent. "Who hurt you?" A cold glint shimmered in her gaze. "Do I need to kill them?"

Samson shook his head, knowing very well that she was serious. "No, it's not like that. It was a little fight. Trust me, he's in much worse shape." When she looked at him uncertainly, he gave her small smile. "Thank you for worrying about me though."

She lightly ran her thumb over his cheekbone. "I'll always worry about you, Samson. You're part of my pack. When I see you or the others hurt, I want blood."

"I know. That's what we respect about you." He straightened and slid his hand through the long part of his hair. He had shaved down the left side of his head again, the black strands brushing his ear on the right side. When she handed him the sunglasses, he slid them back on to cover his black irises.

"Would you tell me if you were in trouble?" she asked as they resumed their trek to the vampire bar.

"I'm not used to relying on people," Samson admitted. He shoved his hands into the front pockets of his jeans, still marveling at the usage of them. The last time he wore jeans was when he was twelve. When he was part of the Dragon Guard in Muir Woods, he wasn't allowed to wear clothes that didn't easily tear apart when shifting.

She gave a soft sigh. "I know, but that's what I'm here for, Sam. The pack, too. We're family."

His fingers flexed at the word. *Family.* He thought he had one back in Muir, but they turned on him when it was convenient for them. Creal made him a scapegoat, and it nearly cost him his life. The fae that reside in the southern portion of Muir had also been like a family to him, but they never came for him, did they?

He glanced at Kee, remembering so clearly how she had come to save him despite being mean to her. She hadn't even known him at the time but still chose to save him because he asked. She had been wounded while rescuing him, both by him and his captor, but she accepted him into her pack regardless.

Was that what it meant to be part of a family?

"It's still a foreign concept to me," Samson eventually said. "But I'm trying."

She smiled at him and linked her arm through his. "You don't have to try. You're doing just fine."

After months of being held captive and abused almost daily, he had trouble accepting touches from other people. He was getting better with his pack touching him but still had moments of weakness. This time, his arm flexed under hers for a second before relaxing.

"Thank you, Kee."

She blinked up at him. "For what?"

He kept his gaze foreword. "For accepting me."

"I should be saying that to you," she said. She was raised to believe that being a shapeshifter was a forbidden taboo that would get her killed. She spent the majority of her twenty-five years hiding what she was in fear of people finding out the truth, so it was strange to have people not only accept her but follow her as their alpha. It's why her pack meant so much to her.

She cleared her throat of the emotion that threatened to bubble up. "You ready to go to Nan's tomorrow?"

He glanced at her. "Your Nana is intimidating."

She laughed. "I know, but she likes you."

Samson's face turned disbelieving. "How can you even tell?"

"I just can, but even if I couldn't, she told me to make sure you came."

"Oh." He stiffened suddenly as he remembered the holiday. "Fuck, she's big on manners, and I didn't get her anything for Yule."

She found it endearing that he kept referring to Christmas as its Pagan counterpart. Her parents raised her as Catholic, but she adjusted to Nana's Wiccan ways when she started living with her. Of course, Nana didn't call it Wicca. She simply believed in the Irish goddess Brigid and relied on the elements to guide her.

"She doesn't expect a gift, Samson. She's more likely to get offended if you do get her something." Kee untangled their arms as they reached Byte's back entrance. She turned to him as they approached the door. "No one expects anything, okay? Let's enjoy the holiday together as a pack."

He nodded, but uncertainty still nagged at him.

"Evening, Miguel!" Kee greeted as the werebear opened the door for them.

He gave her a wide smile, his dark tan skin crinkling around his eyes. "Buenos noches, Senora Quinn! Always good to see you!"

"Visiting the family for Christmas?" she asked.

He nodded happily. "My family is coming to the pack den. We're going to have a big feast."

"That sounds nice. I probably won't see you until after the holiday, but I hope you have a good Christmas, Miguel."

"Feliz Navidad to you and your loved ones!" he chimed merrily as they walked past him.

Kee gave him a wave as they walked into the building. She nodded at the cooks on staff and turned to Samson. "I'm going to get ready in Lucas' room. See you later?"

He nodded. "I'm going to go for a short flight to blow off some steam. I'll see you in the morning."

She watched him go with a frown, knowing something was off with her dragon. She stopped asking him what was wrong weeks ago when he started to get increasingly more frustrated. She couldn't force him to talk to her and constantly nagging him would only push him away.

Shoving the thought aside, she opened the door to the basement and went down the flight of stairs, following the hallway until she reached the last door. Not bothering to knock, she opened the door and was pleased to see her vampire standing near the bed without a shirt on.

"I came just in time." Kee purred as she stalked towards Lucas, her mouth almost watering at the sight of him.

He smirked as she sauntered up to him. He cupped her face in his hands and tilted her head back so he could brush his lips over hers. "Oh, my sweet, you have not come yet."

Heat pooled between her legs at the insinuation. "Yet? So, I'm going to?"

Again, he teased a kiss along her lips. "If you behave."

She huffed against his lips. "You know I never do."

His smirk widened. "But that is the fun of it, is it not?"

"Fun for who?" she grumbled and parted her lips, trying to kiss him.

Lucas dodged her kiss but flicked his tongue over her bottom lip. He felt her arousal spike through their bond, his own responding in turn. "Fun for me will eventually mean fun for you," he answered then laughed when she whined.

"Lucas, if you don't fucking kiss me I'm going to stab you in the balls when you're asleep," she warned.

"Ah, there's my murderous spitfire," he cooed and finally slanted his lips over hers.

She eagerly kissed him back, hands running down his pale, taught chest. They slipped down to the waistband of his slacks before one palmed his erection.

He grunted when she squeezed and broke the kiss, emerald eyes gleaming with desire. "As much as I hate to put a stop to this game, we do not have time to play."

She gave him a sly smirk. "Oh, all of a sudden we don't have time?"

Lucas slid his hand down to cup her jaw. "Not enough for me to fuck you thoroughly," he warned, his accent getting thicker as his cock did. "After our date, however, I plan on ravishing you."

"Promise?" she asked, flexing her fingers around him.

"Yes, you minx." He stepped back before he gave in to the temptation that was his Keira. "Go get ready. I assure you that you do not want to be late."

Kee stuck her tongue out at him as she went to the bathroom to start her hair and makeup. "Are you going to tell me where we're going yet?"

He slid on a white dress shirt and began to fasten the buttons. "I told you that it is a surprise."

"Yeah, but I thought you'd tell me by now. Can you at least give me a hint?"

"I already gave you one."

She scoffed as she began to curl her hair into loose waves. "Telling me to dress formally isn't exactly a hint!"

The vampire let out a soft laugh as he grabbed his suit jacket from the edge of the bed. "I also said that it's something we have talked about before."

"Lucas, we've talked about a ton of stuff. That doesn't narrow it down at all!"

"Well, then you will just have to wait and see, won't you?" he teased. He then checked the inside pocket of the suit, making sure the small box was still there. "Trust me, my sweet, you will not be disappointed."

Two

Lucas watched Keira carefully as she came to an abrupt halt outside the Pantages theatre. Her hair fell in loose waves to her waist as she looked up at the building. He could see her black-lined eyes run along the lit-up sign then to the starburst pattern in the ceiling of the box office. People brushed past them, eager to scan their tickets and get inside, but she didn't seem to notice them.

She had been chatty as they walked from the parking lot, but her words ceased as soon as she saw the theatre. Trying not to take her silence negatively, he put his hand on the small of her back and gently ushered her towards the door. The ushers and staff didn't try to stop him. They knew he was the Lord of Los Angeles County and no doubt knew that he paid handsomely to get their accommodations for the evening.

Once they walked into the vast lobby of the theatre, Keira came to another sudden halt to stare at the interior of the building. Someone behind them cursed at the hold up, but a withering glare from Lucas had them adverting their eyes with a muttered apology. He kept his glare on them until they quickly skirted around Keira and hurried away.

Satisfied that he had scared them off, he returned his attention to his shapeshifter. "Would you like a drink before we take our seats?"

Kee stared at the wide interior of the theatre lobby. The carpet was a dark red that nearly matched the burgundy dress she wore. She took in the golden cream arches that ran along the inside of the building and slightly darker tiled squares around them. Her eyes then went to the multiple chandeliers that hung from more starburst patterns in the ceiling. Directly in front of her were narrow arches with curtain doors that led to the theatre's seats. The west end of the lobby had a long, wide staircase that she assumed led to the upper seating areas. Next to the staircase was a sign for restrooms and the bar.

Lucas shifted his weight on his feet, uncertainty making him anxious. Of course, it was only the person he gave his heart to that could make him doubt himself. He tried to push it down as he watched her. When her head tilted back again to take in the details of the ceiling, his eyes fell on her slender neck. She wore a sleeveless dress that hugged her torso, loosened at her hips then fell in pleats to her shins. The neckline went up to the hollow of her throat, hiding her scars and mating mark from the world.

He lifted his hand and brushed the back of his fingers along her cheek. "If you are displeased, we can leave." Was he completely wrong in taking her there?

She whirled towards him, stunned. "What? No! Why would you say that?"

He blinked at her vehemence but relaxed when he saw the faint traces of tears in her eyes. "Then, you like it?"

"I *love* it, Lucas. I've never been here before. I didn't expect the building to be so…beautiful." Kee grabbed his hands in hers, looking up at him with wide, glassy eyes. "A-are we seeing what I think we're seeing?"

Lucas hummed in his throat as he looked at all the posted signs and banners. "According to the posters, we are seeing *Phantom of the Opera*. Ah, my mistake. I meant for us to see *Cats*," he teased.

She squeezed his hands, ignoring his joke. "You remembered my favorite movie? That was forever ago."

His eyes softened as he looked down at her. He brought her hands to his lips and pressed a soft kiss along her knuckles. "There is very little I forget when it comes to you, Keira."

She was absolutely awestruck by him in that moment. "I can't believe you did this for me," she whispered. "I love you."

Releasing her hands, he gently wiped the corner of her eyes without smudging her makeup. "I love you, too." He placed a chaste kiss on her lips before holding his arm out to her. "Shall we?"

She tucked her hand in the crook of his elbow and smiled happily up at him. "We shall."

—

Lucas found himself watching Keira instead of the performance. There was something truly captivating about observing her. Her range of emotions and reactions was far more enjoyable to him than the actual show.

He loved the way her face lit up in awe and how she lip-synced the words to the songs. He found a soft smile on his lips when she got teary eyed at certain scenes. Watching her experience something she genuinely enjoyed was far more beautiful than anything else.

At intermission, he stood from his seat and offered his hand to her. When she slid her hand in his, he gently helped her to her feet, mindful of her heels.

"Are you enjoying the show?" he asked as he led her towards the VIP lounge.

She rested her hand in the crook of his elbow and beamed up at him. "It's fucking amazing, Lucas. It's wonderful! The sets and costumes are amazing. And the songs, gods! It's so much better than the movie!"

He chuckled. "Did I not tell you that it was?"

"Yeah, yeah, I remember," she laughed as they entered the lounge. She flopped down on a red chaise and watched him as he walked to bar, shamelessly admiring his ass. She lifted a brow when he came back with two glasses of champagne. "You're drinking a glass, too? What's the occasion?" she teased, taking the glass he offered as he sat down next to her.

"We are celebrating." He took a small sip of the liquid, knowing his body wouldn't be able to stomach too much of it.

Kee smiled at him. "And what are we celebrating? Christmas?"

"No, we are celebrating us, of course," he replied and set his glass down on the brown coffee table in front of them. He turned to her and took one of her small hands in his once again. "I have a present for you."

She glanced down at the gold tie clip she got him. She ran her finger over the etched image of a key and frowned. "I thought we agreed on one small thing, Lucas." She gestured at the room around them. "This is already too much. Far too much."

"The show is a date for both of us," he clarified as he reached into the inner pocket of his suit. His fingers wrapped around the box, and he hesitated a moment before pulling it out.

Her eyes immediately widened. Slowly, she set down her champagne flute, lips parting in surprise. And maybe a little bit of shock. Alright, a *lot* of shock. "Lucas—" she cut herself off when he held a hand up to stop her.

"Wait. Will you listen to what I have to say before responding?" When she gave a slow nod, he continued, "I know that our time as a couple has been relatively short. When it comes to marriage, I am aware that many people wait." He brushed his thumb over her knuckles in slow, gentle strokes. "But I *have* waited, Keira. I have waited nearly four hundred years for you."

His eyes dropped to the black velvet box in his hand. "Before you stumbled into my life, I was existing. Night after night I lived to rule and protect my coven. Do not get me wrong, I was not miserable. I enjoyed my life. Giovanni and Dante are my closest friends and I love them, but they are not you."

Kee sucked in a breath when he lifted his emerald gaze to hers. Still, she held her tongue as he continued.

"As you know, I gave up on finding love. I thought I had found it with Janrie, and then with Bridgette. But gods, I was wrong. What I feel for you is not even on the same spectrum, Keira. You fell into my life and filled it with light and meaning. I am no longer existing. I am living." The corner of his mouth tilted up into a smirk. "And that is saying quite a bit coming from a vampire, I would say."

She couldn't help it; she laughed. It was a watery sound, but how could it not be when her eyes filled with tears again. What was with this man making her cry tonight?

"With that said, I am not asking for your hand in marriage." He popped open the lid of the box, revealing three square-cut diamonds set in a band of white gold. He lifted the ring from its cushion and held it out for her. "I am asking you to tell me when *you* are ready for such a leap. This is me promising that I will wait for you. That I will have no other."

Kee watched as he reached for her right hand. She held it out for him, and he slid the band onto her ring finger. She stared down at the princess-cut diamonds admiringly before looking at him again. "Why are you so perfect?"

He let out a startled laugh, not at all expecting that response. "I am far from perfect, my sweet."

"You're perfect for me." She leaned forward and pressed her

mouth hard against his. He met her passion with his own, his tongue demanding entrance. She groaned when his tongue slipped past her lips and rubbed against hers.

He slowly broke the kiss, sucking on her bottom lip for a second as he did. He glanced at his watch and gave her a seductive smirk. "We have twenty more minutes of intermission."

She glanced at the others who had meandered into lounge then back at him with a heated glint in her eyes. "Bathroom?"

A devilish grin had the tips of his fangs showing. "Bathroom."

She took his hand after he stood and led him towards the women's restroom. She casually glanced around to make sure no one was watching before pulling him inside. She locked the door behind them, and he shoved one of the chairs from the vanity against it for good measure. When he turned to her, she met him halfway for a feverish kiss.

Lucas easily scooped her up and set her on the vanity countertop without breaking the kiss. He gathered the hem of her dress in his hands, tugging it up to her waist. He broke apart from her swollen, tempting lips and pressed the fabric against her chest.

"Hold this."

Kee obeyed the command, holding the dress out of the way as his hand slipped into her lace panties. The pad of his middle finger swiped down her slit, coating it in the wetness gathered there for him, before sliding back up to swirl around her clit. She let out a low moan, her hips bucking against his hand in reflex.

"Shh," he shushed her as he undid the zipper of his slacks and pushed them down his thighs. He tugged the crotch of her panties to the side, aligned himself with her opening, and filled her with one swift, hard thrust. Seeing her about to cry out her pleasure, he covered her mouth. At her questioning gaze, he gave her a smirk of pure masculine pride. "As much as I love to hear you screaming my name, I'd rather not get us kicked out. Not yet at least."

She breathed in sharply through her nose when he slid out and quickly thrust back in. A moan vibrated in her throat as he set a fast pace. She wrapped her legs around his waist and cupped the back of his neck with her free hand, trying to hold on while he pounded relentlessly into her.

Lucas kept his hand over her mouth, muffling her cries of ecstasy. His other hand gripped her hip, holding her in place as he drove into her hot, wet heat. He would forever love the way her slick pussy gripped him perfectly. He truly believed she had been made for him. It made all the years of simply enduring life worth it.

Someone knocked on the door when it failed to open, and Kee's eyes snapped open. Lucas was already staring down at her, a brow lifted in question. In challenge. She pressed the tips of her heels against the small of his back, urging him on. There was no way she was going let him stop.

Pleased, Lucas moved faster. The wet slapping sound their bodies made echoing off the tiles of the empty bathroom. He moved his hand between them and found her swollen clit. He pressed his thumb against it before rubbing in firm circles. She bucked against his hand again, her legs quivering.

He slid his other hand down from her mouth to grab her neck. It wasn't hard enough to choke her or completely cut off her air supply, but enough to let her know that he was in control.

Lucas felt her walls flutter and constrict around his cock, and he bit back a groan as his balls tingled with his incoming release. He rolled her bundle of nerves between his thumb and forefinger, rotating the movement until her back began to arch. When her release came, he used the hold on her neck to pull her closer. He covered her mouth with his, swallowing her cry as he grunted his own release. He released her lips after planting a long, gentle kiss on them.

Kee rested her forehead against his after their mouths broke apart. "Mmm," she hummed contently.

"Indeed." He pressed a kiss to her forehead and eased himself out of her. He lifted her off the counter and gently set her on her heels before heading to the sinks. Wetting a paper towel, he handed it to her before tending to his mess.

Someone pounded on the door again, and Kee couldn't help but giggle. "How mad do you think they are?" she asked as they both cleaned up and made themselves presentable again.

"Oh, quite mad, I am sure, but they matter little." He checked his watch and lifted his brows at her. "Less than ten minutes to spare. And, I believe we still have champagne waiting for us."

She grinned and took his hand when he offered it to her, lacing their fingers together. "A man after my heart."

His eyes darkened as he looked down at her. "Oh, my sweet, I am not only after your heart, I am after your entire being."

Kee blushed, the ring on her right hand suddenly feeling a lot heavier. She squeezed his hand, but before she could reply, he kicked the chair out from under the doorknob. After unlocking it, he pulled the door open and casually led her past two seething women and a male security guard. She stifled a laugh when Lucas shot the man a fang-filled sneer, daring him to comment or reprimand them. When the man balked and stepped aside, she let Lucas guide them back to their seats.

By the time they got back to their loveseat, she had lost the words she was going to say. Or maybe it was that she didn't have the courage to say them. Not yet. But there was one thing she could say.

"I love you, Lucas," she said seriously as she stared at his perfect profile. His high cheekbones and sharp jawline along with his elegant nose and long lashes made him beautiful to her.

Swallowing a tentative sip of champagne, he looked at her with a soft tenderness reserved only for her. "I love you too, Keira."

Three

The door to Lucas and Kee's room cracked open, a head of blonde hair poking in. Emilia waited until her golden eyes adjusted to the dark before zeroing in on the bed. Her alpha was still asleep, Lucas unmoving next to her.

With a devilish grin, she charged towards the bed. "Auntie Kee, Uncle Luke!" she called as she flung her small body at the covers.

Kee grunted as her youngest pack mate landed on her. "Mia..."

The seven-year-old gave a wide smile. "It's Christmas Eve!" she exclaimed with excitement. When Kee's eyes slid shut, she let out a tiny growl and shook Kee's shoulders. "Christmas! Eve!" She punctuated each word with a small shake.

"No, no. It can't possibly be Christmas Eve already." Kee felt Lucas shift next to her and suppressed a smile, knowing Mia had woken him from his undead sleep.

"It is! Wake up! We need to—" Her words ended with a shriek of laughter as Kee suddenly attacked her with tickles. Mia rolled onto her back, falling between Kee and Lucas on the bed. "Uncle Luke!" she squealed between a fit of giggles when she saw the vampire was watching them with a tired, bemused expression "Help me!"

Lucas was still adjusting to the nickname, but it made him smile each time she said it. Making sure he was adequately covered under the blankets, he gave her an exhausted smile. "I believe you are at your alpha's mercy, little queen."

Mia fell into another fit of giggles as Kee continued to tickle her. After another minute, the torture stopped and she flopped back against the covers, panting. Recovering her breath, she turned her head towards Lucas and beamed. "Uncle Luke! Are you coming with us today?" Her face fell as she remembered he was a vampire. "Um, I mean tonight?"

Lucas shook his head. "Unfortunately, I must host a Christmas party for my coven tonight."

She pouted at him. "But we're pack. We should be together on Christmas Eve."

Kee's heart warmed. She knew the other members in her pack also considered Lucas, Gio, and Dante to be pack. "His coven is also like his pack, Mia. We can celebrate with Lucas tomorrow on Christmas. We'll spend the night at Nana's tonight and come home tomorrow."

The little wolf sighed dramatically but nodded. "Okay," she mumbled. She perked up at the knock on the door and grinned at her dad when he poked his head in. "Look, Daddy, I got them up!"

Conrad shot Lucas an apologetic look. "Sorry she managed to wake you up, Lucas. I asked her to check to see if *Kee* was awake," he clarified, lifting a questioning brow at his daughter.

Mia smiled innocently. "I checked! She wasn't up so I *woke* her up!" she explained and turned to her alpha. "Auntie Kee, will you do my hair? I want mine wavy like yours."

Kee laughed. "Sure. Why don't you let me get dressed first?"

"Yes!" Mia exclaimed and crawled over Kee to get to the edge of the bed. Before she jumped off, she smacked a loud kiss on her alpha's cheek.

Lucas watched the young wolf disappear through the door with an ache in his chest. He looked at Kee as she sat up, unable to keep his eyes from roaming over her exposed breasts as the duvet fell to her waist. He pushed down the primal need for her and reached out to grasp her right hand instead.

Kee turned to him, but the smile died on her face when she saw how solemn he was. "What's wrong?" she asked as he rubbed the ring on her finger.

"It should have been blindingly obvious from the beginning," he began softly. "But watching you with Emilia reminds me that I cannot give you that."

She tilted her head at him. "Give me what?"

His heart clenched. "A child." Would he lose her over something he had no control over? His undead body was the equivalent to a mortal male being sterile. His sperm carried no possibility of life within them.

Kee laced her fingers with his and squeezed his hand reassuringly. "I don't want children," she told him.

He searched her eyes for deceit. "Are you certain? We could explore other options, Keira."

She shook her head. "After what I went through as a child, I refuse."

He stared at her for a moment, contemplating her words. "You would never harm your child. It is not in your nature."

"I know I wouldn't treat my kid the same as my father treated me, but I don't want them to experience the same hardships I face as a shapeshifter," she mumbled. "It wouldn't be fair to them."

His free hand tucked a strand of hair behind her ear. "It is a pity that the world is so narrowminded. I would love to see miniature versions of you running amuck."

She smiled a moment at the visual of little versions of them both before frowning. She hesitated briefly before asking, "D-do you want children?"

He hummed. "I gave up on the notion many, many years ago since it is not possible," he began. "But if it were possible, yes, I would have many children with you."

Kee's brow creased. "Even though I don't want them?"

"I cannot give them to you," he retorted. "So, it doesn't matter. As long as I have you, the rest is moot."

Her face relaxed into a smile. "If down the line I change my mind, we can look into adoption or donors, okay? For now, I'm happy simply being with you." His eyes drooped as he smiled, and she gently pushed him back towards the mattress. "Go back to sleep, babe. I'll see you after Christmas."

He tugged her down with him and pressed a kiss to her lips. "Until then."

She returned the kiss and repeated his words back to him as he was pulled back into his rest. "Until then."

—

Kee emerged from the basement an hour later, Mia at her side. The two had matching loose curls, sections of it pulled back at the crown. They walked through Byte's commercial kitchen and into the empty club. Conrad was sitting at the bar, Lucy sitting in his lap with their lips locked together.

Kee glanced down at Mia for her reaction. When Mia first met Lucy, the girl wasn't a fan of the werefox. When Kee asked Mia about it, the young wolf had said that she just got her dad back and didn't want to share him. She couldn't blame Mia for feeling that way, especially when her old alpha had forced Conrad and Mia apart for three months. The bastard, who happened to also be Kee's dad, had used Mia as leverage over Conrad's head, forcing him to do his bidding.

After that, Kee had Lucy and Mia venture out with her a couple times, calling them girl trips. She wanted to help close the distance Mia had forced between her and Lucy. Kee tried to take them shopping or to get their nails done, but Mia pointedly ignored every attempt Lucy made at conversation.

The three of them were readers, so Kee mentally smacked herself for not immediately thinking of the Last Bookstore first. The unique store had loosened up Mia enough that she actually responded to Lucy's questions about reading preferences. Kee had snuck away to the second story, letting the pair wander about together.

The second place that broke down more of the wall was the Museum of Death. The disapproving looks Kee received from the cashier had been worth it. Mia, as young as she was, was obsessed with true crime. She devoured the museum, chatting and rambling about random facts when Lucy asked about them. After that day, Mia had started to relax a little more around the werefox.

Baby steps, Kee mused as Mia made a face at the couple.

"Merry Christmas, love birds!" Kee called, causing them to pull away.

Lucy slid off Conrad's lap and went to Kee, hugging her friend and alpha. "Merry Christmas, Kee!" She beamed, pale green eyes gleaming happily. "How was the show?"

"Amazing!" Kee answered, hugging Conrad next. When she pulled back, she glanced around for her fourth pack mate. "Where's Samson?"

"He said he heard something in the alleyway," Lucy said with a shrug. "Conrad was going to go, but Samson said he'd handle it."

Kee furrowed her brow as she ushered her pack towards Byte's back entrance so they could head to Nana's. "When was that?"

Conrad looked at his watch as they stepped in the parking lot. "About ten minutes ago."

"Alright, why don't you guys get the Jeep ready? I'll go find Sam," Kee said, handing the keys to Conrad before heading towards the alleyway. She stepped into the narrow street and approached the dumpsters Samson was crouched next to.

Careful. Came Samson's voice in her head.

She slowed her gait and quieted her steps as she approached him. She expected to see a stray animal, but what she saw instead was a woman leaning against the dumpster, arms crossed over her chest. The girl was short, the clothes she wore much too large for her curvy frame. Her black hair was in a matted bun, loose strands streaked with faded blue falling around her face. Not even the smudges of dirt and healing cuts could take away from the natural beauty of her face.

"Like I said, you're not in trouble," Samson stated to the stiff woman. "I heard the noise and came to check."

The girl looked from Samson to Kee and back. "If I'm not in trouble then why is she here?!" she snapped, jerking her chin towards Kee. "I'm not breaking any laws!"

"Technically this is part of Byte, which is private property, which means you're trespassing," he clarified nonchalantly.

"It's fucking trash. Who's going to miss it?" she hissed. "Look, I already apologized for trying to pickpocket you at—"

He quickly cut her off. "Like I said then, it's fine. This isn't about that either, it's about picking out food from the dumpsters."

Her cheeks flamed red in embarrassment. Defensive, she snapped her head towards Kee, the pupils of her brown eyes turning to slits. "What are you staring at, bitch?"

Samson snarled before Kee could respond, the sound echoing off the bricks of the alleyway. "Do *not* disrespect my alpha," he sneered. "Neither one of us came here to attack you. I already told you that you're *not* in trouble."

The small woman balked, the red draining from her cheeks to

leave her skin paler than it already was. "Alpha," she repeated. "B-but you're a woman. You can't be an alpha."

Kee put her hand on Samson's shoulder to keep him from replying. "I get that a lot," she began. When the woman stared at her again, Kee could see the dark circles under her eyes. "Do you need help?"

The woman blinked and dropped her gaze, but her brow furrowed in defiance. "I don't need your pity," she spat out.

"I'm not offering you pity," Kee clarified calmly. "I'm offering help."

She scoffed but remained in her tense position. "Fuck your charity then."

Samson made a move to lunge at the stray, but Kee tightened her hold on his shoulder. She glanced at the girl and saw that she had pressed herself back more firmly against the filthy dumpster at Samson's move. With a sigh, she patted Sam's shoulder. "Come on, we have to get to Nana's."

The dragon stood but kept his eyes on the stray. "Take it from me, accept help when it's offered before it's too late."

Kee smiled at him when he turned towards her with an unreadable expression. "I'll never regret it," she reminded him. "You needed help, and I gave it." She shot a meaningful look at the girl before leading Samson out the alleyway.

Samson glanced over his shoulder, but the stray had already disappeared.

Four

Lucas straightened the lapels of his suit jacket as he finished greeting another guest at the door. He glanced at the watch on his wrist and held in a sigh. It was barely nine and already he wanted the night to be over.

"You look so happy to be here," Dante commented dryly, coming up to his lord's side. He was in traditional Yoruba clothing, paying homage to his roots in Nigeria. "That bored already?"

"I despise these events," Lucas muttered, looking over his friend's clothes. "Feeling homesick?"

"Sometimes," Dante replied with a shrug. He looked down at the fine material and ran his hand over it. "Although, this *agbada* is much nicer than I would have ever worn hundreds of years ago. It almost makes me feel fake for wearing it."

"You have earned your upgraded status," Lucas insisted. "You have come a long way since your village."

Dante gave him a small smile. "We both have." His dark brown eyes flicked over to Giovanni as the Italian kissed his date for the night. "All three of us, actually."

Lucas followed his gaze, his own lips curving into a smile as

Gio and the other man broke apart but stayed in each other's arms, swaying to the music. "Indeed, but I believe he's making his other part-time lover jealous."

Dante saw Mirabella pouting at the bar, arms crossed over her chest as she watched Gio and his lover. He laughed, the tips of his fangs peeking out from his full lips. "I'm glad I don't have to deal with any of that."

His emerald gaze returned to his head of security. "Do you ever have the urge to be with someone?"

He shook his head, the dim lighting shining on his bald head. "No, not since I was a boy. People expect sex in relationships, but it doesn't do anything for me. I'd rather stay away from it all together and avoid the stress of doing something I don't want to do."

"Do you not get lonely?"

Dante scoffed. "Of course, I do," he answered honestly. "But I have you and Gio, and then Kee and her pack. My family seems to keep growing, and it makes the nights easier."

Lucas gave a small smile. "That is close to something I told Keira."

"Is it?" he said with another grin. "She's good for you, you know."

"Oh? Who is good for my blood son?"

Lucas stiffened, his body going impossibly still as the light, accent-ed voice seeped into his ears like venom. No, she could *not* be here. Not now, not after all these years. He turned back to the door and felt revulsion plummet his stomach. He kept his face impassive despite the fear choking his heart. Not fear for himself, no. Fear for those he cared about. Especially Keira.

"My bleeder has been turned," Lucas replied with a forced air of calm. He was glad his maker could not see that his hands were clenched into fists behind his back. "Dante says she is good for me, but I think not."

Florence looked at Dante with ice in her light brown eyes. "Make no mistake, no one will ever be good enough for my blood son. No one but myself. You would do well to remember that."

"Yes, Lady Florence," Dante said, bending in a low, formal bow.

"It was a joke, of course," Lucas cut in, stepping in front of his friend as Florence continued to give him a calculating stare. "My bleeder was annoying on the best days before I was forced to turn her."

"Did you fuck her?" she asked casually, tossing a strand of dark red hair over a pale, exposed shoulder. She wore a dark green gown, the silk hem fanned out around her feet. Its sweetheart neckline left her shoulders and neck bare while pushing her breasts up high to create ample cleavage.

Lucas gave her the flirty smirk that she loved. "Once was all it took to remind me that she was not you."

She stared at him for a heartbeat before giving him a coy smile. She stepped closer to him and cupped his face in her hands, the metal rings on her fingers like ice. "You were always my favorite. Such a charmer, my little Apollo."

"I aim to please, Lady Florence," he cooed, gesturing behind his back for Dante to leave. His head of security didn't need to be told twice, and Lucas only hoped he would warn Giovanni of the situation.

She pulled Lucas down to her 5'2 height and kissed him hard on the mouth. She nipped at his bottom lip, splitting it open so she could lick away his blood. Breaking apart from him, she gazed curiously at him as she dissected the taste on her tongue.

Lucas lifted a brow at her as she licked her lips and rolled her tongue around her mouth. "Something troubling you?"

"Hm," she hummed. "Who have you fed from tonight?"

His shoulder lifted in a Gaelic shrug. "I had a small snack when I woke, but that human has left. I was saving my main meal for tonight with the other guests. Why do you ask?"

Florence stared at him a second longer before giving him a smile. "Nothing, I wanted to make sure you would be dining with me this evening."

"Nothing would please me more, but you understand that I do have other guests to entertain throughout the evening." He carefully phrased his next words. "Speaking of which, I did not know you were in my city. You would have been the first person on my invitation list had I known."

"Oh, my little Apollo, I longed to surprise you, of course. I have not seen you in ages and I wanted to see this little niche you have set up for yourself here." When she held her hand out expectantly, he took it and placed it in the crook of his elbow. Pleased, she tilted her chin up regally. "Show me around."

Knowing better than to refuse a demand from her, he began to walk her around the bar. Of course, all the tables and chairs had been cleared out to make room for one long dining table. He pointed at the curved staircase that led to the second level containing the VIP rooms and his office as well as the stairwell that led to floors higher up.

"And your coven's quarters?" she asked, looking at all the strung garland and Christmas lights around the bar. The decorations lined the counters, walls, and doors. Red and silver ornaments hung from the garland with tiny red bows mixed in with it.

"On the basement level, naturally," Lucas replied, briefly meeting Giovanni's anxious gaze from across the room. His blood son knew everything that Florence had done to him, had experienced her twisted cruelty for himself. Lucas wasn't surprised when Gio put physical distance between him and his lover.

Florence hummed in her throat and brought them to a stop near the tall Christmas tree. She fingered an ornament that had clearly been painted by a child. "Where is your wolf?"

His gut twisted, but he tried to keep his face and tone neutral. How did she know about Keira? "She is with her pack for the holiday."

She pursed her crimson lips in a pout. "Pity. I very much wished to meet her. You two have caused quite some trouble together, so I hear."

Lucas put on his false bravado. "Me? Cause trouble? I believe you have the wrong son, Lady Florence."

She gave him a knowing smirk. "Oh yes, *you*. Well, you and your wolf. You killed two other lords, my little Apollo. And what was that I heard about you two fighting with fae?"

He clasped his hands behind his back once again when she released him. "Alexander tried to take over the humans. When I thwarted his plans, he almost killed my wolf in retaliation." His voice dropped, and anger swelled inside him. "Then Jada assisted him with draining my bleeder and leaving Giovanni to die. Their deaths were deserved."

"I did not say they were not," she said as she plucked the child's ornament from its branch and studied the crude drawing of what she assumed was an attempt at a wolf. "Does she have a child?"

"No," he answered, watching her flip over the ornament that Emilia had made him at school. "A member of her pack does."

"*To Uncle Luke*," she read. "How charming."

Her tone made the hairs on his neck prickle. "Members of the pack work here," he explained calmly. "So, we have an odd dynamic with her pack."

"I see." She tucked the ornament into the pocket of his suit jacket and gave it a little pat. "You seem to have made a little family for yourself. You should treasure it."

He glanced down at the hand still on his chest, the red nail polish shining. He met her gaze and tilted his head. "You know who my family consists of."

Florence batted her lashes up at him. "I believe I do," she cooed. "Tell me, does your wolf desire you? Have you fucked her too?"

He did not like that he couldn't steer the conversation away from Keira. "My wolf?" he questioned, thinking of how to twist the answer so it was not a lie. "She has a mate, Lady Florence. I would rather not cause havoc between the LA coven and the LA wolf pack."

She held his stare for another moment before smiling. "No, I suppose not." She stepped away from him and set her hands on her hips. "Speaking of family, where is my grandson? And what about my new granddaughter? Giovanni!"

Lucas saw Giovanni plaster on a fake smile as he made his way towards them. "Lady Florence," he greeted, taking her pale hand in his and pressing a kiss to the top of it.

"Ah, there's my other favorite," she cooed, threading her arm through his. "Introduce me to your sister."

"Of course, my lady," he said with a charming smile that made Lucas proud. "Right this way."

"Thank you, my dear." She responded as Gio led her towards the kitchen. Before they walked through the dual swinging doors, she looked over her shoulder at Lucas. "Oh, my little Apollo, do not think I failed to notice that you avoided my question about your wolf."

Fuck. Lucas thought, but simply lifted a brow at her in question before she resumed her walk with Giovanni.

—

After the party, Lucas stood by the door to Byte once again, bidding his guests farewell. He shook the males' hands and the females received air kisses on their cheeks as they left. The humans who were their donors for the evening had already been carted back to their homes in a stylish limo with full pockets.

"A lovely party," Florence commented as she approached him, her silk dress flowing around her feet in a soft whisper. "And I adore your new blood daughter!"

Aubrey stood next to her, the hot pink tulle dress she wore clashing greatly with the dark emerald next to it. "You should have told me about your maker, Lord Lucas!" she gushed, smiling brightly at him, fangs gleaming.

Lucas wasn't fooled for a second. As soon as Aubrey woke up as a vampire, her feelings towards Lucas turned spiteful. She loathed him for making her a *monster*. When he pointed out that it was in the contract, she childishly replied that she never thought it would actually happen.

He never realized how much of an idiot she was until then. Did she not realize that the chance to become immortal was the reason so many humans longed to be bleeders?

"I am wounded that you never spoke about me, my little Apollo." His maker pouted, perfect lips pursed together.

"Of course, I have spoken about you," he corrected. "Whether or not Aubrey was around was an oversight on my part. Forgive me."

Florence batted her lashes at him again. "Always, my pet." She once again pulled him down by his lapels to kiss him. "*Always*," she breathed against his lips.

He forced another smile and waited for her to remove her hands before straightening. "Thank you for attending. Are you planning on staying in the city long?"

She gave him a coy smile. "Well of course. I just arrived, have I not? And I do believe I shall be staying here during my visit. I wanted to come have a look at your coven before deciding, but I found it more suitable for my stay than the hotel."

His façade slipped a little. "You wish to stay here? Lady Florence, I assure you that it is not adequate accommodations for you. It is a night club that humans and other preternatural creatures visit. It is loud and rambunctious."

Her face grew serious. "Are you denying me?"

"Never," he instantly replied. "I simply wish for you to be comfortable."

Aubrey set her hand on the other woman's arm. "Lady Florence, Lord Lucas is right. It's a hot mess here sometimes and there are always wolves around. You know how they smell." She made a sour look before giving her a smile. "But if you have your mind set on it, I will be more than happy to help you move your bags in!"

Lucas gave her a suspicious look before looking at his maker again. "She's quite right. We will move you into a room if you desire it. Aubrey took the last available one in the basement, but we do have rooms on the fourth floor." He would have to tell Keira and her pack to stay away when they weren't on shift.

"The fourth floor?" Florence made a face. "That is *such* a bother."

"Isn't it?" Aubrey agreed with a sigh.

"I suppose it will have to do," she sighed and looked at her blood son. "You will help me with my bags once I arrive, won't you?"

Again, his gut churned uncomfortably, the blood he ingested threatening to bubble back up his throat. "Of course, Lady Florence."

She clapped her hands. "Excellent. I will go back to the hotel and grab my things. Aubrey darling, you will come with me, yes?"

"Yes!" she agreed, giving a radiant smile that showed her elongated canines. "We'll be back soon, Lord Lucas!"

"Safe travels," he murmured as they turned and left the building. Every fiber in his body was telling him that something was wrong. Something was *off*. He wasn't sure if it was the apprehension he felt from Florence being there or the fact that Keira was now in very real danger.

"This is bad," Giovanni commented softly as he came to Lucas' side. Together they watched the pair walk away.

"I know."

He looked at his maker, his friend. "Kee and her pack can't stay here. Not when she's here."

"I know."

Gio set a hand on his shoulder. "Kee's strong."

Lucas closed his eyes. "*I know*." But was she strong enough?

—

Aubrey waited until they were in Florence's town car before dropping the smile from her face. "Convincing enough?"

"A tad over the top, dear," Florence commented and tapped the glass dividing them from the driver. "To my hotel."

Red eyes glanced at her before looking at the blonde next to her. He gave her a fang-filled grin. "Pink, hm?"

Aubrey leaned forward and pressed a hungry kiss to his lips. "You won't be complaining when you take it off me later, Damien."

"You're right," he purred and sent Florence a bored look when she cleared her throat. "Yes?"

"Did you receive the address my bleeder sent you?"

"Yeah, for a house in Riverside. And?"

Her eyes narrowed before they took on a red gleam. "You better watch your tone, fledgling. I may have agreed to this plan of yours, but I am your superior in every way." She flared her aura and both vampires flinched away. "Every. Single. Way. Do you understand?"

"Yes," Damien hissed out. He sucked in a breath when she pulled back her aura and turned back to the steering wheel. "To the hotel then."

"Good boy," Florence praised. She looked at the still cowering Aubrey and reached out to pet her hair. "Oh, child of my child, you have a lot to learn." As soon as Aubrey relaxed, Florence fisted her hair and jerked her head back so sharply that something in the younger woman's neck snapped. "And let me remind you that should my blood son find out about your fling with his former enemy's minion, I will not save you. You do not matter to me, only Lucas does."

Aubrey gagged, her voice not working while her head was bent at that angle. When her hair was released, her head *thumped* against the window, unable to do anything else until the bones in her neck mended back together.

Five

Kee led her pack up the two steps of Nana's porch, but before she got to the door, it swung open to reveal her great-grandma. She was dressed in a green sweater and jeans, red hair pulled into a low ponytail that hung over her shoulder.

"Merry Christmas, Nan," Kee greeted, hugging the older shapeshifter.

"Merry Christmas," Nana replied. As she looked over the small pack, her brows rose when she saw the newcomer Kee had mentioned. She bent to get a closer look at the miniature version of Conrad hiding behind Kee. "Oh? And who is this?"

Kee smiled and put her hand on Mia's head. "This is Conrad's daughter, Emilia."

"Emilia? What a pretty name," Nana said, a rare edge of softness in her tone. "I'm Nanette, but everyone calls me Nana."

Mia shyly stepped out from behind her alpha and held her hand out. "Everyone calls me Mia."

Nana's smile widened as she shook the small hand. "Welcome, Mia. I hope you're hungry."

She perked up. "Auntie Kee says you're the best cook. And that you make really good cookies, too. Can we make some for Santa? Daddy says he'll know I'm here."

Nana nodded. "He will. He's magical like that. And yes, we will make plenty of cookies for him and his helpers. I think I have a few carrots for his reindeer too. Why don't you head inside and start thinking of what kind you want to make?"

"Yay!" Mia beamed and hurried inside.

Conrad smiled and gave Nana a hug. "Thank you for humoring her."

She patted his back affectionately. "You did well, boy. She's beautiful."

His smile turned into a grin full of pride. "Thank you."

Lucy let out a little excited squeal as she hugged Nana next. "Thank you so much for having us!"

Nana let out a huff of a laugh as they parted. "I wouldn't have it any other way." She turned to Samson and patted his shoulder. "Glad to see you here, not that I had any doubts that Kee would take you into her pack."

Samson's smile was small but sincere. "Good to know one of us didn't have doubts."

She scoffed at him and waved at the pack. "Well, come in. No point standing out in the cold." She waited until the members of the pack walked by before stopping her great-granddaughter. She reached for her right hand and held it up to inspect the ring. "Don't think I didn't see this," she commented. "The vampire has taste."

Kee smiled fondly down at the ring. "He does."

Naha hummed. "Why is it on the wrong hand? If he wants your hand in marriage, then it should be in the correct place."

"That's my fault. He's waiting for me to be ready. It's my call on when I move it to the other side." She continued to stare down at the ring, eyes softening. "He said he'd wait for me."

"And why are you waiting? You love him, Kee. You're the happiest I have seen you. Waiting is pointless if you know he's the one."

Kee lifted her eyes to stare at her grandmother. "You don't object?"

Nana snorted. "Object? Girl, who do you think gave him the blessing?"

Kee's lips parted in surprise. "Wait, wait, wait. Lucas asked for your blessing? To propose?" Of course, her vampire would take that extra traditional step before asking her to marry him. It didn't dawn on her at first to consider what Nana thought of Lucas, but now that she had Nana's approval, she realized how much it meant to her.

Gods, he really is perfect.

"A man as old as he knows better than to go against such traditions," Nana pointed out with an approving nod.

Kee hugged her again, tighter this time. "Thank you, Nana."

Nana stroked Kee's hair affectionately then pulled away. "Enough sappiness," she chided. "Let's go in. I need to check on dinner."

Kee followed her into the two-story house, smiling at her pack as they stood in the living room and argued as to who would sleep where in the guest house. When Nana led her to the kitchen, she was surprised to find it empty. "No Christopher or Gabriel?"

Nana shook her head as she went to the stove and stirred the pot of beef stew. "No, I didn't want to deal with Christopher whining about your alpha status. We don't need drama on Yule."

"I'm sorry, Nana. Are you still going to see them for the holiday?"

"Yes, I'll be seeing them on New Year's," she said. "And don't apologize. I invited you and your pack first. You are my blood, Kee. Christopher and Gabriel are not."

Kee knew when her great-grandmother was done talking about something, so she didn't press the issue. "Well, I hope you have a good time when you do see them. I really like Gabriel—he's a good kid."

"Cut that," Nana gestured at the fresh loaf of bread sitting on a cooling rack. "And Gabriel *is* a good boy. He wants to go to the preternatural college in LA when he graduates high school. I fully support his decision. He needs to get away from the pack."

"I think my brother also wants to go there when he graduates." Kee replied, smiling a little at how well she had come to know her brother. They texted almost daily, trying to make up for the sixteen years they missed out on. "You'd like him, Nan. He may look like Liam, but he's nothing like him."

"Good. We don't need any more alpha-holes." She glanced at Kee as she laughed and did a quick double-take as Kee tied her hair up in a bun. She instantly closed the distance between them and pressed her fingertips to the four white scars on the back of Kee's neck. "Keira Marie Quinn, what in the goddess is this?"

Kee winced at both the cold tone and the use of her full name. She really should have told Nana about her mating mark before tonight. She turned towards her with a sardonic expression. "Oh, didn't I tell you Cain and I are mated? Surprise."

Nana scowled. "I don't understand."

"Liam," Kee said his name as if it was the answer for everything. "He ordered Cain to mark me, Nana. I was a 'gift' to Cain for winning the alpha fight. Cain couldn't say no. He tried, I know he did, but fuck it sucks being tied to him."

"I can only imagine how it would feel to be bonded to your ex-boyfriend while being in love with another," she murmured. "It's incomplete though, yes? You need to physically mate for the bond to snap in completely."

"Right," Kee agreed. "Which is never going to fucking happen because I won't go back to Cain. I love Lucas. I just want a way to break this stupid bond."

Nana frowned. "I wish there was something I could tell you, Kee, but there isn't. The only way to break a bond is through death."

She sighed. "I can't kill Cain, so I guess we're stuck with it. Luckily Lucas has been pretty understanding with the whole thing. He's not too fond of the bonding dates Cain and I have to go on every two weeks, but he knows I wouldn't do it if I didn't have to."

"That's because he's a good man, your vampire. He knows a treasure when he has one," Nana said as she stepped back to the stove.

With a wide, silly grin, Kee turned back to the bread and began cutting it in even slices.

—

"What did you do to your face?"

Samson looked up at the sound of the Irish accent. "Nothing." Nana rolled her eyes and sat next down next to him on the couch, handing him a plate of apple cake. He gently took the plate and fork from her but kept his gaze on the cake.

She clicked her tongue at the lie and poked him in the cheek. "Who did you get in a fight with?"

His shoulders hunched. "Just some guy."

"Why? What was the cause of it?" she pressed.

Samson sighed and set the plate down on his lap. He glanced over at his pack mates, watching as the four of them played some board game with colorful cards and cars. "Because it helps," he murmured.

Nana tilted her head at him, her ponytail falling over her shoulder. She flicked a glance at Kee then back to the dragon. She stood from the couch and jerked her chin towards the door. "Come have a smoke with me."

Knowing better than to argue, he set the cake on the end table and stood. Before he left the room, he looked over his shoulder and saw Kee giving him a questioning look. He reached out to her mind, connecting to it as easily as he had the first time.

Everything's fine. Just going to have a smoke.

You sure? I can go with you.

No, play your game. He gave her a small, reassuring smile. *I'll be alright.*

I'm here for you, Sam.

That warm feeling of belonging spread throughout his chest again. *Thank you.* When she smiled and returned to the game, he went to the porch to meet Nana.

She handed a cigarette to him, a lit one already between her fingers on the other hand. She waited for him to take it and light it with his own flame before harassing him. "So, speak, dragon. What is helping with what?"

He took a drag from the cigarette and let the smoke out through his nostrils. "The fighting."

"You fighting for sport?" she asked.

He nodded once. "There's an underground fighting ring for preternaturals."

Nana was silent for a moment. She took a long inhale from her cigarette and exhaled the smoke before speaking. "You're getting paid for this?"

"Yes," Samson replied quietly, a spark of shame crawling up his spine.

"Didn't Kee's man get you a job at the club? Why do you suddenly need this money?"

He ran his hand through his hair and avoided eye contact. "Kee taught me how to make drinks, so I was hired on at Byte as a bartender. I don't need the money, that's not why I do it."

"Ah yes, you said the fighting helps. What exactly does it help with?" she asked as she flicked ash off the end of her cigarette.

He chewed on his bottom lip for a second before answering. "With the anger." When she didn't comment, he quickly added, "Not anger at Kee, of course."

She scoffed. "Do you think I'm dumb, boy? I know it wasn't about Kee. Because if it was, I would beat your ass."

He had no doubt that she would. "I have no reason to be mad at her. It's more like the world that I'm angry with."

"For what happened to you?"

He nodded but was still unable to meet her gaze. "My so-called family in Muir abandoned me like I was nothing. They gave me to the Ringmaster like I was worth nothing." He crushed the cigarette in his hand, not caring that the ember burned his palm. "They made me endure months of torture like I meant *nothing*." A different smoke billowed from his nostrils. It came from the fire that settled in his chest, the fire that was like a second heart to every weredragon.

"And fighting someone makes you feel better?" Nana questioned.

He ran his uninjured hand down his face. "It's an outlet for my anger. I get to take out all my rage during a fight, leaving me empty. It gives me room to feel something—*anything* else instead."

She stubbed out her cigarette on the porch railing and flicked the butt into her lawn. "I understand how you feel," she began. "When my mate died, I was hollow. There was this giant hole inside me, and all these negative feelings filled it. Anger, hurt, sadness. All of it welled up inside me until it was too much to take. I wanted to feel something else, or nothing at all."

"What did you do?"

She turned to lean against the railing, arms crossed over her chest. "I almost ended it. Almost took the cowardly way out. I know my mate would have chewed me out in the next life, but I didn't care at that point anymore."

His black eyes widened slightly. He couldn't imagine this strong woman committing suicide. "What stopped you?"

"Kee," she answered simply. "My daughter called me saying her daughter was dead because of her granddaughter. She was bawling on the phone, so I didn't make out all she was saying. But I heard the word shapeshifter, and it was enough to jolt me out of my darkness. I didn't get the full story until I met up with them.

"I hadn't seen my real daughter in almost two decades. Had only seen my granddaughter Trinity a handful of times when she was a child. That's how long those bad feelings had their claws in me." She sighed. "I know Kee told you her story. Her father's alpha ordered him to kill her and her mother. An alpha's order is almost impossible to resist, so he carried out his mission. My daughter blames Kee, but it's my fault."

"How is it your fault? I don't understand." Samson shook his head. "I was in the foster care system by the time I was twelve, so I don't really understand family dynamics."

Nana rubbed her arms. "Because I never told them what I was. My daughter was six when the genocide of shapeshifters took place. She shifted into a wolf that month, so she was safe from the hunt. I had no reason to tell her about my heritage. Even when she had Trinity, I didn't tell them about the gene. Trinity shifted into a wolf, so I thought it was gone."

He furrowed his brow. "They had no idea you were a shapeshifter?"

"I think perhaps my daughter suspected it. It explains why she called me the night Trinity was killed." She clenched her jaw. "If I had told them what I was, what was lurking in our blood, maybe Trinity would still be alive. Maybe Kee would still have her parents." Her voice quieted. "Maybe she would have never been attacked."

Samson frowned. "Maybe," he began. "But then Kee wouldn't have us, her pack. She wouldn't be half-engaged to someone who truly gets her. And then, maybe you wouldn't be here. Kee gave your life a purpose, so what would that have meant for you if she hadn't needed you?"

She let out a dry laugh. "Point taken, boy."

A small smile curved his lips. "I'm just saying."

"And I'm saying that things get better," she stated. "It may take a long time, but you have something now that I didn't have."

His brow arched. "Kee?"

"More than Kee. You have a pack that cares about you. You five are so close knit despite your short time together. Lean on them, Samson. Let them help pull you from this void. I know it isn't easy, but that's what a pack is for." She cupped his shoulder. "Fighting isn't going to help you. All it's going to do is worry the people around you."

"I don't want them to worry. That's why I haven't told anyone what I'm doing."

"Yes, but what if something happens to you?" she pressed. "How is that fair to them?"

Samson knew was she right, but it was so hard to let go of something that erased all the dark emotions in him. Even if only temporarily. "I have two scheduled between now and New Year's Eve."

"Two?" When he nodded, she squeezed his shoulder. "The *last* two?"

He reluctantly agreed. "Yeah, it'll be the last two."

Nana gave his shoulder another squeeze before letting go. "Good boy. Your pack will help you through this, Samson. Is there anyone else you have met that you can lean on? Maybe a romantic interest?"

The image of a certain stray came to mind. Not necessarily in a romantic way since he didn't know her, but she did interest him. He had seen her a few times outside the building the fights were held in. Instead of picking discarded trash from the dumpsters, she had been picking the pockets of the drunk bystanders. After a fight where he received a rather nasty blow to the head, he had stumbled along the back wall towards the exit. She had mistaken him for a drunk, her hand reaching for his pocket when she didn't think he was paying attention.

He, on the other hand, had thought she was trying to touch him. Self-preservation kicked in, and he immediately grabbed her wrist and twisted it behind her back before shoving her against the wall. She had been wild in response, thrashing and bucking her small, lush body against his. She spat curses at him while simultaneously apologizing for trying to lift his wallet.

Despite the pain from the blow to the head, he had laughed. She reminded him of a pissed off kitten. When he released his hold, she spun around to face him. He was going to ask her what her name was but instead had to protect his balls when she abruptly lifted her knee to them. While his hands were busy shielding his junk, she ducked around him and disappeared into the crowd.

"I'm not dating anyone," he eventually said, but a smirk tilted his lips.

"Well, maybe you should. I'm not saying to go out and make someone your life's purpose, but maybe a distraction will be good for you. Something joyful, however small, can do wonders for your soul."

"I'll keep that in mind, Nana," Samson said.

"Good." She pushed off from the railing and jerked her head towards the house. "Come, we have to prepare a visit from Santa Claus."

Samson followed her back into the living room but stopped when he felt the tension in the room. His head tilted as he looked at his alpha, her hand clenched tightly around her phone. "What happened?"

"Lucas," Kee growled. "He texted me and told me not to come back to Byte. He gave me zero explanation, and now he's not answering me."

Conrad took her phone away before she broke it. He cupped her face in his hands and gave her a little shake. "Calm down before your anger gets ahead of you," he began, trying to steady her rage. "You know he wouldn't say something like that if there wasn't a reason."

She put her hands on his wrists and took a deep, steadying breath. "You're right. Sometimes my worry translates to anger. I'm trying to be better about it."

"We know." He laughed when she pouted. He released her face and slung an arm around her shoulders. "Come on, let's go make some cookies." With a cheer from Mia, the small pack made their way to Nana's kitchen.

Six

Lucas knew Keira had questions for him. To abruptly tell her not to come back to Byte without any explanation last night probably angered her. Especially when he denied her call and deleted her text messages. However, he would not risk Florence snooping through his phone. She would stoop to that level; of that he had zero doubt.

Right as he went to put his key in the lock of the alpha house, the door swung open. He looked at the startled Samson then down at his watch. "It's one in the morning, Mr Richland. Where are you off to?"

Samson blinked out of his surprise and adjusted the duffel bag slung over his shoulder. "Out."

He lifted a brow at him. "It looks to me as if you are _sneaking_ out like an adolescent would."

"I'm not sneaking out," Samson said as he straightened his spine. He knew Kee loved the vampire and that the two were practically engaged, but he would always have reservations about him. He didn't forget that Lucas had pushed Kee away from him. "Everyone's asleep, and I didn't want to wake them."

Lucas shot him a disbelieving look. "I do not care what you do in your spare time so long as it does not come back negatively on your alpha."

Samson's grip tightened on the strap of his bag as he narrowed his eyes. "It won't."

"Good," Lucas simply responded before brushing past him. He made his way to Keira's room, not looking back to see if the dragon had locked the door behind him.

And why would he? Lucas was more dangerous than anything that may break in.

He silently slipped into Keira's room and closed the door without a sound. He stepped to the foot of the bed and stared at his shape-shifter. She lay on her stomach, the blankets resting at the base of her spine and exposing her bare back to him.

Even now he truly could not believe that she was his. Could not fathom how he had developed such deep feelings for her.

With a ghost of a smile, he toed off his shoes and climbed on the bed. He felt her stiffen as his weight dipped the mattress, but as he began to crawl up her body, she relaxed. When he got to where the blankets stopped, he bent and placed a soft kiss to her skin. Slowly, he traced up her spine with feather-light touches of his lips. When he reached her neck, he brushed her hair aside and placed a kiss on her mating mark.

Cain may have forced his mark on her, but she wore his ring willingly.

He placed a kiss to her head before rolling over so he was lying next to her. She instantly moved closer to him, molding herself into his side and nuzzling his chest. He closed his eyes as a wave of contentment settled over him.

"You okay?" she murmured.

"Yes," he started but then thought better of it. "Physically, yes."

"Mentally?" Kee moved her head up to his shoulder so she could look at him. "What happened?"

His lips pressed together as he debated how much to tell her. All of it, he decided. Withholding information from her worked out poorly for both of them last time.

"My maker showed up at Byte yesterday," Lucas began. "She is staying at the coven during her stay."

It took a second for Kee to digest his words. When the meaning finally clicked, she quickly sat up and looked down at him. She held his face in her hands, thumbs stroking his cheeks. "Are you sure you're okay? I know what that bitch did to you."

He looped his arm around her waist and pulled her back down to his chest. "I will be so long as she stays away from you."

"Do you think she will?"

He let out a sigh. "No. She was already complaining that she has not had a chance to meet you. She wants to meet the bonded wolf that has been causing trouble with me."

She snickered. "We have been troublesome, haven't we?"

Lucas smirked. "I prefer to think that we were the ones who *stopped* the trouble."

She let out a tired laugh and snuggled against him again. When she first got his text message, she had immediately been on the defensive. She wanted answers and had been irritated when he failed to give her any. "Thank you for coming tonight and explaining it."

"I know better than to leave things like that and induce your wrath." He chuckled when she lightly smacked his chest. "But in all honesty, seeing you has eased my anxiety about Florence being here."

"Because of what happened to your past lovers," she stated. "You think she'll come for me?"

"As of right now she only knows that you are my bonded wolf. I told her you were mated to the LA alpha in an attempt to throw off any suspicion she may have, but I am not sure she is convinced." He ran his fingertips along her arm. "As much as we hate it, Cain's mark may be what saves you from her. She will not potentially start a war with a wolf pack."

Kee closed her eyes and fisted his shirt tightly. "Are we going to have to stay away from each other?"

He remained quiet for a second. "I do not want to, but I will do what I must to keep you safe, Keira."

She frowned, brow furrowing. "What about when she finally demands to meet me? Will we act like we did at The Street?"

"We may have to, my sweet. I will not risk her harming you."

Her eyes drooped with drowsiness. "We'll make it work though, right? No matter what?"

"Yes," he promised. "No matter what."

"Love you," she murmured as she began to drift back to sleep.

"I love you, too." He stroked her arm lazily, listening to her pulse slow as she fell deeper into sleep. He held her to him, only releasing her when he had to return to Byte. He slid out from under her, tucked the blankets around her, and went out into the early dawn before the sun could light up the horizon.

—

Samson let out a soft sigh of relief as he approached the four-story gym several blocks away from the alpha house. Part of him had worried that Lucas would snitch to Kee. He had gripped his phone tightly the entire way to the building, anticipating a ring at any moment. He had only come tonight to train, but Kee would have asked what he was training for, and he didn't want to lie to her more than he already had.

As he approached the double glass doors, he saw a familiar spitfire lurking around the trashcan outside on the sidewalk. "Anything tempting in there?" he asked as he approached.

She jumped at his sudden proximity, almost dropping her battered backpack. She pushed tangled strands from her face before lifting her chin haughtily. "Oh yeah, trash is *so* tempting. You should try it, really. It's a new diet trend."

He took in her appearance and tried not to frown at how much dirtier she had become overnight. Had there been nowhere for her to go on Christmas? Even through the grime, he could see how pale she was. Did she spend the holiday alone in the cold?

He adjusted the bag hanging on his shoulder, concerned about her situation. "Do you want to come in?"

Her eyes darted from him to the gym and back. "There's no fight tonight so the public can't go in."

"I'm a member," he stated casually. "I can have a guest with me."

She turned back to the trashcan, rifling through it for anything she could use. "And why would I go in with *you* of all people?"

"Besides the fact that you tried to pick my pocket, smash my balls, and trespassed on my work's property?" he listed, finding a small joy when she hunched her shoulders. "How about the fact that it's warm and has showers?"

She perked up at the mention of showers but bit her lip in hesitation. "What's in it for you?"

Samson tilted his head. "Does something have to be in it for me?"

She scowled at him. "People aren't nice just to be nice. They always have a hidden agenda."

His mind traveled back to his fam—acquaintances in Muir, but he quickly shoved the thought aside and focused on how Kee helped him without any expectations. "Not everyone."

"Well then if it's just pity, I don't want it. I don't *need* it! I'm fine on my own," she hissed, hands balling into fists around the straps of her bag.

Hadn't he felt the same way when Kee had offered to give him money for clothing and other necessities? "You want to earn your shower then?" Even in the dark, the dim streetlamp doing nothing in terms of light, he could see her cheeks grow red. "Not like that," he cut her off when she was about to yell at him. "I need a sparring partner."

"Sparring partner?" she mumbled, flicking her gaze back to the brick building. "If you expect me to fight like you did in the ring…"

"All you need to do is hold the punching bag and pads. But I suppose if you don't want to, that's fine. You can stay out here," Samson said as he turned and headed to the doors of the gym. He grabbed one of the sleek metal handles and smirked when he heard her soft footsteps behind him. He held the door open for her, resisting the urge to grin at her. "I'm Samson, by the way."

She shot him an appraising look before storming past him, slinging the bag onto her back. "Tori," she threw over her shoulder as she stalked inside like she owned the place.

He followed her with a smirk.

After two hours of Samson beating the shit out of a punching bag and hitting the gloved mats on her hands, the two sat down on a metal bench off to the side. He handed her a water bottle and protein bar from his duffle bag before opening his own.

"Your kick is mean," Tori commented around a mouth full of granola bar. "My arm went numb there for a second."

He let out a quiet laugh, surprised by her willingness to talk. They had exchanged a few words throughout the workout but mostly focused on what they were doing. He had a sneaking suspicion that she had been trying to feel him out. He couldn't blame her; he had done the same. "Thanks. I'm working on it for my next fight."

She swallowed a gulp of water then quietly picked at the label on the plastic for a few seconds before speaking again. "Why do you fight? Do you want to do it professionally?"

"No," he answered.

"What does your pack think about you fighting?"

He tensed. "They don't know. And I don't want them to know either."

"Then why fight?" she repeated.

"It's…cathartic." He just had this conversation with Nana last night and wasn't ready to tell it again. When she angled her head in question, he shook his head. "I don't want to talk about it. Not now."

She lowered her tone. "People die in the rings, you know. I've seen it."

"I have too," he agreed. "But I have two more fights I've already committed to."

"You should stop."

Samson's ire prickled, but he tried remained calm. "And you should stop eating trash and living on the streets, but here we both are."

Tori bristled and abruptly stood from the bench, pupils turning into slits. "Fuck you! You think it's easy? You think I *like* living on the streets? You know nothing about my situation!"

He held her gaze, making sure she saw that he wasn't judging her. "I know that you've been offered help, but I think you're too stubborn to take it. Don't be like me, take the help. My alpha's offer still stands." She chucked the water bottle at him, but he easily caught it before it hit him. He looked at it with mild interest. "Well, that was rude."

"You're rude!" she seethed, gaining the attention of the guy curling weights next to them. "Why should I trust some random person I've never met?"

He looked up at her again and met her brown gaze. "Because I did, and it saved my life."

Her lips pressed hard together at the open honesty in his expression and tone. She wanted to know more, to ask what he meant. However, she was too miffed by his earlier comment to respond rationally. "Your *precious* fucking alpha? Fuck that, fuck her, and fuck *you*."

His eyes narrowed as he crushed the water bottle in his hand, the pressure popping off the cap and spilling water everywhere. His nostrils flared as his inner flame burned with his anger, smoke billowing out of his nostrils. He could handle her disrespecting him, but Kee was another story. "Go take your shower and get out of my sight before I rip out your throat."

The low, cold tone made the hair on the back of her neck stand up.

Without being told twice, Tori turned and hurried to the female locker room at the back of the gym. Once she was safely away from Samson, she went to the showers and stripped down. She set her backpack and dirty clothes on the counter by the sink before turning to the nearest stall. Turning the water to hot, she stepped in and nearly moaned at the comfort. She didn't have any soap or hair products, but she didn't care. Simply bathing in the hot water would get the dirt off her and do wonders for her soul.

She was jerked out of her enjoyment when she heard the locker room door creak open. Did Samson change his mind? Her pulse pounded in her neck at the thought of him following up on his warning.

She didn't dare look.

But soon she didn't have to.

His scent, earthy with a twinge of sweat, filled the bathing part of the locker room. She held her breath as she heard his footsteps head closer towards the showers. She was certain he would break down the stall door and follow through with his threat, but she would be damned if she didn't go down without a fight. She curled her hands into fists, ready to defend herself in the small, tiled enclosure.

Instead, she heard his faint footsteps by the sink. They paused for a second before retreating the way they came.

When the door squeaked again, she rushed to finish her shower, not giving him any more time to change his mind. A part of her mourned the loss of the hot water when she turned off the nozzle, but she needed to go. Stepping out of the stall sopping wet, she cautiously made her way to the sink where her clothes were. She blinked in surprise to find that he had left her the black hoodie he had been wearing with a stack of protein bars and a bottle of water resting on top of it.

Seven

"Why are we packing our stuff? Did you and Uncle Luke get into a fight?" Mia asked as the pack made their way down the final flight of stairs from the fourth floor of Byte, duffel bags in hands.

Kee shook her head. "No, he has some people visiting from out of town who may need our rooms."

She frowned up at her alpha as they walked across Byte's empty dance floor. "Does Uncle Luke not want us around them?"

Perceptive, Kee mused.

"You could say that. Lucas wants to keep us safe, so staying at the pack house is the best way to do that for now," she said, stopping at one of the larger round tables.

"What about Daddy and Sammy? And Lucy? They work here. Are they going to be in danger?" Mia asked as she set her bag down.

"We'll be okay, baby girl," Conrad replied as he stroked the top of her golden hair. He agreed with Lucas and Kee that if they all stopped showing up to work it would raise more suspicion from Lucas' maker.

At Mia's frown, Lucy chimed in, "We're safe at work. Lucas won't let anything happen to us. Plus, Gio and Dante will be on shift too. We're practically untouchable!"

Unconvinced, the youngest pack member simply nodded and climbed onto one of the bar stools. She gave Samson a weak smile when he pat the top of her head in reassurance. "What's for lunch, Sammy?"

"Chinese," he replied. "We haven't had it in a while."

She brightened, amber eyes widening with delight. "Did you get chow mein? And fried rice? Lucy likes white rice. Did you get that, too? What about orange chicken? Broccoli beef?"

He let out a soft chuckle. "All of that plus more."

"Yes!" she cheered, previous troubles forgotten.

"Thanks for ordering it, Sam. How much do I owe you?" Kee asked, placing her bag with the others. A frown curved down her lips when he shook his head at her. "I'm not making you pay for a pack meal. I know how much we eat."

"It isn't a big deal. I don't mind," he replied as he pulled out a chair next to Mia, per her request.

Conrad sat down on the other side of his daughter and tied his shoulder length hair back into a bun. "At least let us chip in. We want to help."

Samson waved his hand. "Really, don't worry about it. It's my treat to the pack."

"Samson, are you sure?" Lucy pressed, sitting next to her boyfriend and putting her hand on his knee.

The dragon sighed. "*Yes*. Please, all of you, stop asking." He knew they meant well, but he liked being able to help provide for his pack. It brought him some small piece of pride and helped him really believe that he was a part of the pack.

Feeling the shift in his mood, Kee ruffled his hair affectionately. "Thank you, Sam. At least let me tip the delivery person when they get here, okay?"

"Fine," he acquiesced. He abruptly tilted his head to the side when he heard a bang from the outside alleyway. Shooting Kee a knowing look, he got back to his feet and headed towards the kitchen.

"I'll go," Conrad offered as he began to stand, but Kee gently waved him off.

"We got it, Con," Kee stated as she followed Samson, not giving the dragon a chance to rebuke her. If it was the same girl, she would offer help again. Something about her pulled at Kee's alpha's side. It wasn't like Samson, who had literally broadcasted a cry for help, but she could hear it with her instincts regardless.

Samson led the way through the kitchen and out the back door. He had a split second to realize Miguel wasn't there before he heard Tori shouting. Not waiting for Kee, he took off towards the alley. When he got there, he saw Miguel holding Tori's arm up at an odd angle, causing her to thrash and squirm like a snake.

Kee barely had time to grab Samson's shirt before he launched himself forward. The power behind his movement had her staggering and stumbling before she anchored her feet and tugged him back. Even with that, his shirt began to tear as he tried to get out of her grip.

She cursed before shouting at the security guard. "Let her go, Miguel!"

The werebear looked at Kee then at her fuming pack mate. "But she was trespassing, are you sure?"

"Yes, she's fine. Let go." When the werebear looked at her uncertainly, she pushed authority in her tone and flared her aura. "*Now,* Miguel!" When he abruptly did as told, Kee released Samson.

Samson quickly ran to Tori's side, snarling at Miguel as he did. It wasn't until the security guard held up his hands and backed away that Samson relaxed his face and looked down at the scowling woman. "You alright?"

Tori smoothed her shaking hands down the sweatshirt he gave

her. "I don't need your help."

"That's not what I asked, is it?" he growled.

She tucked a strand of clean hair behind her ear and turned away from him. "I'm fine," she mumbled.

She may have put on a front of being calm, but the trembling in her hands gave her away. He didn't think it was possible, but she looked even paler than she did last night, dark circles under her eyes. He reached out but hesitated, wondering if his touch would be welcomed or not. Considering he had threatened her last night, he decided against it.

"Are you hurt?" he asked instead, dropping his hand back to his side.

Tori had seen his movement out of the corner of her eye. She was both relieved and upset that he didn't follow through. She wasn't sure what to expect after what happened at the gym. "I *said* I'm fine."

"That's good," Kee commented, stepping up to stand beside Samson. She too had seen Samson reach for the girl. His obvious protectiveness for her made her earlier decision that much easier. "I don't believe we properly met. I'm Kee Quinn."

Tori lifted a brow, expecting the declaration to come with a handshake, but the other woman simply gave her a smile. "Tori Zheng," she answered in a soft mumble.

"It's nice to meet you, Tori." She gestured at Byte's building. "Would you like to join us for lunch? We're having Chinese food."

She gave Kee a deadpanned expression. "Are you asking me because I'm Asian?"

Kee lifted a brow. "No, I'm asking you because you're hungry and that's what we ordered. Unless you prefer the trashed leftovers from last night?"

Tori's cheeks heated in embarrassment. She wasn't proud of her chosen situation. "I—"

"There's no catch, Tori. It's just a hot meal to put in your stomach." Samson cut her off. "Remember what we talked about."

Tori shot him a withering glare. "You mean, before you threatened me?"

He held her gaze without remorse. "Yes. Accept the help when it's offered. And I meant what I said about Kee."

She huffed and looked at Kee again but avoided making direct eye contact. Alphas didn't like that shit, right? "Do all your pack members threaten bodily harm if they talk poorly about you?"

Samson growled in warning, but Kee simply laughed. "I wouldn't be surprised if they did. We're all protective over each other." Her tone grew serious. "But make no mistake, I'll kill anyone who hurts my pack."

"Isn't that how alphas are supposed to be?" Tori asked, crossing her arms over her chest as a shiver ran through her.

"Supposed to be, yes, but in my experience, not many are." She shrugged. "My pack is small, but they're mine and I would do anything for them."

Tori's lips reluctantly curled into a smile. "That's good to know."

Kee offered her another smile and stepped aside, sweeping her hand out. "The invitation still stands for lunch."

This time Samson held out his hand to Tori. "Don't be stubborn." He could feel Kee's eyes on him, but he kept his eyes on the short woman in front of him.

"Don't call me stubborn." Tori smacked his hand away, but before he could drop it back to his side, she snagged it within her own. She refused to look at him, her cheeks blushing. "Lead the way."

Pleased with her murmured answer, he wrapped his fingers around hers and guided her from the alleyway.

"By the way, I like your sweatshirt," Kee commented lightly. When Samson glanced over his shoulder at her, she gave him a wicked grin.

Did he think she wouldn't notice his favorite hoodie? Yes, it was plain black, but it was also saturated in his scent.

Tori kept her gaze on the broken asphalt under her feet. "Thank you," she muttered. "Someone let me borrow it."

"That someone gave it to you," Samson corrected, not caring that Kee knew. "It's just going to get colder, and you looked half frozen last night."

Tori frowned but couldn't make herself tell him just how much the sweatshirt meant to her. Not only was it a rare act of kindness in today's age, but it may very well have saved her life. The hoodie dwarfed her, but the extra material was perfect for keeping her warm.

Due to the type of wereanimal she was, she was extremely sensitive to the cold. More than once she had woken up in an alleyway stiff and dizzy. She had curled herself into a small ball, trying to conserve all the heat she could when she slept, but it didn't help. She would wake up sluggish and numb, forcing her body to move so she could find heat or at least bask in the winter sun.

"Thank you," she bit out instead, flexing her fingers around his. When Samson shot her a surprised look, she scoffed at him. "Shut up."

Kee smiled when her pack mate laughed, her heart warming for him. She wasn't a fool; she knew Samson had been struggling, could feel it in his aura. But she also knew better than to coddle. He didn't like when she fussed over him.

When they approached the door, Samson lifted the corner of his lip in a silent sneer. The werebear raised his hands to show he meant no harm. He didn't wait for Miguel to open the door, instead pushing it open for him and Tori. Once she was through, he tugged her aside and held the door open long enough for Kee.

"Thank you, Miguel. Don't worry about Sam," Kee said as she walked by the security guard.

"Yes, ma'am. I'm sorry, I didn't know she was a friend," he explained with a frown.

"You know now and that's all that matters." She gave him a reassuring smile. She thanked Samson for holding the door then led the way through the kitchen to the empty club. The remaining members of her pack were already looking at them in question.

Tori's steps faltered when she saw the other three people staring at her. Samson's hand tightened around hers, keeping her grounded and steady. Why was that a thing? Still, she stayed behind him as they approached the table laden with food.

There was a moment of quiet consideration as the pack surveyed the newcomer.

Kee gently nudged Samson with her elbow. "Introduce your friend, Sam."

He pulled Tori so she was standing next to him. "Pack, this is Tori," he began. "Tori, this is Conrad, Lucy, and Mia."

Lucy stood from the table and approached the three. "Hi, Tori! It's so nice to meet you! Are you joining us for lunch?"

Tori blinked at the girl with white-blonde hair and nodded as they shook hands. "Um, yes. I was invited."

Lucy clapped her hands together. "Excellent! Samson ordered way too much food."

"That's because you eat enough for three wereanimals," Conrad teased, coming up to his girlfriend's side and giving Tori a nod in greeting.

Lucy's pale green eyes narrowed before she shoved him. "Oh yeah? Someone's not getting lucky tonight."

Conrad's lips pursed together before a wicked grin split them. "Oh, we'll see about that."

"What does *getting lucky* mean?" Mia asked from the table, head cocked to the side.

Kee snorted a laugh as she took a seat at the table. "That's a conversation for you, Con."

"Nope, no. Not yet. I refuse," Conrad replied as he steered Lucy back to the table. He pressed a quick kiss to his daughter's hair and squeezed her shoulder. "I'll tell you when you're older."

Tori watched the entire exchange with a bemused expression. Were all packs like this? This… comfortable?

Samson pulled out a chair at the table and gestured to Tori. When she lifted a brow at him, he sighed. "You're impossible to do nice things for. Sit the fuck down." She grumbled but did as told, making him snort. "If I knew bossing you around was all it took, I would I have started with that."

"Screw you," she snapped, crossing her arms over her chair. "I do *not* like being bossed around."

"I don't know, sometimes a girl just needs a man to take control. Isn't that right, Kee?" Lucy hummed, staring at her friend knowingly.

Kee choked on her water, a blush burning her cheeks. "Hey, leave my love life out of this."

"She *does* submit to him, doesn't she?" Conrad mused as he grabbed the container of white rice for Lucy.

"She does," Samson agreed. "Although she gives him a run for his money."

Kee pointed her chopsticks at him. "Like hell if I make anything easy for him," she said. "Besides, he likes the challenge."

"And you like submitting," Conrad added innocently.

"I'm going to break your kneecaps, Beta," she threatened, tossing a wrapped fortune cookie at him.

Samson laughed as he handed Tori a takeout carton of some sort of spicy chicken. When he saw her smiling with an actual, real smile, it tugged at something in his chest. He glanced over at Kee, who was already studying them with a knowing smile. Holding her gaze, he jerked his chin ever so slightly in Tori's direction. Her smile simply grew before she gave him a noncommittal shrug and turned her attention to Mia, who was asking for soy sauce.

He wasn't sure what that meant, but he had a better idea of what he wanted. "After lunch we're going to the pack house for games. Do you want to come with us?"

Tori froze, her chopsticks halfway to her mouth. She looked at him with wide eyes then at the other people at the table. Each one was simply smiling at her without a trace of contempt. Were they all so quick to accept her? Why? They didn't know her.

"Um, I don't want to impose. I appreciate lunch though," she mumbled.

"But with you we'll have an even number of players!" Mia protested. "You *have* to come! Please?"

Tori hunched her shoulders as they continued to stare at her. "I-I guess, if you don't mind." She smiled tentatively when Mia cheered then looked at Samson when he cleared his throat. "You don't have to do this."

"What do you mean?" he asked innocently.

"You know what I mean," she muttered under her breath.

He leaned towards her, lips by her ear. "I'm selfish. I fully expect you to be my training partner again tonight."

There was no sexual underline to his words, but his deep voice whispering in her ear had her pressing her thighs together.

Eight

"I really like your pack," Tori admitted as she sat cross-legged on the roof of the alpha house wrapped in a thick blanket. She couldn't believe she had spent a second night with them. Couldn't believe that they seemed to want her around.

"And they really like you," Samson replied from his spot next to her. "Which just makes me like you more."

He had said it so casually that she didn't know how to take it. She frowned and picked at her nails, not knowing what to say. "So, are you going to tell me what kind of wereanimal you are?"

"Are you going to tell me yours?" he shot back with a lifted brow.

Her cheeks flushed. "Maybe."

He laughed and leaned back to stare up at the stars. "Telling you what I am comes with a story of why I'm here."

She bit the inside of her cheek. "And that has something to do with why you fight?" When he nodded, she drew her knees to her chest. "You don't have to tell me. I can tell it's a sensitive subject."

Samson remained silent for a second, contemplating his choices. "Can I trust you?"

Tori blinked. "I don't know, can you? We hardly know each other."

"True," he hummed. "But there is something about you."

She snuggled deeper into the blanket. "I won't tell anyone if you don't want me to. Besides, who would I tell? It's not like I'm drowning in friends."

He closed his eyes as he decided. "I was an orphan by the time I was twelve. I went on a field trip to Muir Woods with some classmates and was attacked by a dragon guard for trespassing into their territory. Thanks to the full moon, I was infected with the gene and never left.

"It took me a long time to come to terms with what I was. I didn't believe it until the next full moon when the change was forced on me. I accepted my beast, but the people around me were still the enemy. Until they weren't, you know? I trained and rose through the ranks, making friends along the way. I had very close ones." His hands balled into fists. "Again, until they weren't."

Tori stared at him, listening intently as he spoke. When he didn't continue, she gently prodded for more, bumping her shoulder against his. "What happened?"

He let out a heavy sigh. "I stuck my nose in the wrong business. Someone in power was working with our supposed enemy, and I wanted to know why. I followed him and saw crates of wereanimals being delivered to his house. At the time I didn't think he saw me but turns out he did. The next day I was 'exiled'. Some bullshit excuse that I fucked his wife and committed treason. My so-called friends and family did nothing to intervene."

"Exiled for screwing his wife? Really?" She snorted at the pettiness of it.

"It wouldn't have been so bad if I had truly been exiled, but I wasn't. I was given to the same person who was delivering the wereanimals. Turns out she's a dealer for The Street. She specializes in exotic monsters. Sold bits and pieces of them—of *us* just to make a profit." His voice softened. "I was there for two months, Tori. Barely given enough water and food to survive. I was in a silver cage barely big enough to fit my dragon form. Apparently, it made it easier to gouge out my scales."

Tori stared at him in horror, mouth floundering for something to say. "What the fuck…" Not exactly eloquent, but all other words failed her.

"Yeah." He sat up and looked at her with a small smile. "Then Kee found me. At the risk of her own life, she broke me out. Her fiancé helped too."

"That's why you told me to accept help when it was offered," she mumbled. "Why it saved your life."

"Exactly. And, in doing so, I found a real family. We are a pack of misfits, all of us different breeds and with different pasts, but I think our differences make us closer," he said.

She reached towards him but froze when his eyes instantly darted to her hand. She curled her hand into a fist and dropped it back to her lap. "You don't like being touched, do you?"

"No." He tilted his head. "Well, it depends. I prefer to initiate the contact, but there are exceptions. My alpha, for example. I'm getting better with my pack, but I have my moments."

"Moments like when we first met? Is that why you almost popped my arm out of its socket?" she accused, batting her lashes at him in mock innocence.

"Hey, you were trying to pick my pocket," he pointed out, but a laugh lingered on his words. "But yes. I didn't know you were going for my pocket. I had just gotten out of a fight and was still a little dazed from getting punched in the head. I saw someone reaching for me and my self-preservation kicked in before I could stop it."

How could she blame him? "I'm sorry." She furrowed her brow. "For all of it. It's not fair, what happened to you."

He gave her pointed look. "Life isn't fair, Tori, but somehow we find a way to make it through."

She could have nodded and left it at that, but he had confided in her. She wanted to do the same. "I live on the streets by choice," she admitted, unable to meet his gaze. "I have a family that would take me in. In fact, they would literally fall to their knees and cry if I did. But I won't. Isn't that crazy? *I'm* crazy, right? You can say it. Say I'm stupid while you're at it."

He shook his head. "I would never," he said. "There's more to your story than that."

She pulled the hem of the blanket up over her head, covering her cold ears as well as hiding her face from him. "My family worships me. I don't mean it figuratively, Samson. They actually *worship* me. I tried to get them to stop, purposefully acted out to show them I'm not worth it, but they refused to be swayed."

Samson scooted closer to her. She was rubbing her hands together anxiously, so he gently took them into his own, offering her both strength and warmth.

"Have you heard of the Legend of White Snake?" she whispered. "It's a Chinese folktale."

"No," he answered softly.

"There are a bunch of interpretations and versions of it, but this is the basic concept of it. There were once two snake spirits, one white and one green. One day they transform into two beautiful women and go to the human world. White snake falls in love with a man named Xu Xian and they get married. Together they open a medicine shop, giving aid to everyone.

"Then there is a monk named Fa Hai. Depending on what version you read, he was a different spirit who was wronged by white snake or just a human who detected what she truly was. Anyways, he convinces Xu Xian to have his wife drink a wine that will expose her. It works and a massive white snake takes her form causing her husband to die of a heart attack in shock.

"Pregnant, she goes to Mount Emei to get some resurrection grass to save him. He comes back to life and still loves her despite what she is. In some retellings green snake helps her because she's indebted to white snake or Fa Hai continues to try and separate them. There are also a few where she controls water and breaks a whole temple." She twisted her hands in his so that she could lace their fingers, a sardonic smile titling her lips. "Some people believe that white snake was evil, can you guess what side my family is on?"

He squeezed her hands back. "But why do they worship *you*?"

"Bai Suzhen, white snake's adapted name, wanted to help people, hence the medicine shop. She helped all people with her medicine, even if they couldn't afford it. My entire family thinks of her as a healer of sorts." She shook her head. "Anyways, my parents were in a really bad car accident when my mom was full term with me. She supposedly wasn't going to make it, but she still went into labor. She popped me out, flat lined, and the doctors brought her back. The *doctors*, Samson. Still, they think it was me. That, somehow, I saved her."

"Did they know you were a white snake when you were born? Are they weresnakes too?" he asked.

"Basilisk," she corrected. "That's the actual term weresnakes prefer. And no, they didn't. They're both human, but I was bitten by a snake when I was little. The virus stayed dormant in my system until I was eight. Then the full moon came and *BAM*, hello giant ass white snake. My mom claimed I was special when I was born, that I saved her, so when I shifted for the first time, she just took it to an extreme."

Samson mulled over her words. "By chance, was it a green snake that bit you?"

Tori shot him a pointed, surprised look. "You're catching on.

My grandparents on my mother's side are from China and take our folktales very seriously. They taught my mom to be that way too. So, once I turned into a white snake, my mother went on and on about how the green snake that bit me was from the folklore. That Bai was reunited with her friend after all these years."

"So, they threw themselves at your feet?"

She shook her head. "You don't understand, Samson. It wasn't just that they threw themselves at my feet. I had to raise myself because they wouldn't go against me. It was so stifling. I could do no wrong in their eyes.

"They kept me sheltered in the house for years. *Years*! I was home-schooled to keep myself pure from humanity's toxicity. I was given any and everything I ever wanted without question. They praised my name at every single fucking opportunity. When it got to the point that I was suffocating under their attention, I demanded they let me leave the house. And just like that, they agreed. Because they didn't want to upset Bai.

"I wanted them to punish me, as twisted as that sounds. I drank in excess, smoked weed, snorted white lines, brought home both men *and* women. Shocker, they did *nothing*. I wanted them to scold me and tell me I was fucking up. To tell me I was wrong. I needed some new emotion from them, but they refused. They just smiled and bowed. Fucking *bowed*. I couldn't do it anymore."

He heard her breath hitch and rattle. He leaned closer to her and hesitantly put an arm around her shoulders. When she stiffened, he was going to pull away, but then she fell into his chest and cried. He pushed the blanket back from her head and gently stroked her hair as she silently sobbed against him.

Tori peeled herself off his chest a few minutes later, using the edge of the blanket to wipe her nose. "Gods, I'm such an ugly crier."

He smirked at her. "I won't disagree."

She shoved his chest indignantly. "Rude. What, you don't think snot is sexy? Doesn't do it for you?"

His smirk grew. "You do it for me."

Tori scowled at him, but the heat in his eyes softened it. "Shut up, I do not."

"Didn't I just say otherwise?" he asked as he tucked her hair behind her ear.

She stared at him, anticipation warming her chest as he held her gaze for a long moment. "A-are you going to kiss me?" she whispered.

"Yes," Samson said simply. "Unless you and your snot don't want me to."

She quickly wiped her nose again and sniffled before nodding. "I want you to—" She couldn't finish her sentence, not when his lips were already pressed against hers. A needy sound echoed in her throat, and she kissed him back.

Gods, he was so warm.

Samson growled when she climbed into his lap and straddled him. When she leaned back, making to move off him, he looped an arm around her waist and held her in place. "Don't."

"But I know you don't like being touched," she panted. "I-I'm sorry. I just acted instead of asking."

"You don't have to ask. I want you to touch me, Tori," he rumbled as stared at her lips.

She stared at him for a second before slowly lifting her hand to gingerly trace the scar that cut through his brow and reached the very top of his cheek. "This okay?"

His lips tilted up in a small smirk. "I'd rather feel your lips." His arms loosened around her waist as he reconsidered her words. "Unless you want to go?"

Her tongue slipping past his lips was all the answer he needed.

Nine

A couple days later, Kee stared at her reflection in Lucas' bathroom mirror. She wasn't exactly sure what she should be wearing to meet his maker. She decided on a pair of black slacks and a low-cut charcoal blouse. For her makeup, she did a smoky cat eye and debated on lipstick. When her vampire called to arrange this meeting, she knew Florence was near him. His tone was bored, sentences short and detached. She didn't even try to ask questions when his maker was in earshot.

But now the problem was that she didn't know what to do.

During their short call, he had told her she was permitted to get ready in his dwelling, so she had gone straight to his room when she got to Byte. He wasn't there and a pang of yearning hit her hard. She hadn't really spent time with him since their date. Yes, he came to see her Christmas night to explain what was going on, but she had fallen asleep in his arms before they could spend time together.

She didn't get to tell him what she decided.

Gods, why did Florence have to show up now of all fucking times?

"Are you angry with me?"

Kee lifted her head, not realizing she had been staring at the counter. She turned to the door and a wave of warmth rushed over her at the mere sight of Lucas. She glanced over his shoulder, looking for a deadly shadow following him.

"She is upstairs getting dressed," Lucas explained when he saw her guarded expression. When she relaxed and gave him a smile, he closed the distance between them. She melted into his arms, and he held her tightly to him. "My sweet," he sighed contently.

"I miss you," she mumbled into his black dress shirt. "So much."

"I miss you as well." He pulled back and ran a thumb across her bottom lip. "I am trying to get rid of her, but she is scheming. She claims to have come just to see me, but I do not trust her. Something is amiss."

Kee stared at his lips longingly, her body swaying towards his. She had to force her next words out. "What do you think she wants?"

"I am unsure," he answered. He tilted his head, making sure he didn't hear anyone approaching before pressing a quick kiss to her lips. "Stay on guard, Keira. She will be dissecting everything you say, everything we do. Do not give her reason to doubt anything I have said."

She nodded even as her stomach clenched with disappointment. "I won't."

"I am sorry to put you through this," he began. "I only wish to keep you safe. You know that, yes?"

"Yeah, but I don't like it. I'm bitter," she admitted. "I just want to be happy with you without anyone or thing getting in our way. We've only had a month of peace."

His eyes softened. "I know, Keira. I am not pleased with this situation either. You simply need to survive until we are rid of her. Then we can spend many years together in bliss." He bent towards her, pressing another kiss to her lips before they brushed the shell of her ear. "I love you. Never forget that."

"I love you, too," she whispered. Her anxiety spiked as the words she wanted to say at Pantages bubbled up. "Lucas—"

They both tensed at the light footsteps nearing his door. If they jerked apart from each other now, it would look suspicious. He wove his hand into her hair, gripping it as he tilted her head back. "Remember what I said," he breathed before he tugged her head back further, exposing her throat to him. His fangs brushed along her tender skin. "What was that, wolf?" he asked in a mocking tone.

She swallowed once, slipping into the role she had while at The Street. "I'm sorry."

"Oh? And what is going on here?"

Kee couldn't see the owner of the voice with the European accent, but she could feel them. Florence was strong, her presence filling the bathroom with a thick tension.

Lucas drew back from Keira's neck but didn't release his hold as he looked at his maker. "My wolf was late. I sought to remind her what happens when she displeases me." He felt irritation surge through their bond and had to aim the smirk that tilted his lips towards Florence. "It is so hard to keep pets in line sometimes."

Florence tossed her hair over her shoulder, thick lashes batting at her blood son. "I know that better than anyone, my little Apollo. You have often fallen out of line."

"Me?" he asked coyly, acting affronted. "My Lady, you wound me. I simply like to remind you that I am worth the trouble."

Florence laughed, the sound both harsh and sensual. "That you are," she cooed. "Now, let the poor wolf up before you snap her neck."

Lucas released his hold on Keira's hair but kept his face impassive as she straightened on her heels. He watched as she rubbed her neck, though they both knew he hadn't hurt her in the slightest. "Keira, this is Florence, my maker. Florence, this is my bonded wolf, Keira."

Kee gave a dip of her head, refusing to bow. "A pleasure." She looked over the short woman. Her luscious hair was crimson and fell in perfect waves over the off-white sheath she wore. The dress was silk and hugged each dip and curve of her body, especially the hard peaks of her nipples. Kee was pretty certain that if the woman stood a certain way, the outline of her sex would also be apparent.

Glad I went for the modest approach, Kee mused.

"Indeed, a pleasure," Florence hummed, looking over the wolf in front of her.

Kee felt as if she was standing in front of Warren once again. The vampire was scrutinizing every inch of her from head to toe. The difference was that she wasn't nervous or scared. She knew who she was, what she capable of, and Lucas' maker wouldn't change that. The only twinge of discomfort she felt was when the woman's eyes fell on the scars peeking out from her blouse.

"Broken is drawn to broken, I see," Florence murmured.

Oh, fuck no. She did not just call my man broken. "Excuse me?" Kee snapped out before she could stop herself. Apprehension shot through their bond, but she couldn't stop herself. "What was that?"

A slender brow lifted at the challenge in the wolf's tone. "I believe you heard me. Broken is drawn to broken. Or is it, marred drawn to marred? Imperfect to imperfect?"

Kee's hands balled into fists. "You're right, I'm not perfect. I have scars because I was, in fact, broken. But I don't care what the fuck you think of me. What I *do* care about is what you say about Lord Lucas." She relaxed her hands at her sides. At the worry in the bond, she tried to phrase her words carefully. "He saved my life and in doing so made sure my mate didn't break. My pack and I owe him."

Florence swept her gaze over the wolf once again. "Indeed." She looked at her blood son, studying his bemused expression before holding her hand out to him. "It seems like you have a guard dog instead of a wolf."

"Is that so bad?" he teased as he put her hand in the crook of his elbow. "Having someone to defend my honor?"

She scoffed. "What honor? Are you some innocent maiden?"

Lucas gave her a devious grin. "You know best of all that I am not."

"Indeed, I do." Florence flicked a glance at her son's bonded wolf, but the wolf was looking at her nails with a bored expression. "So, wolf, Lucas tells me some of your pack works at the bar. Are any of them here now?"

Kee lifted a brow at her. "Does it matter?"

She delicately sniffed at the disrespect. "I am simply trying to make conversation with you to get to know you better. Really, what are you teaching her, my little Apollo?"

"Do not disrespect my maker a second time, wolf. Answer the question," Lucas warned.

Kee sighed. "Yes, one of my wolves is working security at the front door tonight."

"Your wolves?" Florence pressed. "Not your mate's?"

Fuck. "Mine, his, ours." She shrugged. "What does it matter? My mate and I rule our pack together."

"I see," she commented and turned her attention to her blood son again. "Come, I want to find a snack at your bar." Without looking at her, she addressed Keira. "You will join us as well, wolf."

"Of course," Lucas said and began to lead Florence out of his room and down the hallway of the coven. He wanted to turn to Keira and check how she was doing, but he could feel the irritation still thrumming through their bond. He needed her to hold out for them.

The three of them stepped onto the main floor of Byte, and Kee immediately noticed the attention that turned towards them. She could practically feel Florence bask in the looks she received from the patrons of the bar. Men of all species looked at her as if she were something to be devoured, woman looking at her with a mix of jealousy and longing.

Kee was on the team with the ones who looked at her with contempt. Of course, her reason for that feeling was because Florence was practically hanging on Lucas.

"Lord Lucas, Lady Florence," Dante greeted as he approached them. "I have saved a table for you off to the side of the dance floor. Unless you would rather have a VIP room upstairs?"

"I think I rather like watching all the sexual tension of the dancers up close," Florence said with a sly smile, squeezing Lucas' arm as she did.

"Then right this way, my lady." Dante led them over to the high-top table mentioned, pulling out Florence's chair for her as Lucas took his seat next to her. "Would you like me to send over a human for feeding? Any preference?"

Florence watched as Lucas' wolf sat in the third chair. "As a matter of fact, I do."

Kee stiffened at both the stare and the innuendo. "I'm not on the menu."

"But, why not? Are you not Lucas' bonded wolf? Surely you have been on his menu?"

She scowled. "I was at one point, but we've come to an understanding. My man doesn't like to share."

"Ah, yes, your *mate*." She leaned back in her chair, draping her arm along the back of the cool metal. "What does your mate think of your bond with my Lucas? That you work here with him? That you fucked him before? He must be quite jealous."

Kee kept her face neutral. "Is that what my lord told you?"

Florence's eyes narrowed at her. "Not in so many words, but I know it to be true."

"Do you?" She shot back.

"Neither one of you are denying it."

"Maybe we don't like to kiss and tell. Or maybe past mistakes are none of your fucking business."

"Keira!" Lucas scolded sharply, but he was quite relieved that she handled that so well. If she had been too defensive, it would have raised suspicion. Flaunting it would have just been bad for them both.

Kee, back in her role, automatically submitted and dropped her gaze to the polished table. "My apologies, Lord Lucas."

He rubbed his temples. "I told you to behave, but you have been disobedient all night."

"Then you should punish her," Florence suggested with a cocked brow. The three looked at her in surprise. "Discipline your pet, my little Apollo. Draw blood from her like you almost did earlier."

Dante twitched with restraint. "I do not think doing so in public is the best course, Lady Florence."

"Did I ask for your opinion? Did I say you could even speak?" Florence spat before turning back to her blood son. "Bleed her, Lucas. Show me how you discipline your pets when they disobey you."

"Florence, I cannot just draw blood from the alpha's mate in public," Lucas said slowly, making sure to stay calm. "I will handle her in private."

"Bite. Her," she demanded through clenched teeth. "Or I will do it for you."

Kee pushed back her chair and stood up before looking at Lucas. "If you need to do it to make a point, then do it, but I'm not going to let your maker touch me, Lord Lucas." She pulled her hair over one shoulder and looked at him expectantly.

Lucas fluidly stood from his chair without making a sound. He didn't want to break his word to Keira again, but if anyone was going to bite her it would be him. Still, fear gripped him. What if he fell prey to blood lust? What if the unique scent drew Florence in? Would he be able to stop his maker?

Kee's kept her gaze locked with Lucas' as he closed the distance between them. His cool fingers brushed along the side of her neck, but she didn't flinch. She felt his anxiety but didn't feel any herself. She trusted Lucas and tried to tell him so with her eyes.

"Ah, sorry to interrupt," Dante cut in, a finger pressed to his earpiece. He ignored Florence's warning hiss and turned his attention to Kee. "The front door just paged. Apparently, a pack member is there saying it's an emergency."

Kee blinked and stepped away from Lucas as her alpha side kicked in. "Who? Conrad?"

He shook his head. "Conrad is the one who sent the message over the headsets. He told one of us to come get you."

"Then who is at the door? What is the emergency?" she asked quickly.

Dante relayed the information to her. "The person is Tori, and Samson is the emergency.

Ten

Kee turned to Lucas, eyes wide with fear for her dragon. "I have to go."

He nodded once, face impassive. He wanted to go with her, to make sure she was safe. Last time the weredragon was in a predicament, Keira was harmed, and he had to leave her in Riverside. Their shared anxiousness swelled in the bond, making both of them a little shaky as they parted.

"You are just going to let her go?" Florence sneered.

"I will not interfere with pack bonds, Lady Florence," he said firmly.

Kee could have kissed him for that. Instead, she turned and made her way to the front door, heels clacking against the floor. She hated not being able to at least hug Lucas goodbye, but she could hold him once his bitch of a maker was gone.

"This is real right?" Kee whispered to Dante as he kept pace next to her through the crowd. "Not just some ruse to save my ass?"

"It's real," he said. "But don't be mistaken, it did indeed save your ass back there."

Kee scowled. "I hate her."

"Me too."

They reached the front doors and she saw Conrad standing on the sidewalk, a distraught Tori next to him. The girl was wringing her hands together, teeth biting on her bottom lip. Kee left Dante at the door and approached Tori. "What happened?"

Tori flinched at Kee's stern tone. "I-it's Samson."

"What *about* Samson?" she pushed.

Her brows knitted together as her bottom lip trembled. Samson had told her he didn't want his pack to know, but after spending the last couple days with him and the pack…it didn't feel right. She saw how much they cared about him, and they deserved to know that he was risking his life for no fucking reason. Still, her heart ached at the thought of betraying him.

"Tori, please. Where is Sam?"

Swallowing her pride and the fact that Samson would hate her, she told the alpha the truth. "He's fighting."

Kee's brow furrowed. "Fighting? Fighting who? Why? What happened?"

She shook her head. "No, you don't understand. He's been fighting for a couple of weeks now." She nervously tucked her hair behind her ears. "It's an underground fighting ring for monsters. He gets fights scheduled and then makes money based on the odds and time he spends in ring."

Kee's hackles rose, her muscles going taught with disbelief. "What?" she whispered.

"T-the gym he trains at has a basement level to it! When it's fight night, it's kind of open to the public if you know the right word to get inside. They don't really try to limit who goes in because it's all potential for more money." She was blubbering, her nerves pushing her on. "I'm worried about him. He's fighting a vampire tonight who is a mean-looking mother fucker and—"

"Take me there," Kee demanded, cutting off her rambling.

Tori flinched again. "Yes, ma'am," she said, head bowing.

Kee fished her keys out of her back pocket and began walking around Byte's building to get to the back parking lot, Tori silently following behind her. When she got to the Jeep, she unlocked it and climbed into the driver's seat. She waited for Tori to get in before starting the engine. "Where?"

Tori recited the directions and grabbed the handle above the door, clinging to it for dear life as Kee peeled out of the parking lot and down the street. Cars blared their horns at them, slamming on breaks to avoid collision, but the alpha didn't stop. The basilisk should have been terrified, but all she could think of was how angry Samson was going to be with her.

He had accepted her despite the situation she put herself in and didn't judge her on it. He had opened up to her, trusted her with his story. He had let her caress and kiss him, despite not liking to be touched. She knew he didn't want his pack to know he was fighting and trusted her not to tell them.

But she did it anyways.

She took the kindness he showed her and betrayed him.

Took his trust and broke it.

"You did the right thing, Tori."

She lifted her head and looked at Kee miserably. "Did I?"

"Yes," Kee stressed. "I know Samson hasn't recovered from what he went through. We offered therapy, but he refused. He said he was handling it on his own, so I let him. I didn't think it was going to be like this. Putting himself at risk like this." She tightened her hand on the steering wheel until her knuckles were white. "I should have known better."

"He didn't want to worry you guys," she whispered. "Please don't punish him."

She whipped her head towards Tori. "What? Punish him? I would never. Am I going to yell at him? Fuck yeah, I am. We all love him too much to let him do this to himself. We will help him overcome his trauma, but this isn't the way."

"He's going to hate me," she stated, tears welling in her eyes. "We just connected and I'm going to lose him."

"No, you're not," Kee said as she turned back to the road. "I promise."

"You can't promise something like that," she argued as she furiously wiped away a tear with the sleeve of his hoodie.

"I can," she argued. "Because you can't lose a pack mate. And if he even thinks about leaving this pack, I'll whoop his ass."

Fresh tears spilled down her cheeks. "Wait, a pack mate? *Me*?"

"Yes, I'm sorry the circumstances aren't better, but you have a place in my pack should you want it." She parked the Jeep along the curb a block away from the gym, the street already packed with cars. She cut the engine and looked at Tori. "That is, if you want it, Tori. I know we all met a few days ago, but I know it's the right call. However, it's up to you."

"What if he doesn't want me in the pack after tonight?" she asked meekly.

"It's not his decision." Seeing Tori about to argue, she continued, "*I* am the alpha, not him. He may have introduced you to us, but it is *my* choice to bring you into *my* pack. Don't forget that. You have a home with us."

"Thank you." She wiped at her eyes. "Yes, I want to be a part of your family."

"Good." Kee unbuckled her seatbelt. "Now, let's go get our dragon."

Tori wiped at her face again, took a deep steadying breath, and slid out of the Jeep. They met on the sidewalk, both moving briskly towards the gym. "I know the door guy," she explained. "I pickpocket when I'm here and give him a cut." She winced at how bad that sounded. "Does that bother you?"

"Everyone has a past, Tori. I'm no one to judge, trust me," Kee explained as they approached the gym entrance.

Tori cleared her throat and lifted her chin in greeting to the tall bouncer. "Hey, how's the crowd tonight?"

"Big and the alcohol is flowing, little girl. Pockets ripe for pickin'." He glanced at Kee. "Who's this?"

"A friend. First time to the fights," Tori explained. She crossed her arms as the guy continued to look over Kee, his eyes traveling from her heels to her cleavage. "Don't ogle her tits, you jackass, let us in."

The man started to deny it, and Kee knew exactly what he was looking at. "The person who gave me these scars had their head blown off."

The guy balked and stepped aside for them, muttering something about crazy bitches as they passed by him.

"Was that true?" Tori questioned as she led the way to the stairs that would take them to the basement. "About the head being blown off?"

"Like I said, we all have a past," Kee said, following behind her newest pack mate.

The smell of blood, sweat, and booze made Tori's nose wrinkle as they began their decent into the basement. No matter how many times she had come down here, the foul scent hit her just as hard as the first time. She swept her gaze over the large crowd then to the ring. She abruptly stopped on the fifth stair from the bottom, dread filling veins. "Damn it, we're too late."

Kee's gaze cut over to the fighting ring and sure enough there was Samson. He was shirtless and barefoot, black jogging shorts the only clothing on him. He had his fists raised in front of him, his bulky opponent bouncing on the balls of his feet. The vampire swung at

Samson, but the agile weredragon swayed to the right and dodged it, swinging his own fist into the vamp's gut.

Tori panicked as Kee brushed past her down the stairs, walking straight towards the ring. Kee couldn't stop the fight, not without serious repercussions to her and Samson. She quickened her steps, trying to catch up to the alpha. *Her* alpha. A part of her warmed at the declaration.

"Kee, wait," she said, grabbing a fistful of the other woman's shirt and tugging her to a stop. "You can't stop the fight. You'll both get in trouble."

Kee snorted. "Let them try."

Her brow furrowed. "No, Kee, you don't understand. Every person here will turn and jump you guys. Abandonment of the ring is ruthlessly punished here. We can't take all of them."

Kee's resolve faltered as she glanced around the wide basement. There were a ton of people. Would they really all join in? She wanted to rip Samson from the ring, but if it meant taking on all these preternaturals, she'd just have to wait.

"Well, we'll just have to get closer to cheer him on, won't we?" Kee asked as she pushed through the crowd.

"Yes?" Tori agreed hesitantly, not liking the tone the alpha had used. She kept a hold on Kee's shirt as she followed behind her through the mass of people.

Once they got to the elevated boxing ring, Kee shoved a man out of the way when he refused to step aside for her. She reached for Tori and pulled her to stand next to her. From this angle, she had to look up to watch the fight. Despite her anger at him, she felt pride when Samson slammed his fist into the vampire's throat, making him drop the floor and hack.

Tori was a jumble of nerves as they watched Samson fight. She was worried for his safety, but also for their very new relationship.

She didn't want to lose him before she even had a chance to have him.

Kee knew the moment Samson realized she was there. Whether it was from her scent or the feel of her aura, he recognized her. His body visibly stiffened before his head whipped in her direction. When their eyes met, she could see the terror there.

Oh, yeah, he knew he fucked up.

"Kee—"

The call of her name was cut off when the vampire's fist collided dead center with Samson's face. There was a hollow pop before blood spurted from his nostrils. Kee watched helplessly as Samson staggered back, blinking rapidly. He dropped to a knee and started to shake his head. Her gaze went to the vampire as he snickered and approached Samson's delirious form.

"Get up, Samson!" she demanded as his body swayed in its kneeled position.

Tori covered her mouth with her hands, eyes wide with panic. Tears stung her eyes as Samson's opponent swung his foot hard into the side of the dragon's head. Samson fell onto his side from the force of the kick and just barely got his hands up in time to cover his face as the vampire pounced and began wailing on him.

No, no, no! This was exactly what Tori had been scared of!

Kee snarled and moved to crawl onto the elevated mat, but Tori yanked her back again. "You *can't*," she stressed in a watery tone.

Kee swore and slammed her hand down on the mat. "Get up, Sam!" she repeated, her tone sharp. "Up! Get the fuck up, damn it!"

Samson suddenly caught his opponent's foot as it sailed towards his ribs. With a hard pull forward and a sweep of his leg, he had the vampire falling forward. The weredragon used the momentum to switch their positions. Samson straddled the other male's chest once he had him on his back, pinning him down.

"Yeah, Samson!" Tori cheered as he began to punch the shit out of the vampire's face.

Kee remained silent as she watched her dragon turn the fight around, blood steadily beginning to cover his fists as the assault continued. Finally, his opponent slapped the mat twice and Samson immediately stood and backed away. A referee climbed into the ring and went to Samson, announcing him as the winner.

Tori was grinning like a fool, clapping her hands and shouting his name. She turned to Kee, ready to gush about his comeback but froze when she saw a cold mask had settled over the alpha's face. Abashed, she lowered her hands and tucked them in the front pocket of the sweatshirt. "Sorry," she mumbled. "I got caught up in it."

"I suspect that's a similar reason as to why he fights," she replied, eyes still on Samson. When he finally had the balls to turn and glance at her, her chest constricted at his broken nose and the blood covering the bottom half of his face. The left side of his face was puffy, a nasty discoloration adorning his cheekbone. She wouldn't be surprised if he had fractured it.

"Kee—" he began.

"No. Get out of the ring, get your shit, and get your ass outside. We'll be waiting by the doors." Kee then simply turned her back on him and made her way back to the stairs.

At the implied 'we', Samson's eyes shot to Tori as if he had just noticed her presence. Why did that sting? She didn't have time to dwell on that particular feeling because his expression turned to one of complete disgust. Her heart clenched as his eyes narrowed on her, the shape of his irises thinning into slits. She tried to work up the courage to call his name, to apologize, to say anything, but before she could, he turned his back to her.

She had been right to worry. He hated her now.

Eleven

Samson's nerves were wound so tight, his muscles hurt. Then again, they could just be aching from the fight. He had been concerned when he found out who his opponent was. The vampire was huge, both in height and in stature, and fast as hell. Samson had been staying out of the vamp's reach, calculating when to strike when Kee's scent had caught his attention.

He had been terrified, but not of her. No, it was what her presence meant that he feared. He knew she would be angry with him if she ever found out what he was doing. What he had been hiding from her. But how far would that anger stem? Would she hate him? Turn against him? Banish him from her pack?

He wasn't sure he could handle another family abandoning him.

Panic welled in him, filling his veins with ice even as his chest flushed and constricted with his rise in blood pressure. Kee hadn't said a single word to him after leaving him in the ring, and it only made his anxiety mount. He sat ramrod straight in the backseat of the Jeep, trying to control his breathing as they drove home.

He could feel Tori stealing glances at him, but he was too conflict-ed to even raise his eyes to her. He was so incredibly *pissed* at her. Had he been wrong to trust her? He thought after sharing their pasts that they had been on the same page. He didn't tell her why he fought, but why would that matter? He told her he didn't want his pack to know, but she went and tattled to Kee anyways.

Samson jolted out of his thoughts when the Jeep shook from a door being slammed. He saw Kee walking up the driveway and seeing her back to him, seeing her retreating, broke a small piece of him. Flashes of Flynt, Creal, and Bay walking away from him flooded his mind. Memories of being locked in a silver cage, being poked and prodded like cattle haunted him. The scars from the scales that had been gouged out of him throbbed with a phantom pain.

He didn't want this to be like Muir.

Couldn't handle being left behind again.

He threw open the car door, almost smacking Tori with it, and stumbled out of the Jeep. He ran after Kee, his breath wheezing past his lips. "Kee," he croaked, fear seizing his throat. Still, he forced out another word, "*Please.*"

Kee stopped at the plea. She turned towards him and crossed her arms across her chest. She didn't say anything, just stared at him expectantly.

His knees cracked as they hit the concrete, but he felt no physical pain. "Please," he rasped again.

"Fighting pits, Sam? *Really?*" she began. Seeing him like this hurt her though. It was so out of character for her dragon to show such emotion. Her protective side wanted to hold and comfort him, but he had to understand that what he did was not okay. "This is what you've been doing behind my back?"

Tori looked between the two of them and fisted her hands. "Kee, maybe—" She stopped talking when the alpha simply held up her hand.

"Why? Why put yourself at risk like this? After what Lucas and I went through to save you?"

He hung his head and stared unblinkingly at the ground. He couldn't go through this again.

"You died in front of me, and I brought you back. *This* is how you repay me?" Kee was keenly aware that she was being unfair, but the fear she had felt for him in that ring still lingered around her like a cold fog. She had been helpless to help him. Even now, she felt like she failed him as his alpha.

Samson braced his hands against the cold pavement as he bent forward, his body shaking with anxiety. "Don't abandon me."

Kee's weak resolve snapped at his broken whisper. She couldn't handle him suffering, especially not at her own hand. She closed the distance between them and kneeled in front of him. He flinched when she reached for him, so she kept her touch gentle as she wrapped her arms around his shoulders and pulled him to her.

"I will never abandon you, Samson," she said softly as she pet his sweat matted hair. "*Never.*"

His body stiffened for a few seconds before it simply collapsed in her embrace. He pressed his face to her shoulder, not caring about the pain it caused his broken bones.

"I'm sorry," he breathed.

She let out a soft, defeated sigh. "At least tell me why."

He squeezed his eyes shut. "It helps with the rage," he said quietly. "It makes everything bearable. I'm not over what happened to me. I'm still angry, Kee. It haunts my dreams, my thoughts. I can't escape it."

"Except when you fight," she corrected.

He nodded once. "I can't explain it."

Kee smoothed her hand along his hair and down his back. "I understand, Sam. Believe me, I do. When I woke up from my attack, I craved violence. I wanted blood and death. Killing my attackers and the one who planned it was my sole mission. I didn't care much about anything else.

"Once they were all dead, that was it. I got my vengeance and felt better. Do I still have some anger issues? Yes. Do I occasionally get nightmares from it? Yes. But I had an endgame, Samson. What's yours? When is your stopping point? What will it take?"

His hands balled into fists. "I don't know."

"Fighting is a temporary distraction," she reminded him. "You have to find something else to help you."

"My mom," Tori began timidly. "She's a therapist in Huntington Beach. She specializes in trauma and a lot of her patients are preternatural. I could ask her to see you."

Samson lifted his head from Kee and looked over his shoulder at her. Despite the anger he felt for her turning against him, he knew the implications of her offer. She would risk seeing her obsessive mother for him.

The sentiment helped balm the burning resentment.

When he didn't respond to her, Kee pinched his ear. "You should thank Tori," she said.

Samson sat up and returned his attention to Kee. "I don't want to see a therapist."

"You don't have to. No one will force you to do anything you don't want to, Sam. I will help you get through this, but you have to let me," she explained. "But that's not what I'm referring to. You should thank her for caring about you." At his puzzled look, she scoffed. "She risked upsetting you to come to me about endangering yourself."

He glanced over at Tori again. "Yeah?"

The basilisk swallowed as she met his gaze. "Yeah."

"She's also your new pack member, so you better get rid of any hard feelings." Kee stood and dusted off her slacks. She put her hands on her hips as Samson climbed to his feet as well. "No more fighting?"

He nodded once. "No more."

"Thank you," she said. "I'll see you guys inside after you patch things up." She gave Tori a wink before turning and heading to the front door. She lifted a brow at the remaining pack members, Conrad included, spying from the slim window adjacent to the door. With a smile, she rolled her eyes and met them inside.

Samson took a deep breath and turned to face Tori. He stepped towards her, flexing his fingers at his sides. When she stiffened and started to back away, he grabbed her.

She let out a startled yell and began to struggle until she realized he was hugging her. "S-Samson," she whispered. Her hands lifted and tentatively rested on his back, feeling his strong muscles through the thin tank top. When he squeezed her reassuringly, her bottom lip trembled. "I'm sorry. I was just worried about you."

Samson pulled back slightly, but her hands fisted in his shirt, keeping him close. "Tori."

"I know we just met, and this may sound corny as fuck, but I feel like I've known you longer. I know it's stupid. That *I'm* stupid. But I can't help that I feel this way. My mom would say something along the lines that we are kindred souls, or have met in a previous life, and I'm not sure I believe that shit, but something has to explain why—"

He pressed his lips to hers, sealing off her rambling.

Tori let out a shaky breath when their lips parted. "You're rude," she mumbled. "I was talking."

"You spout nonsense when you're nervous," he stated as he framed her face with his hands. "And when you're scared. I don't want you to be afraid of me."

She looked up at him, staring into his nearly black eyes. Even with his nose currently crooked and bloodied, he was handsome. "I'm not scared of you," she clarified. "I was scared of what I did, of what you think about me now."

The dragon let out a soft sigh. "I'm not going to lie, I was pissed. I told you about how I was betrayed, what it did to me, but then you went and did it." When her eyes misted over, he bent to put his forehead against hers. "The difference is that you didn't do it out of spite."

She nodded. "I didn't," she agreed. "And I knew it would break your trust. That I would ruin whatever it is that we were starting"

"You didn't ruin anything, Tori. You did this genuinely out of concern for my well-being, and I didn't see it that way until Kee pointed it out." He tucked a piece of her hair behind her ear before cupping the back of her head. "I need you to understand that it's not something I'm used to. I'll try to be better but be patient with me."

Tori gripped his shirt tighter and gave it a tug. "You idiot," she hissed without venom. "I should be the one to say that! I'm fucked up, Sam. Truly messed up in the head because of how I grew up."

He fisted her hair and gently tugged her head back so he could place a kiss to the hollow of her throat. "Then we'll be fucked up together."

She shook out of his grip and put her hands on his shoulders, using them as leverage to jump up and wrap her legs around his waist. Samson cupped her ass, easily supporting her weight as her mouth met his. She let out a keening whimper in her throat as their tongues tangled.

Samson squeezed her ass and carried her towards the front door. He looked over her shoulder as they neared the door and saw his four pack mates grinning at him through the window. He cleared his throat and set her down, chuckling at her disappointed huff. "We have an audience."

Tori's brow furrowed as she whirled around to see the other members of the pack. They shot her innocent looks before disappearing. With cheeks burning, she crossed her arms over her chest. "Nosy, much?"

He laughed again. "Welcome to the pack." When she tried to hide a shy smile, he held his hand out to her. "Come on, since Conrad is home, I need him to set my nose."

She slid her hand into his, smile widening as he led her into the pack house.

Twelve

Kee sat on the couch, watching her pack with a content smile on her face. Lucy and Tori were chatting in the kitchen as they got out snacks and glassware. Samson was teaching Mia how to defend herself, and Conrad was wrestling with a bottle of champagne. When Conrad finally popped the cork out, Kee laughed as Mia squeaked in surprise at the sound and jerked, kicking Samson in the groin.

"And we're done for the night," Samson wheezed through the pain in his balls. "Back to watching movies."

"Sorry, Sammy!" Mia said. "I didn't mean to!"

"I know, kid," he replied, patting her head once he could stand straight again. He shot Kee a look when she tried to muffle another laugh. "I swear she hit me harder than the guys I used to fight."

"Looks like you've met your match. And to think she was here at home the entire time," she laughed.

He laughed too, but she wasn't stupid. She knew he wanted to go back to the ring. Could see it when he rolled his shoulders and absent mindedly cracked his knuckles. Who was she to chastise him for fighting when she went on a killing spree when she was hurting? She felt like a hypocrite, but she was his alpha and she worried about him.

Still, she was happy that he was sticking to his word to not go back.

Despite the happiness she felt, there was still that twinge of disappointment. Lucas, Gio, and Dante were at the impromptu New Year's party that Florence insisted on, and Kee felt their absence like a physical ache. She missed all of them.

"Here."

Kee tore from her thoughts to see a wine glass of champagne and orange juice hovering before her. "Mimosas at night in a wine glass? Fancy."

Tori grinned as she sat down next to her alpha, Lucy sitting down on the other side. "Fancy as fuck."

Lucy snickered. "We're classy bitches."

"So classy." Kee laughed and sipped her drink before looking at Tori. "How are you liking pack life?"

A small, shy smile curved up Tori's lips. "Well, I only actually joined the pack yesterday."

Kee smiled. "Yeah, but I met you a week ago. I think I knew then that you were going to be mine."

"You mean *mine*," Samson clarified as he squeezed in next to Tori on the couch and stole her glass to take a swig of her mimosa.

Kee grinned. "That too."

Tori snatched her drink back and punched Samson square in the chest. "Get your own, dick!"

He rubbed his chest, a smirk tilting up the corner of his lips at his feisty snake. "But then it wouldn't taste as good."

Tori's cheeks turned pink as she stared down at her drink. "Dick," she repeated lamely and swatted his hand away when he pet her hair.

"Gods, you two are so cute!" Lucy gushed as she watched the new couple. She then zeroed in on Conrad when he came into the living room with a beer in one hand and sparkling apple cider in the other. "Ah, talk about *cute*," she murmured.

"I heard that," Conrad said as he handed Mia the apple cider. He sat down on the floor next his daughter, his back against the couch where Lucy's legs were. He kissed the top of Mia's head before turning and pressing a kiss to Lucy's knee. "My girls are the cute ones."

Kee smiled, but her hold tightened on the glass. She missed Lucas. Seeing her pack with their couples made Lucas' absence that much more painful. She only hoped she wouldn't have to deal with it for too much longer.

She lifted her phone from her lap with the intention of texting her vampire but stilled when she saw she had a missed call from a number she didn't recognize. When she went to tap the number to call it back, the phone began to vibrate with an incoming call. She smiled when she saw her extended cousin's name.

"Hey Gabriel!" she said as she answered the call. "Happy New Year."

"*Kee?*" came her cousin's response.

"Yes, it's me," she laughed. "How's Nana's? What did she cook for din—"

"*Kee,*" Gabriel cut her off.

Kee's hackles rose at the wobble in his voice. She sat up, her back going perfectly straight with tension. "What is it? What happened?"

He sobbed into the phone. "*It's Nana.*"

Ice crept into her veins. "What about Nana?" Someone took the glass from her hand, but she was too honed on the call to pay attention to who did it. She slowly stood from the couch, her muscles tight with apprehension. "Gabriel, gods damn it, what happened? Where is Nana?"

"*I'm so sorry,*" he cried

When he finally got out his explanation, said those horrible words in her ear, her hand dropped to her side, phone tumbling to the carpet.

Conrad and Samson shot to their feet.

Conrad went to Kee as Samson picked up the phone. "What is it? What happened?" Conrad asked her. When she just continued to stare unblinkingly ahead, he put his hand on her shoulder. "Kee?"

"Who's Nana?" Tori questioned.

"Her great-grandma," Lucy explained softly, a worried frown pulling down her lips. "She raised Kee."

Conrad frowned when she didn't respond. "What happened to Nana?"

Kee finally blinked and slowly looked at her beta. "She's dead."

"What? What do you mean?" Conrad squeezed her shoulder, brow furrowing as Kee's face remained blank. "Kee?" he called, but she had gone quiet again.

"Gabriel says he and Christopher went over to spend New Year's Eve with her," Samson said, relaying the information to his pack as Gabriel told him. "When they got there, she didn't answer the door. Gabriel thought she had fallen asleep, but Christopher said he smelled blood. He broke down the door and they found her in the kitchen." His eyes darted to Kee, and he softened his tone. "There was blood everywhere, but not all of it was hers. She put up one hell of a fight."

Conrad paled and quickly looked at Kee again. "Oh gods, Kee. I-I'm so sorry." When she continued to just stare off into space, he pulled her into a hug. What could he possibly say to her? How did he fix this?

Mia approached her dad and alpha, a whine in her throat at the tense energy. "Auntie Kee, I'm sorry about Nana." She gently grabbed Kee's hand in her small one and rubbed her cheek against it.

Kee blinked again and pulled away from Conrad's hold. Her brain felt fuzzy, a dull buzzing blocking out any thoughts that attempted to form. She robotically looked down at her smallest pack mate when she heard her sniffling. She squeezed Mia's hand back before freeing her hand so she could pet the young wolf's hair.

Lucy went to Conrad, latching onto his arm as they stared at their friend in concern. "Kee? Do you want to talk about it?" she asked softly.

Kee glanced at the couple but quickly looked away at the worry there. Her gaze fell on Samson and Tori, but again she found something too similar to pity on their face. She didn't want to see their concern. Why would they worry about her? She didn't need it. It wouldn't change what had happened. It wouldn't bring back—*fuck!*

She stumbled back from Mia as the roaring in her ears grew, blocking out any other sound around her. She squeezed her eyes shut, but that had been a mistake. As soon as her lids dropped, her mind tormented her with graphic images. Samson had told her what Gabriel discovered, and her mind decided to paint a crude picture.

She could see blood splattered along the white cabinets of Nana's kitchen, smears of it on the brown granite countertops. Were the smears from Nana's hands? Did she try to use the counters as leverage to haul herself up? No, she didn't. Because she was lying on the wood floor in a puddle of her own blood. Nana was—

Kee choked on a sob, her throat constricting with the sudden wave of grief that pulled her under. Her lungs heaved as they tried to pull in more air, the grief turning to anxiety as her lungs worked overtime. She thought she heard her pack members calling her name, but the rushing in her ears and the heavy breathing made it hard to tell.

Nana was dead.

Her stomach dropped as her brain repeated the ugly three words over and over again. No, it couldn't be true. The world couldn't be that cruel, could it? To take away her great-grandmother? To take away her only parental figure? To take away the only other person she knew who was like her?

It wasn't fair.

It wasn't fair!

Her chest felt like it splintered, her heart gushing and hemorrhaging within. Pain oozed from the internal wound and drowned her already struggling lungs. Her knees buckled, but strong arms wrapped around her before she could fall.

"I have you, Keira," Lucas murmured into her hair as he easily supported her weight. "I have you."

She sank into the security only his comfort gave and let the remaining part of her break. She clung to him as she sobbed, tears staining his black dress shirt. "Nana—" she cried. "She's gone."

He cupped the back of her neck, holding her tightly to him as her wails pinched at his heart. "I am sorry, my sweet. I know how important she was to you."

"It's not fair," she wheezed.

"No, it is not. Death rarely is." He tightened his hold on her neck when she sucked in a sharp breath. He was reminded of when she woke up after her attack, and when she came back from killing Cain's friend. "You need to breathe, Keira," he cooed, trying to calm and soothe her as she gasped. "Take deep breaths."

Conrad carefully approached them and put his hand on Kee's left shoulder. "You're not alone, Kee. We're here for you." He gave Lucy a small smile when she and Mia came over. Lucy pressed her cheek to the side of Kee's shoulder Conrad was holding while Mia nuzzled her alpha's side.

Lucas nodded at them as she began to suck in and hold her breaths before slowly, shakily letting them out. "There you go. Deep breaths," he praised, thumb rubbing circles into the side of her neck. "Be an alpha and draw strength from your pack. Take it from our bond, my queen."

Samson grabbed Kee's other shoulder. "You know Nana would be chiding you for this," he said gently. He nodded at Tori when she tentatively touched Kee's back. "You know, she taught me to mind my manners. Gods help me if I ever forget them again."

Mia closed her eyes as she rubbed her cheek against Kee's side. "Like when you tried to take one of Santa's cookies, Sammy?"

"It was *one* cookie," he stressed. "I didn't know they were all for him. I'll forever fear the wrath of her wooden spoon because of that."

"I'll never drop any sort of cake on any carpet," Lucy added in a watery voice.

"I thought Christopher was going to shit his pants when she turned on him," Conrad snickered.

Lucas stroked Keira's hair. "I felt real fear when I asked her for your hand in marriage. She was so stoic. She just looked at me with a dismissive blankness when I asked, but it felt as if minutes passed before she answered. Even when she finally did agree, she merely told me that she would castrate and then stake me if I hurt you. Somehow, I knew she was not exaggerating."

Kee choked on a laugh; she couldn't help it. It was weak and watery, but it was still a laugh. "I love you guys," she murmured into Lucas' shoulder. "All of you. Thank you."

Conrad squeezed her shoulder again before each of the pack members stepped back. "That's what we're here for, Kee. We're your pack, your family. We won't let you fall."

"And if you do, we'll happily fall with you before picking you back up," Tori said softly before looking at her pack mates for help. "That's what a pack does, right?"

Samson pressed a quick kiss to Tori's lips when she looked for reassurance. "It is," he agreed. "Although I'm also new to this family thing so I could be wrong."

Lucy hummed. "Honestly this is my first pack, too. Is this something that they do? If not, then ours will be different."

"*Continue* to be different, you mean. We fit together, but not like other packs," Conrad mused.

Kee smiled a little. "Pack of misfits."

Tori grinned. "The LA Pack of Misfits. I like it."

Thirteen

Lucas released a somewhat defeated sigh as he walked into Byte. Giovanni and Dante seemed to have handled the party, and hopefully Florence, in his absence. It had been risky, leaving Florence at the club unattended, but Keira mattered more to him.

When he felt Keira's panic and desperation through the bond, it was so sudden and overbearing that it had made his knees buckle. He had looked at his two vampires, hoping he conveyed everything he needed in that look, and disappeared from the club.

He didn't regret his decision. Especially not when he barged into the alpha house and saw her crumbling under her grief. He wrapped her up in his arms and immediately she cried, making his heart hurt for her. Her pain hurt him, and not just because of the bond they shared.

After her pack had consoled her, she built up a tentative dam to keep her emotions in long enough to ask Conrad to go to the scene of the crime in her stead. She wanted to go, but they all knew she was in no state to do so.

Once Conrad set off with Samson in tow, Lucas took her to her room. He wasn't fooled. He had observed his shapeshifter this past month with her pack, and he knew when she was putting on a mask of strength for them. Just from the bond alone he knew she wasn't done letting out that initial grief.

Sure enough, when he laid down with her, she buried her face in his chest and sobbed again. It was selfishly pleasing to him that she let down all her walls with him. He coveted and cherished the fact that she let herself be bare and transparent with him when the world only ever saw what she wanted them to.

"What am I supposed to do?" she asked.

"Remember her and cherish the times you had. The pain will always be there, but the sting of it will not always be so sharp," he told her.

She didn't say much afterwards, and he would not force her to. When she wanted to talk about Nanette, she would. But for now, he understood that the wound was still raw and bleeding. So, he did what he could. He held her until the tears dried up, until the time came when he had to head back to Byte. Normally he would have stayed overnight with her, but with Florence scheming, he wouldn't dare.

"I am sorry I cannot be here with you," he said softly, brushing the hair from her face as she drifted in and out of a fitful sleep.

"I hate her for taking you away when I need you," she mumbled.

His stomach twisted with guilt. "I know." He pressed a long, lingering kiss to her temple. "Forgive me."

"I don't blame you. I know you're enduring it for us; it just really sucks. Especially right now." She sighed, eyes fluttering open to look at him. She cupped his cheek in her palm and gave him a weak smile. "I love you, Lucas."

He turned his face into her palm and kissed it. "I love you, too."

And so it was with a heavy heart that he had to leave her. He would not put a bigger target on Keira's back by staying the night with her, no matter how much it pained him to leave her in such a state. No matter how much he felt like he was failing her.

Lucas clenched his hands into fists as a wave of resentment hit him, and not for the first time. This wasn't from Keira's side, no. This was him. It stemmed from the fact that he had to be away from Keira when she needed him most. He already hated his maker for taking away two women before, but this was worse. What he had felt for them was but a fraction for what he felt for Keira, and this forced distance was weighing on them both.

Florence needed to go.

He flung open his bedroom door with more force than necessary and wasn't at all surprised to see Dante and Giovanni waiting for him. They each looked at him expectantly, their bodies tense and unnaturally still as they waited for the bad news.

"It's bad," he confirmed, loosening his tie with jerky movements. "Keira's great-grandmother was killed."

Giovanni sat down on the bed with a sad sigh. "Oh no. How is she?"

Lucas clenched his teeth and threw his tie at the floor. "Not well," he bit out. "Damn it! I should be there with her!"

Dante nodded in agreement. "Florence needs to be dealt with. Have we discovered what she wants?" he asked calmly, trying to soothe the rising anger in his friend.

Lucas shook his head, jaw clenching again. "Not yet. I cannot tell what she has planned, but every part of me is sure that it has something to do with Keira."

Giovanni grimaced, crossing his arms over his chest. "Do you think she had something to do with the murder? I mean, she showed up late as hell tonight to the party *she* demanded we have. I know she has a flare for the dramatic, but what if she was killing Nanette?"

Lucas' spine straightened as he stiffened, realization dawning on him. "She had to. It is too much of a coincidence." How would he break it to Keira? She would want blood, and he wasn't sure he could stop her even if he wanted to.

Dante frowned. "But why? Why go after Kee's great-grandmother instead of her?"

"Because of me," Lucas replied bitterly. "I think she knows that I will defend Keira. She is not stupid; she knows Keira is important to me. She suspects our relationship is more than what we let on."

"Why would she suspect it at all then?" Dante asked, brows furrowing. "You both have acted marvelously uninterested in the other."

Gio perked up. "Didn't you say she immediately started to ask about you and Kee when she showed up at Christmas?"

Lucas nodded. "Yes, but that could simply be because of the rumors. I killed a reigning lord and a vampire who used to be one. There was no way the other lords wouldn't speak of it. Especially after I was contacted by the Lord of California regarding the kills."

Gio paled. "I didn't know that," he murmured. "What did Abraham say? Why didn't you tell us?"

Lucas ran a hand through his hair as he sighed. "I did not wish to worry you two. After explaining the situations and why I retaliated, he agreed that I was in the right. However, he ended our conversation telling me to tread carefully from here on out."

"You're on his radar." Dante shook his head. "That's not a good thing, Lucas."

"I know," Lucas agreed. "But that could be why Keira is, in turn, on Florence's radar. Unless someone else told her of Keira, but who?"

Gio sputtered a curse in Italian before suddenly standing from the bed, eyes wide. "Aubrey."

"What?" Dante asked is disbelief. "You think that dunce is behind this?"

Gio gestured wildly with his hands. "No, listen," he began. "When Florence asked me to present her to her new granddaughter, I did.

When I introduced them, there seemed to be an air for familiarity about them. I thought perhaps it was just because they had already heard about the other, but what if it wasn't? What if they met before?"

Dante continued with the image Gio was painting. "Didn't you say Florence made a show about how you never told Aubrey about your maker? What if they were both lying?"

The anger that had been simmering in Lucas' veins went to a full boil. He could practically feel the fire pulsing in his body. "They did become suspiciously close during the night. When has Aubrey ever freely offered to help someone?" He felt his fingertips heat, his golden fire begging to be released. "That *wretch*."

Dante traced his goatee as he pondered the information. "But how would Aubrey know to contact Florence? And why?" he scoffed. "I mean, despite the fact that she hates being a vampire?"

"Because I chose Keira over her," Lucas growled, irises bleeding red as it all clicked into place. "I do not know how she knew to do so, but it doesn't matter. I will kill her for this."

Gio quickly put his hands on his maker's shoulders, stopping him. "You *can't*," he stressed. "You just told us that the Lord of California is watching you. What do you think killing your blood daughter will do? You can't risk it."

Lucas' mouth tightened at the truth of Giovanni's words. Still, he craved blood and ash for this betrayal. "She cannot go unpunished. She brought Florence here to punish me and put Keira's life in danger. It is unacceptable!" he sneered the last part with a surge of his power, making Giovanni and Dante both duck their heads. He tried to swallow down his rage, not wanting to affect them any further. "Apologies."

Dante shook his head. "There is nothing to apologize for. We're angry with you, Lucas. We don't want any harm to come to Kee either. Most of the coven feels the same way."

Lucas rubbed the bridge of his nose as his eyes shifted back to green. "Aubrey has to be dealt with."

"Oh? And what did my precious granddaughter do?" Florence cooed.

The three males snapped their heads to the door, taking in the red head that leaned against it. The fact that none of them heard or felt her approach was alarming. How long had she been eavesdropping?

Lucas took in the smug, knowing smile on her face and felt his anger flare again. He couldn't help it, his aura pulsed out in response to his resentment. "You know *exactly* what she did." He felt Giovanni and Dante tense behind him, but there was no stopping his rage now.

Florence's smile only grew as she gracefully pushed off the door and stalked towards him with feline grace. "My little Apollo," she tutted as she stood in front of him, hands pressed to his chest. "Did you think I would not know?" She splayed her fingers out before curling them in, sharp nails tearing through the fabric of his shirt and biting into his skin. "Did you think I would let another woman have you?"

He didn't flinch as the nails dug deeper into his flesh. "I am *not* yours," he growled, the anger in him destroying his filter and patience. "It has been centuries since I laid with you, even longer since I harbored anything remotely resembling soft feelings."

Her eyes turned glacial, an ugly snarl marring her face. Before he could react, she slapped him hard across the face, drawing blood. "You dare speak to me that way?" she screeched, nostrils flaring. "You *dare*?!"

Giovanni and Dante made to move, ready to defend their lord and friend, but Lucas held up his hand to stop them. When he waved it at them, they both reluctantly stepped back, heeding his command to stay away.

Lucas calmly lifted his hand to touch the four gouges along his cheek. He looked down at the blood coating his fingers and rubbed them as if bored. "Tell me, Lady Florence, did you kill my wolf's kin?"

She straightened, smoothing her hands down her loose black dress before looking at him with a coy, knowing smile. "You mean, did I kill your *shapeshifter's* kin?" When her blood son went still, she laughed. "I did. I killed the older shapeshifter and drank as much of her as my stomach could muster." She sighed with disappointment. "You think I would have known to pace myself after draining so many of them two hundred years ago. But I will say that the bitch did a number on me in the process, so I got to drink more than the last one all those years ago. It takes a little extra to heal wounds, you know."

Lucas couldn't breathe. As the undead, he didn't need to, but when he reflexively went to do so, he found he couldn't. Of course, his maker had been a part of the genocide of shapeshifters. He should have guessed it, especially since she reveled in carnage, but during that time he had tried to create as much physical distance between them as possible. He never cared to hear what she was up to because he didn't want to draw her attention to him in any way.

But now that he knew for certain that Florence had helped wipe out Keira's ancestors, her heritage, it infuriated him. His own maker had made it so that Keira had to spend her whole life hiding what she was in fear of monsters like Florence hunting her down. But Florence did not hunt them down to kill them. She hunted them to drain them.

Just like she did Nanette.

As if reading his thoughts, Florence's smile widened. She framed his face in her hands, making sure one slid through the blood dripping down his cheek. "Each shapeshifter I drank from, I told myself I would keep them alive so I could have an unlimited well to drink from. The other preternaturals refused to let any of them live, however. They saw the spike of power the shapeshifter blood gave us. It was a rather large reason the others agreed to end the shapeshifters.

"Oh, but I *tried* to keep them, my little Apollo. Each shapeshifter I drained, I tried to stop. I told myself that I could have unlimited power if I kept just *one* alive. But it's so addicting." She shuddered as a violent wave of need crashed through her. She then looked at him with a cruel smirk. "Then again, you know that, do you not? You have tasted your shapeshifter. I tasted it in your blood that first night. It was a great surprise to have that slumbering hunger jolt awake within me."

Lucas bared his teeth at her, irises bleeding to red again. A deadly combination of panic and fury thrumming through him. "What do you want?" But he already knew.

She giggled and continued as if she hadn't heard him. "Oh, and do not get me wrong. You initially had me fooled, darling. About her being a wolf that is. I already knew you were fucking her." Her fingers dug into the cuts on his face as her own anger wiped away any humor in her expression. "Of course, I had to discipline you. However, her being mated to the LA alpha threw a wrench in my plans. Naturally I planned on killing her just as I did your other two. I even bought *very* expensive silk sheets for you! But alas, I could not risk a fight with the alpha." She clicked her tongue in a displeased manner, eyes rolling. "Politics, you understand."

Lucas snarled as she pressed her nails deeper into his cut once again, but he didn't feel the physical pain. All he could feel was the burning heat in his veins, but he wasn't sure if it was his rage or his flame. Either way, both responded to the image of Keira's dead body joining the ones of Janrie and Bridgette.

"I understand nothing," he seethed, his bloodied fingers pressed hard together at his sides, ready to ignite. "*What* do you want?"

A smile spread her painted lips again, her fangs gleaming. "I am getting to that, my darling." She ran her bloodied fingertips over his lips. "You see, Aubrey and her lover contacted me about your little whore. When I learned that I could not kill her, I wanted to know everything about her instead. How could I destroy your harlot without directly landing a finger on her? Any pack member was too risky, again because of the LA alpha, but what about her kin?

"You see, I had already been in Los Angeles, planning what to do, before your Christmas party. I am so glad that I did too because lo and behold we discovered her kin in Riverside. Naturally I wanted to be the one to dole out the punishment. How else would I feel better about your treachery?

"Anyways, imagine my surprise when I spilled that woman's blood and found out she was a *shapeshifter*! The scent is unmistakable, even after two centuries. Plus, I was just reminded of it when I tasted the lingering traces of it in your blood." She tilted her head innocently. "It was very easy to conclude that your pet is also a shapeshifter."

Lucas' rage swelled again, his body all but shaking from it. He felt a pull on the bond from Keira's end, a flare of worry sparking along it.

Shit. He had forgotten to shield his emotions from her as Florence told her horrendous tale. Of course, she would feel the fury that had been building in him. He could only imagine what she was thinking as he abruptly tried to throw up a wall between them. He did not want her to feel anything else that may come of this night. It would not end well.

"And so that brings us to your question," she purred. "It is quite simple, my little Apollo. I want you in my bed and your pet collared. I want us to drink from her together, revel in the power then make her watch as you fuck me. Maybe with you I can control myself long enough to not drain her in one go. We could share her for decades, my love. We will be unstoppable together."

Lucas had heard enough; his anger had passed its limit. The mere image she painted was enough make his stomach roil and his rational flee. He shot out his hand to grab her throat, squeezing it hard enough that bones cracked. He snapped the fingers on his other hand, his golden flame eagerly answering his call.

"No," he seethed, fangs elongating. "You cannot have me, and you especially cannot have her. I would rather die than let you sink your fangs into her."

She managed a broken laugh from her damaged windpipe. "Fool."

Then, faster than he could comprehend, she stabbed something into his chest. Abruptly his flame flickered out, the blood in his veins coming almost to a complete halt. He looked down and saw a wooden stake sticking out of his chest right above his heart.

Where the fuck had this thing come from? How did he miss it? And gods, was this thing blessed?

She knocked his hand away from her throat, the bones already healed. "Did you miss the part in my story where I said I drained a shapeshifter tonight?" she asked, batting her lashes up at him. She twisted the stake in his chest, pleased when blood spurted from his mouth. "I am brimming with power." She rose on her tiptoes and licked at a trickle of blood running from the corner of his mouth. "I am *untouchable*," she breathed against his lips before kissing him.

Lucas crumbled to his knees when she released him, and that infuriated him more. The stake ground everything in him to a halt, making him almost as still as a corpse. This would not kill him, no. She wouldn't be so foolish as to kill her prize, but it made it impossible to fight back. How could he have underestimated her so much? Better question, how could he have forgotten the power of shapeshifter blood?

"Run," he managed to growl out.

The two vampires who were rooted to the spot in terror jumped into action. They split up, each heading towards the door from either side of Florence. One of them had to escape. One of them had to protect the coven.

One of them had to tell Kee.

Florence sighed at the inconvenience and turned away from Lucas. With her enhanced speed, she lurched forward and grabbed both of them by the back of their shirts. Putting all her strength into it, she yanked them towards each other. They crashed hard together, skulls cracking against skulls followed by a pop of a shoulder being dislocated.

Gio's shoulder screamed with pain, but he managed to stay standing. Dante had fallen to the floor, but Gio could see the determined look in his eyes. When their eyes met, a silent understanding crossed between them. Dante was the best bet to get help.

As dazed as he was from his head injury, Gio turned to Florence. "Lady," he cried, forcing a wobble to his voice. He would use her twisted version of love for him against her. "I'm so sorry. Please."

Florence held her arms out to her trembling grandson, cooing as he stepped into her embrace. "Oh, my Giovanni," she purred, stroking his hair back from his face. She looked down into his glazed eyes and clicked her tongue. "You should not have made me do that. I do not wish to harm the blood of my blood." She cradled his face in her hands and forced him to bend his head so she could flick her tongue over the blood dripping down over his brow. As she did, her eyes caught the other vampire making a break for the door. With a sneer, she moved to push Giovanni off her, but his arms suddenly cinched around her waist, holding her tightly in place.

Snarling, she brought her elbows down hard on Giovanni's shoulders, snapping both his collar bones from the force. After he collapsed at her feet, she looked up, but her blood son's head of security was gone.

She grabbed the bottom of Giovanni's jaw and forced his head up so they were making eye contact. "What did you think to accomplish besides angering me, Giovanni?" She jerked his head towards the clock on the wall. "It is already dawn and thus he has nowhere to go." She roughly released him, and he fell back to the floor, groaning as his broken bones rattled.

Lucas met his blood son's painful gaze and managed a brief nod of approval. She did not need to know that the clock was ten minutes ahead. Dante could get far enough away in that time to at least hide from the sun for the day. It was now up to his friend to get help.

He could only hope that help wasn't Keira.

Fourteen

Kee woke up from the dark void of sleep the next morning, her body feeling heavy. She stared up at the ceiling with swollen eyes, blinking groggily at it. Her mind was fuzzy, almost numb. A part of her hoped it would stay that way, but then yesterday caught up with her.

When her throat tightened, she rolled over and buried her face in Lucas' pillow. She unleashed a muffled cry of anguish as thoughts of Nana filled her head. Her brusque, blunt, but loving great-grandma was dead. Her only parent, gone. The only other shapeshifter she knew of wiped out. Murdered brutally in her own home.

She barely heard the bedroom door click shut, the sound almost drowned out over a sob, and pressed her face harder into the pillow. She tried to stop the tears as the mattress dipped next to her, a warm hand cupping the back of her head.

"I'm here," Conrad said softly, stroking her hair.

Without looking, Kee reached out a trembling hand to him. When his hand found hers, she squeezed it tightly, trying to siphon some of her beta's strength for herself.

He waited until her shoulders stopped shaking to speak again. "I know words are useless, but I really am sorry, Kee. We loved Nana like our own."

She forced herself to sit up next to him, wiping at her eyes and nose. "She loved you guys too," she said, sniffling. With a heavy sigh, she leaned against him, setting her head on his shoulder. "I don't know what to do, Con."

He rested his head against hers. "You take it one step at a time. Just don't forget that your pack is with you each step, okay?"

Kee closed her eyes as tears stung them again. "Thank you."

"You don't have to thank me," he replied, rubbing his cheek on her hair.

After an agonizing moment, she forced herself to ask her next question. "How was it?"

Conrad wasn't going to tell her about Nana's house until she asked. "I had Samson go with me. When we got there, the Riverside pack had it blocked off. They tried to make us leave, but we were prepared to fight. Luckily, Christopher remembered me and vouched for us."

"Surprising," she murmured. "Since he doesn't like me much."

"I think he knows Nana would smite him from the grave for denying you anything," he chuckled softly. "We met Dan, the Riverside alpha, and he let us view the scene. Samson and I took pictures and tried to take in all the scents before they became too stale."

Kee pursed her lips together. "Anyone suspicious?"

He shook his head. "There was definitely a new scent, but it wasn't one we knew."

Her hands balled into fists. "I should have gone with you. That way I can help hunt down the fucker who did this to Nan and rip them apart."

"You were grieving, Kee. You wouldn't have been able to think straight, let alone process anything. You had me handle it, and I did."

She nodded. "So, what did this Dan have to say?"

"He said they were going to transport Nana's body to the mortuary that works with preternaturals. Since it's a murder investigation, he said they're going to hold off on cremating her. Apparently, he also has Nana's will to give you."

She scrunched up her face. "Why the fuck does he have it?"

He gave another short laugh. "Samson asked him literally the exact same question."

"I knew I loved Sam for a reason," she commented with a weak smile.

"Dan said that Nana entrusted him with it since she was a lone wolf in his territory. If anything happened to her, it automatically falls under his rule as alpha." He shrugged. "He said he was her mate's beta when he was still alive and that his respect and loyalty to her never ended, even when she refused to stay as part of his pack."

"I guess that makes sense," Kee murmured. "So, what now?"

"I gave him your phone number and told him that any decisions about Nana needs to go through you. He looked incredulous when I said you were my alpha, but Samson warned him that it wasn't the time to pick a fight." Conrad smirked. "I don't think I've seen an alpha look so affronted before."

That got another soft laugh out of Kee. Gods she loved her pack. "What did he say?"

"Nothing in response to that. But he did say that he would text you with details and before any decisions are made going forward."

"That's good to know, I guess," Kee mumbled.

When her phone began to ring, Conrad reached for it and handed it to her. She straightened up with another sigh and looked down at her screen. "Sorry Cain," she said as she denied the call. She assumed he probably felt her turmoil through the mating mark, but she didn't want to verbally explain herself. She didn't think she could without crying.

Looking through her notifications, she frowned at all the messages waiting for her. Cain had tried to call her several times last night and this morning, his texts asking what happened and if she was okay. She sent him a text informing him that Nana died before checking her other messages. She had a few from Gabriel, one from Zach wishing her a Happy New Year, and one from an unknown number.

She clicked on Gabriel's messages and pressed her lips hard together as she read them.

Hey Kee. Again, I'm so sorry. Please call when you can.

Grandpa wants to talk to you about the funeral plans. Nana also has a will he wants to go through.

Kee's hand clenched around her phone as her anger spiked. "Gods, what a fucking douche! She *just* fucking died!"

Huffing, she checked the unknown number.

Hello Keira, I'm Dan, the alpha of the Riverside pack. We had the mortuary pick up Nanette, but in respect to her, I want to wait for you before making any decisions about cremating. Do you want to be there today? Also, what would you like us to do about her house? We have already examined the scene and are working to find out who did this.

Kee rubbed hard at her face. Naturally, she knew these were things she would have to eventually deal with, but not now. Not so soon after.

Conrad read the messages over her shoulder and sneered. "I hoped he would have given you at least a day to mourn."

"Guess not," she grumbled.

Yes, I want to be there. I don't know about the house yet. She read her lame message and sighed as she sent it. "Fuck, I don't know what to do."

He squeezed her shoulder. "We support any decision you make, Kee."

She nodded mutely as her phone vibrated with an incoming response.

We will clean it, if you want. She put me in charge of her will, which we can worry about when you're ready, but it includes her final wishes. She specifies where she wants to be scattered.

Kee closed her eyes against the sudden sting of tears. Conrad rubbed her back, silently supporting her as he aways had. "Will you go with me? To see her?" she whispered.

"Of course," he answered without hesitation. "Lucas will understand if I'm late."

Lucas.

Her grief for Nana had momentarily eclipsed the stress for her vampire. The pure blinding fury she felt from him last night terrified her. Even when the two of them had fought, she never experienced a rage like that from him. Of course, as soon as she started to worry, he blocked her off, but that just stoked the embers of her own anger.

She tried multiple times to call him, but every time it rang through to his voicemail. Even her texts went unanswered. She almost drove to Byte, but by the time she stood from the bed and grabbed her keys, it was already dawn. Regardless of what may have happened, the chances were that he was already asleep.

Plus, she had to consider Florence and what Lucas had been trying to do since his maker arrived. Kee couldn't let her anger undo everything he did to protect them.

Kee had spent the last month trying to sooth and calm the easily riled rage inside her. After her ambush, the fire that was her anger had been lit and nothing could douse it. Not completely. She thought avenging herself and killing the fuckers who had a hand in her attack would settle it, and it *did* help, but it still existed.

Working out several nights a week with Dante and having reading dates with Lucas in bed also worked. She had a better control of it, brushing off things that didn't matter, but sometimes the fire could still flare to life.

Swallowing the spark of anger, she turned to Conrad. "I think something happened at Byte last night."

His brows furrowed. "Like what?"

"I don't know. I felt Lucas' fury through the bond, but he shut it down before I could feel more." She rubbed at the spot under her left collarbone, a lingering ache had settled there since last night.

"Do you feel him now?" he asked.

Kee closed her eyes and concentrated on their bond. She couldn't feel any emotions from him since he was sleeping, but she could feel him. "Yeah, he's there."

"Lucy works the bar tonight," Conrad stated. "I'm sure she can tell you if something is wrong when she gets there. I can too, but I'll be outside most of the night."

Kee bit at the skin on corner of her thumb, thinking. "No," she finally said. "I'm going to ask Lucy if I can be her."

Conrad blinked before his eyebrows knitted together once again. "Kee, holding Lucy's skin for her entire shift is going to be hard."

She shook her head. "I'm not going to work her whole shift. I'm going to have her call in and tell whoever is working that she's going to be a few hours late."

Conrad rubbed his chin. "What if you get tired?"

She perked up at him as an idea hit her. "Maybe I'll have Sam work a chunk of her shift instead. So, he can go in for the first part of her shift and I can finish it? If I get too tired, Samson can stay and cover while I leave."

Her beta nodded. "You'll have to ask him, but that's probably the better solution. That way you don't piss off the other bartenders by leaving them hanging."

She smiled and turned her attention to the bedroom door. "Well, Sam? Lucy?"

There was a brief moment of silence before the door clicked open, the two pack members in question giving her sheepish grins.

"You can totally use my skin. I've always been curious as to how I look to other people," Lucy commented as she walked over to the bed and flopped down on it, lying on her stomach.

"I don't mind working the bar," Samson added, sitting down on the edge of the bed facing his pack. "You think something happened with Florence?"

Kee absorbed the comforting feeling of her pack around her before giving a single nod. "I think so, but I'll find out tonight if Lucas doesn't answer me."

"*We*," Samson stressed. "You don't have to do shit alone."

She gave him a smile, remembering the talk she had with him on the driveway. "I know." She glanced at the open door and raised a brow. "Where are the other two?"

"Eating breakfast and watching cartoons," Lucy replied. "We wanted to make sure you were okay. Well, not okay, but you know…"

Kee pat Lucy's head as the other girl trailed off. "It's going to be a process, but I'll get there." She looked at her two boys. "And I didn't say it last night but thank you guys for going to Nana's for me. I-I don't think I could have handled it."

The dragon offered his hand to her. When her palm met his, he wrapped his fingers around hers. "We understand."

Her eyes stung once again. "Thank you," she repeated.

"Oh, what? A dogpile and we weren't invited?" Tori chimed from the door, hand clutched to her chest in mock offense.

"Rude!" Mia called from beside her.

Kee gave a watery laugh and patted the blanket. "Well, what are you waiting for then?"

The two hurried to the bed, Tori climbing onto Samson's lap while Mia curled up on Kee's other side.

Kee's smile widened as her whole pack surrounded her, their presence soothing the ache deep in her soul. "I love you guys."

Fifteen

Conrad pulled into a parking spot at the mortuary and turned off the Jeep. He pulled the keys out of the ignition and turned to look at Kee. She sat frozen in the passenger seat, hands anxiously wringing the seatbelt across her chest. Her eyes were fixated on the seemingly innocent, two-story building in front of them, but he had a feeling she wasn't seeing it at all.

"Do you want to come back later?" he offered, keeping his voice light as he tied his hair back into a small bun at the base of his head.

She blinked twice before looking at him. "No, I can do this. I just—I just need a second to get my shit together," she mumbled in response, tightening her hands around the belt. "I know Dan is waiting for us, so I won't take too long."

He scoffed. "You take all the time you need, Kee. He's not the one who lost a family member."

She nodded once then took several deep, relaxing breaths before unclicking her seatbelt. "Okay, let's go," she said, forcing a calm into her voice that she didn't feel. When Conrad met her at the front of the car, she straightened her spine and walked towards the entrance to the mortuary. Her hand lingered on one of the doors' handles for a single heartbeat before she mustered the courage to pull it open.

Conrad followed in after her and immediately wrinkled his nose at the strong smell of lavender. He wasn't sure if it was to mask the scent of the dead behind the next set of doors by the reception desk or to soothe the grieving visitors. Maybe both.

Sensing the other two wolves as they stepped further into the building, he turned his attention to the waiting area on the right. He gave a single nod to Christopher then to the Riverside alpha. "Dan, this is my alpha, Kee."

Kee walked towards the alpha as he stood to greet her. He was about 5'7 and had short brown hair that was neatly styled back from his face. She didn't shake his hand when he offered it, but if he was offended, he didn't show it. Honestly, she didn't need any more skin files floating around in her head, and he probably wouldn't appreciate her using his image anyways. Better to avoid it all together.

She gave him a small, forced smile. "Thank you for taking care of Nana in my stead."

"It's no trouble. I'm sorry for your loss," Dan replied solemnly, his light brown eyes softening. "She may have been a lone wolf, but I was once her mate's beta. John and I had years of friendship between us before he died. Looking after his mate was the least I could do."

Christopher butted in before she could reply. "Dan has Nanette's will. We should go over it as soon as possible so we can lay her to rest properly."

A tendril of rage slid down Kee's spine, making the hairs on the back of her neck prickle as Cain's beast roused. She turned her eyes on Christopher and found great satisfaction when he took a step back at her glare. "Nana *just* fucking died, you greedy mutt. Why don't you try letting her soul rest for a moment before trying to pick her clean?"

Christopher sputtered with indignation as Conrad snorted then looked at Dan for help. "This is why Sasha should have been left in charge of the will! Tell her, Dan!"

Kee turned her glare on the alpha, daring him to contradict her. The alpha held her gaze for a long moment before looking at his pack mate. "It's to my understanding that Nanette raised Kee as her own child. Yes, Sasha is her actual daughter, but the two had a falling out after John died. That is why Kee is the beneficiary of the will. So, the call is hers to make." His voice lowered an octave as the power of his alpha status wrapped around the next words. "You need to respect her wishes. Especially when she is grieving."

Christopher ducked his head, cheeks coloring with embarrassment at the indirect reprimand. "Yes, sir."

Dan kept his gaze on his pack mate a moment longer before returning it to Kee. "I'm sure your pack told you, but there was a scent on Nanette none of us could pinpoint. The fact that your pack didn't recognize it either could mean that it's someone we've never met, but you spent more time with her so maybe you will be familiar with it."

Doubtful. Her sense of smell wasn't as strong as theirs, but she wouldn't tell him that. "Maybe," she said and glanced at the door by the reception desk when a tall black man with greying hair came out. The name printed above the pocket on his plastic apron was Kenan Theodore.

"Ms Quinn, I'm presuming?" the mortician asked as he approached. "I'm sorry about your loss. Whenever you're ready, Nanette's body is ready for you to view."

A pang of fear hit Kee square in the chest. Without having to ask or reach for it, Conrad's hand slid into hers for support. She squeezed her fingers tightly around his and swallowed thickly before forcing out her next words. "I'm ready."

No, she wasn't. How could she ever be ready to view the lifeless body of her great-grandmother? Of the person who raised her?

"It's alright if you need to take some more time," Kenan said in a kind voice. "I have been doing this for a long time and have learned that everyone has their own grieving process."

Kee shoved down the knee-jerk reaction to snap at him. It wasn't the nice mortician's fault that she could barely handle her shit right then. "I'm ready," she repeated, not able to keep the bite from her tone.

"Alright," Kenan said, not calling her out on her bullshit. "Right this way then."

"Mr Theodore handles all our pack cremations," Dan explained as the four of them followed Kenan. "He was the first to come forward and open his services to us when the Monster Movement went into effect."

Kenan nodded. "The way I see it, everyone dies. Even the preternatural who have very extended lifespans will eventually die. It didn't seem right to turn someone away just because they're different."

Conrad kept Kee's hand in his as he addressed the mortician. "How did your fellow humans like that?"

He laughed dryly. "They didn't, but that was okay. Any business I lost was replaced by the preternatural seeking our services."

"So, you don't just work with werewolves?" Kee asked curiously.

"I work with *everyone*," he clarified. "It's been very interesting to see how different every race celebrates death." At her puzzled expression, he continued. "We are both a mortuary and funeral home. We kind of expanded to do both so that it was easier on our preternatural clients."

Dan looked at Kee as Kenan brought them to a stop outside the room. "We can also host Nanette's wake here, if you'd like."

Kee stiffened. "I haven't thought that far ahead," she admitted in a soft voice. "All I know is that she wants her ashes scattered somewhere specific."

Christopher released a heavy sigh. "I'm sorry you're going through this, but you're not alone. You're being selfish."

Kee squeezed Conrad's hand when he growled low in warning. "No, I'm not alone. I have my pack to support me," she replied tersely before leveling him with another glare. "I know you want answers, and to plan all this shit out, but I'm still reeling with the fact that I lost my only parent. I'll have her cremated as is custom and spread her ashes where she wants them, but other than that *I don't know*. That's going to have to be good enough for you right now. If it's not, well, quite frankly, I don't give a fuck. You're nothing to me Christopher. I love Gabriel, but that doesn't mean I feel shit for you. So do as your alpha told you and back off before I make you."

The wolf in Christopher rose to the surface, his eyes gleaming with the beast's presence, but Dan immediately grabbed him by the back of the neck and yanked him away. "Go back to the car and wait for me," Dan commanded, the echo of power in his voice making the hairs on Kee's arms stand up.

Christopher cowered at the order before turning on his heel and heading back the way the group came.

Dan sighed and looked at Kee again. "I apologize for my pack mate."

She gave a single shoulder shrug before looking at Kenan. "I want to see Nana now so I can go home."

The mortician gave her a nod before leading them all into the sterile-smelling room. "Now, her body did sustain quite a few wounds, Ms Quinn. I want you to be prepared for that before I pull back the sheet."

Kee shuffled into the room, her heart hammering in her chest as she approached the stainless-steel table in the middle of the room. A white sheet was over the body, hiding it from view. Her breath kicked up a notch when she realized this was actually happening. Logically she knew it was real, but seeing it in person, having it *visually* be true, was completely different. Her hand tightened on Conrad's again as she came to a halt a few paces from the table.

Conrad pressed his shoulder against hers, holding her hand back just as tight. "I'm right here," he told her. "And we can still come back another day if you want, Kee."

She tried to swallow past the lump in her throat. "It won't be any easier on a different day," she whispered, eyes still locked on the white sheet.

"No, it won't," he agreed. "But no one is going to force you to do something you're not ready for."

Kee released her beta's hand, cutting that tether of support, and cautiously approached the table. She stood beside it, peering down at the outline of the body beneath the sheet. Out of her peripheral, she saw Kenan pull on a pair of gloves. He then walked to the head of the table and grasped the edges of the material covering Nana. She felt his eyes on her, heard the unspoken question in his gaze. Her head felt like it weighed a hundred pounds as she let it dip into a nod.

Kenan pulled back the sheet to right below Nanette's chin and Kee let out a high-pitched keening sound.

Her knees went out and hit the grey linoleum with a soft thud. Her chest constricted and tightened as the sight of Nana's lifeless face burned into her brain. The pale and waxy pallor of Nana's skin was all wrong, the freckles along her nose and cheeks too stark. Her face should have been warm and vibrant and full of life, not this empty, stiff shell. Even her red hair looked dull and limp. Nana's body looked like nothing more than a husk, and that was how Kee knew she was really gone.

A sob broke free, but it came out as a loud gasp as she struggled to normalize her breathing. She braced her hands on the table and pressed her face against her arms as tears began to fall. Squeezing her eyes tightly shut, she tried to take in deep breaths and hold them. She could almost hear Lucas in her head, instructing her breathing as he had so many times before.

Gods, she wished he was there with her.

As if he could hear her, she felt a burst of warmth from their bond. His comfort and love coming through to sooth her aching soul, reminding her she wasn't alone. With the warmth came the same, familiar ache in her chest, but then it all disappeared as quickly as it came. She would ask him about it later, but for now it was enough to pull herself together.

Feeling Conrad behind her, she shook her head. "Give me a second," she rasped.

"Take whatever time you need," he said softly before stepping back to give her space.

With a last deep breath, Kee gripped the ledge of the table tightly and pulled herself to her feet. She wiped her cheeks dry and looked at Kenan when he presented her with a pair of latex gloves. "What are these for?"

"In case you want to examine the body closer. At Dan's request, I haven't cleaned or fixed any wounds." He gave her a sympathetic look. "I suppose that's also my way of warning you. She's in the same state as she was when found."

Fucking fuck, Kee thought as she took the gloves from the mortician and slid them on with shaking hands.

The alpha of the Riverside pack approached the table on the opposite side. "I wanted to preserve any scents that may be lingering."

"Okay," she murmured in response. She flinched when the sheet was rolled down to rest right above Nana's breasts, exposing the damage done to her neck while keeping her modest.

"What's your first guess?" Dan asked.

Kee moved closer, bending down to examine the jagged slash across Nana's neck. "It looks like her throat was slit with claws," she frowned. "So, my first suspect is a wereanimal of some kind." She glanced over at Conrad. "I want to say my sperm donor, but you know his scent."

Conrad nodded. "I initially thought that too, but neither Samson nor I could pick up his scent. That doesn't mean he wouldn't have someone else do it though."

"True," she said. Her brow furrowed when she saw a slight discoloration on just one side of Nana's neck. She very gently tilted Nana's head to the side, trying not to notice how the skin gaped open as she did. She noticed that part of the skin was torn higher there along with the bruising. Having been bit and fed on twice, she was familiar enough to recognize it.

"Do you see it?" Dan pressed.

Kee looked up and met his gaze. "A vampire?"

A flare of his aura pushed at her. "Know any?"

She didn't care for the sarcastic jab. "I don't know what Christopher told you, but my fiancé would never do this."

"And your fiancé's coven?" he asked. "Piss anyone off lately? I've heard the rumors that you two leave quite the trail of bodies behind you."

She didn't realize she called Lucas her fiancé until he repeated it back to her. "His coven wouldn't do this either. If you've heard the rumors, then you know the people we pissed off are dead. I suggest not putting yourself on that list."

"Don't threaten me, Quinn. I'm trying to find out what happened. You can't blame me for searching all avenues," the alpha growled.

Kee snarled at him. "You don't think I want to know what happened to my great-grandmother? Of course, I do. And you can bet your ass that I'm going to kill the person who did this." When he lifted a brow at her, she bared her teeth at him in a very werewolf-like manner.

Conrad cleared his throat. "The next obvious reason as to why we know it's not the coven is because we don't recognize the scent. Our pack is always at Byte, and I'd say that most coven members visit there at least once a week."

"*Most.*" Dan echoed.

Kee growled again. "Trust me, if someone from Lucas' coven *did* do this, they won't be spared just because I love their lord. In fact, I know that Lucas would help me get my revenge on them. Better yet, the coven *knows* that. That's why I know they didn't do this."

Dan stared at her for a long moment, assessing her words and the truth in them. "Fine, but that still leaves us with nothing."

"It's not nothing," she said as she took the sheet and raised it back over Nana's head, not able to stomach the sight of her anymore. "I know it's a vampire and that's all I need."

Dan sighed as he stepped back from Nana's body. "I was already planning on questioning the Riverside coven. It's not a stretch to think that they did it in revenge for you two killing their lord."

"They would probably have some wounds from when Nanette defended herself," Kenan offered. "She has dried blood under her fingernails, and a few are broken."

Kee shook her head and pulled off the gloves. "They would be healed already." Especially since they fed off a shapeshifter, not that she would say that out loud. She glanced at Dan as they gathered at the door. "You'll let me know what you find?"

"Yeah," he replied, tossing his gloves in the trash by the door. "I hope you'll do the same."

"I will," she agreed and turned to Kenan when he offered her a small, clear bag. She didn't have to ask what the pearl earrings and necklace were. It was the jewelry Nana wore every day; the necklace having once belonged to her mom. The pendant was small, only about an inch in circumference. It had a five-pointed star and two long, mirrored knots below it, the tails of the knots curling up on either side of the star.

Tears filled her eyes again. She clenched the bag tightly in her fist and gave the mortician a watery, grateful smile. "Thank you."

He gave her a kind smile and nod in return. "Of course." His smile waned. "Are you ready for me to proceed with cremation? Or would you like me to wait until you catch who did this to her? Preternatural crime is so different from humans. I know the higher-ups are in talks of forming a special branch for monster crime specifically, but in my experience, packs tend to want to solve their own cases."

"We do handle our own issues," she agreed. She took in a shaky breath and slowly let it out. "Y-yes—" She took in another breath to steady herself. "You can proceed."

Conrad rubbed her back as he saw her bottom lip tremble and ushered her out the door. When they were all back in the hallway, he met Dan's gaze. "Is there anything else that needs to be discussed?"

"Not at the moment," he said, eyes returning to Kee. "I know you went ahead with the cremation, but we don't have to go through her will until you're ready."

She snorted, the sound a little wet with her tears. "Try telling Christopher that."

"You let me handle him. I won't tolerate another outburst like that." He put his hands in his pockets as they headed back to the waiting room. "His father would have been disappointed in him."

Kee shrugged. "I wouldn't know. I never met him."

Dan gave her a smirk. "John would have liked you. You take after Nanette a lot."

Another watery smile. "Thank you." She rubbed at her nose then looked at Conrad. "I'm ready to go home. We have a busy night ahead of us." She turned back to Kenan and nodded again. "Thank you for taking care of Nana. I'll be the one to collect her ashes when she's ready."

"Of course, Ms Quinn," he said, opening the door to the waiting room for the group. "I will be in contact." With that, he disappeared back behind the door.

"I'll also be in contact." Dan led them towards the front door and out into the winter afternoon. "I know I already said it and it doesn't help, but I'm sorry again for your loss. Nanette was an amazing woman."

Was. "Thanks," Kee forced out. "Well, I guess we'll talk later." With that awkward goodbye, her and Conrad made their way to the Jeep. After sliding in and buckling up, she opened the baggy and pulled out the pendant and slipped it on over her head.

Sixteen

"Kee, you need to read this." Conrad appeared in the doorway of her bathroom, holding out his phone to her.

Setting down her brush, she took the phone from him and read the group text message that had been sent out from Gio's phone. "Byte is closed for the evening. Enjoy the night off," she read aloud and looked up at him. "Closed without warning?"

He leaned against the doorframe. "Because that isn't suspicious as fuck."

She handed the phone back to him and grabbed her own phone from the counter. She shot Lucas another text, this time asking about the closure. When it once again went unanswered, she clenched her jaw. Her worry shifted to anger and back.

"I should have gone last night," Kee sighed as she turned and leaned against the counter. "I didn't want to ruin the image Lucas created of us to appease Florence, but something is wrong. It's fully night and all the vampires should be awake. So why isn't he responding? Why is Gio writing everyone and not Lucas?"

"We'll figure it out, Kee," Samson said, appearing next to the pack beta. "We'll get to the bottom of this."

She rubbed at her temples. "I know, it just makes me anxious not knowing."

"It makes all of us anxious," Conrad stated. "None of us want anything to happen to the coven."

Kee nodded but tensed when she heard the doorbell followed by a series of hard, rapid knocks. She looked at Conrad and Samson, who both looked equally tense, before making her way to the front door. Tori poked her head out of the kitchen while Lucy and Mia looked up from their puzzle on living room floor.

Conrad and Samson stood on either side of Kee as she looked through the peephole, their muscles taught with the anticipation of a fight.

"What the hell?" Kee muttered as she quickly unlocked the door and flung it open. "Dante?"

Dante was hunched over, body trembling. His hand shook as he held it up to her, stopping her from approaching him. "*Don't,*" he rasped with a voice like sandpaper. "Need. Blood." He choked out each word as if it pained him to do so.

Samson bolted to the kitchen as Conrad and Kee stepped out onto the porch, blocking the door to protect the other pack mates just in case blood lust took over.

"Here." Samson came back with two of the bags of blood they kept in the fridge for when Lucas stayed over and handed him one. When the vampire bit into the bag and drained it, he handed him the second. "Do you want me to get another?"

Dante downed the second bag and squeezed his eyes shut as it quenched the thirst and soothed the pang radiating from his stomach. He forced himself straight and rubbed the skin of his head before looking at the three of them. "I'm alright now."

Kee frowned at him, her brow pinched with worry. "You sure? What the hell happened?"

He smoothed his beard down with shaking fingers. "Florence fucking happened," he responded.

Kee's hackles shot up. "I knew it," she cursed. "What did she do? Is everyone okay? Is Lucas?"

Dante shook his head. "No. No one is okay, Kee. She's a monster." His hands balled into fists. "I always knew she was, but she's gone completely off the rail."

"What did she do?" Kee repeated forcefully, her aura snapping out. When Samson and Conrad both flinched back from her, she took in a long breath before gently touching their arms. "Sorry."

Dante hesitated. "You may want to sit down."

"I don't need to sit down," she said but accepted Conrad and Samson's support as they stepped closer to her. "I need to know what's happening."

Byte's head of security rubbed his face, effectively messing the beard he had just fixed. "Florence, she—" he cut himself off as he tried to think of where to start. "She staked Lucas."

Kee blinked once in shock. "*What?*" She instantly honed in on the bond her and Lucas shared, pulling insistently on it with her worry. When she felt nothing in return, she lifted her lip in a snarl. "I know he's alive, but what did it do to him?"

"When older vampires are staked, especially if the wood is blessed, it can render them immobile. I don't know if she did anything else to him because Giovanni gave me a chance to escape last night. I took it so that I could get help."

Kee just shook her head, trying to wrap her mind around what he was telling her. "But why did she stake him?"

"He tried to kill her," he answered with a heavy sigh. "But in the worst way. He wasn't thinking. He was too consumed by rage to think clearly about what he was doing. I've only seen him that angry once or twice in the centuries I've known him."

She put a hand to her chest. "I felt that anger," she murmured. "But what got him so riled?"

He paused again and looked from Samson to Conrad before looking at her again. "She had a hand in wiping out your ancestors," he began. "And…she told Lucas that after admitting that she killed your grandmother."

Conrad sucked in a breath and turned to Kee to see shock light her features before her face fell into a blank mask. "Kee—"

"Tell me everything," Kee demanded, her voice low and cold.

Dante did. He recited everything Florence said to Lucas. The shapeshifters, Nanette, and her plans for both Lucas and Kee.

She let out a dry, humorless laugh. "This bitch killed Nana, my only parent, and now she wants to take my man? Let her try. I'm going to slaughter her."

Samson put his hand on her tense shoulder. "Wait, didn't you hear what Dante said? She wants you to. She probably knows that you're going to come for revenge. She'll be ready."

"Not just that, but she knows that you and Lucas are together. Aubrey has told her everything," Dante added, crossing his arms over his chest. "She closed the bar tonight because she knows I came to tell you. Whether it's for Nana or Lucas, she's expecting you to come, Kee. You'll play right into her hands."

"I don't give a fuck," Kee seethed. "She has no idea what she's unleashed. She's taken too much from Lucas, too much from me. It ends tonight."

Samson cracked his knuckles. "Well alright then. Let's get a new plan going."

Conrad stopped Kee before she could protest. "*No.* We're going with you. Florence is insane; you're not facing her alone."

"And she has the coven at her mercy. I don't know if they'll answer to her, but she has Aubrey and her boyfriend on her side," Dante sighed. "You can't win against three vampires. You'll need all the help you can get."

"I'm in!" Tori suddenly said, appearing in the doorway behind them. When they turned to look at her with surprise, she grinned. "Let's kick some vampire ass."

Kee shook her head. "Tori, I can't ask you to do that."

"You're not asking for me for shit," she answered, crossing her arms across her chest. "I'm a part of this pack now, right? I want to help." She scowled at her alpha when she started to shake her head. "I want to prove that I'm useful to you. I want to prove that I'm an asset to the pack, Kee."

Samson stepped up to Tori, resting his hand on the top of her head. He ignored her attempts to bat his hand away and smirked at Kee with pride. "We've all felt this way at some point, Kee. My girl is no different."

Kee let out a heavy sigh. "I know." She leveled a cool look at her newest pack member. "You don't have to prove anything to me, but if you really want to go with us then I won't stop you."

Tori cheered triumphantly. "Fuck yeah! Let's get this game plan going then!"

Samson wrapped an arm around Tori's shoulders and pulled her into his side. "We'll be Team Scales."

Kee rolled her eyes when Tori snickered in approval and looked at Conrad, who had his brows lifted in expectation. "How about Team Revenge?"

He gave her a deadpanned expression. "That's terrible, Kee."

She threw her hands up. "Then you think of one!" she huffed as she pushed past them into the house.

Some of the stress on Dante's shoulders eased. He knew the seriousness of the moment hadn't changed, but the pack's easy banter helped calm the worry he felt. He knew he came to the right place for help. No one would fight harder for Lucas, Gio, and the rest of the coven than their pack.

And they *were* all pack. All family.

Seventeen

"I'm sorry, but this is still so weird," Tori stated, looking at the man next to her then at the one across from her in Byte's alleyway.

Conrad raised his brows at her. "You're taking this all pretty well considering it was just sprung on you."

"I mean, everyone knows shapeshifters were a thing in the past, so it makes sense that they're still around hiding. It also explains how you're the alpha of a pack of misfits," Tori murmured, still whipping her head back and forth to stare at both versions of Samson. "But fuck, it's so uncanny."

Samson let out a quiet laugh. "Yeah, it's a bit weird to see myself."

Kee tugged at the hem of Byte's security shirt. "You sure you're okay with me using your image, Sam? I know when we first met you weren't a fan of the idea."

He waved his hand as if brushing off the concern. "That's before I knew you."

She gave him a thankful nod and looked at Dante's furrowed brow. "We still okay with the plan?"

Dante shook his head. "No, not really, but I don't see another alternative. She's expecting you to come so maybe your pack mates showing up instead will throw her off enough for me to sneak down to Lucas and Gio."

"Hopefully, but either way I plan on killing her," she said.

"The best way to kill her will be with fire," he began. "I've seen Lucas' fire enough times to know that it'll get the job done, but I don't know if he'll be in any shape to use it."

Kee's heart twisted in pain for her man. Her fiancé. She rubbed the empty spot on her—Sam's—ring finger. "He'll be okay," she stated confidently. He had to be. "And if not, I'll find a way to do it myself, even if I have to burn Byte down in the process." She grinned sheepishly at Dante's indignant sputter. "I mean, I'll try not to, but I make no promises."

He let out a little sigh that was only a tad sarcastic. "I suppose that's all I can hope for."

The five of them tensed when they sensed someone approach, their attention snapping to the two vampires as they casually strolled into the alleyway.

"My, my, what a totally expected surprise!" Aubrey cooed in an over-dramatic tone as her and Damien walked further into the space between the buildings. "The bitch's pets are here! Where's your little alpha female? I told Lady Florence that she's too scared to come without her vampire to fight her battles."

"That's rich coming from the backstabbing whore who got her ass kicked by that same alpha." Conrad pointed out with a smirk. "Or did you forget I was there when she slammed you against the door by your throat? If it weren't for Lucas, I'm not sure you'd be here right now, Aubrey."

Her cheeks tinged pink. She glanced at her boyfriend, straightened her spine, and tossed a lock of hair over her shoulder. "That's when I was human, flea bag! Things are different now."

"Yeah, keep telling yourself that," Samson scoffed as the two got closer.

Aubrey narrowed her eyes at Samson, but the retort fizzled off her tongue when she saw the second Samson. She blinked at one and stared at the other in shock. "You—"

She didn't get to finish her statement as Tori struck, slamming her fist into the other woman's face. Using the surprise to her advantage, Tori leapt at the girl to tackle her to the asphalt by the dumpster.

When Damien snarled and reached for Tori, Samson shot forward and grabbed his arm. He held the arm tightly to keep the other man in place before driving his knee up into the vampire's stomach to double him over.

"Go on," Tori said to Kee and hissed as Aubrey slapped her, scoring her nails across her cheek to draw blood. "We'll *gladly* handle these two." She slapped Aubrey back, snickering when she wailed.

"Feel free to kill them," Kee said and gestured for Conrad and Dante to follow her out of the alleyway.

As they passed Samson and his opponent, her eyes fell on the vampire struggling to free himself from Samson's hold. When the two locked eyes, she realized he looked familiar but couldn't place how. When she had more time, she'd think on it, but there were more pressing matters at hand.

The trio rounded the building, heading straight for the back entrance to Byte. Dante tried the handle and nodded at the pack members before flinging the door open. They were instantly greeted with the sight of Mirabella and Brent standing beside the entrance to the basement.

"Oh, thank the gods, you're here!" Mirabella cried in her British accent as she closed the space between them to hug Dante. Her brow furrowed when she looked at Samson and Conrad. "Wait, where's Kee?"

Brent snorted. "Probably cowering with her tail between her legs."

Kee snapped her fist out and punched him in the nose, feeling satisfied when she heard it crunch. "That's from Kee," she said in Samson's voice.

Brent shouted in pain and covered his face with his palms. "You fucking asshole!" he snapped, but the words came out muddled and slurred.

"Now is not the time," Conrad interjected when Brent removed his hands from his face and balled them into fists. "Can you tell us what's going on?"

Mirabella rubbed her arms. "Florence has the coven under her thumb. We can't disobey her orders and are afraid to try."

"How's Lucas?" Kee asked, glancing at the door over Mira's shoulder. "And Gio?"

She shook her head. "We don't really know. She's kept them from us." Her nails bit into the pale skin on her arms. "I wanted to check on him and Gio, but we were ordered not to go down in the basement." Her face twisted a bit. "Gio's lover tried to go down to help him, and Florence ripped his spine out."

"Wait, so where is the coven? Where have you guys been staying?" Kee asked.

Mira sighed. "Anyone who doesn't live at Byte is barred from coming in, but those of us who are here have been banished to the rooms upstairs."

"How are you supposed to feed?" Dante questioned. "She can't starve an entire coven."

Brent wiped the blood from his nose. "She said her fucking minions were going to bring us humans."

Conrad jerked his thumb towards the alleyway. "You mean Aubrey and that guy?" When Brent nodded, he snorted. "They're a bit busy right now."

Mira pursed her lips together. "Well, I guess we'll depend on the bagged blood then."

Dante grimaced but moved Mira aside so he could get to the basement door. As soon as his hand enclosed around the knob, Brent barreled into him, knocking him away from the door. Dante steadied himself on his feet and bared his fangs at Brent. "What the hell was that for?"

"It's compulsion." Brent grunted, his tone somewhat remorseful. "I have to guard the door."

Mirabella sighed. "She planted the command in our heads with compulsion to not let anyone through. She's not stupid; she expects Kee to come for Lord Lucas."

Kee's upper lip twitched as a wave of anger hit her. "Where is Florence?"

"In the main club," Mira replied, jerking her thumb over at the door through the kitchen. "She's made herself quite at home."

"Of course, she did," Kee muttered and turned her attention to Dante. "Can you handle him?"

Byte's head of security snorted and bent his head so that his neck cracked. "Don't insult me. I trained Brent. He won't be an issue."

Mirabella frowned. "Wait, I also have the order! I don't want to fight Dante."

"You won't," Kee clarified. When the blonde relaxed, she gestured at Conrad. "You'll have to go against Conrad."

"I don't think that's much better," Mira sighed as she looked at the wolf. "Can you try not to damage my face?"

"I'll do my best," Conrad said before looking at his alpha. "I don't like that you'll be out there alone."

She put a hand on his shoulder. "Then you two will just have to hurry, won't you?" When Conrad frowned, she squeezed his arm before dropping her hand to her side. "Focus on rescuing Lucas and

Gio, okay? I can hold her off until then."

"We will," Conrad agreed.

"Be careful," Dante added before facing his opponent once again.

"I'll try," she replied and then made her way through the kitchen. She paused at the doors leading to the main area of the club to take a steadying breath before pushing through them. Immediately, she felt the tension in the air, and it took her a second to focus.

"Oh? And who are you?"

Kee's focus finally zeroed in on Florence when she spoke. She had cleared the tables and chairs from Byte's floor, shoving them all against the club's main entrance. To replace them, she had moved one of the overstuffed chairs from the VIP rooms upstairs to the direct middle of the dance floor. Florence was wearing one of her slinky dresses, the neckline dipping deep between her breasts to stop at her navel. Red waves framed her pale face and accentuated her dark lipstick.

"Well?" Florence prompted.

Kee chose not to respond immediately, instead scouting the club for any other vampires. She saw one standing off to the side of the bar, fidgeting anxiously. She briefly recognized him as one of the bartenders.

"You can go," she said to him.

He jumped when addressed and blinked unsurely. "Samson?"

"You think you can overrule my standing and orders?" Florence asked, a disbelieving scoff in her tone. "Quite bold of you."

Once again Kee ignored her. "It's been stated that we're all pack, correct?" When the vampire gave a shaky nod, she continued, "In this pack I'm ranked higher than you so listen to me when I give you an order."

He shot her a grateful look before taking off towards the rooms upstairs.

Kee waited until she heard the door to the stairwell slam shut before turning her attention to Florence. "I'm sorry, you were saying?"

Florence's eyes held Samson's, her delicate face blank of expression. When the man didn't look away from her, her eyes narrowed. "So, you're part of my Apollo's pet's pack, hm?"

"I am," Kee responded. "And you're the one who's weirdly obsessed with her son."

Florence elegantly swung her legs off the arms of the cushion to cross them in front of her. "I find it odd that a werewolf pack would be so willing to consider a coven of vampires as brethren." She tilted her head to the side. "That goes for one not a wolf either."

Kee lifted her shoulder in a shrug. "Maybe my alpha is just that inspiring."

The vampire rose to her feet and shoved her foot back, sending the cushioned chair skidding back against the bar. "And what about the pack and vampires? What hold does the alpha bitch have over my son's vampires?"

"None," Kee replied. "She and Lucas are bonded." She let petty sarcasm trickle into her next words. "The two of them are quite close, as you know. Why wouldn't the pack and coven be?"

Fury broke through the vampire's cold mask. "And where is your alpha bitch, hm? If she is so close to my Lucas, then why is she not here?"

"Because that would be the obvious thing to do, wouldn't it? Maybe she didn't want to give in to your ploy," Kee responded as she slid into a defensive position, fists raising near her chin.

Florence sneered, a corner of her painted lips lifting. "Then she clearly does not care enough to try and save him."

"You really talk too much." Kee laughed dryly. "It's embarrassing."

The vampire hissed and lunged.

Samson's body was bigger and heavier than Kee's. She was only using his skin, so it was harder to adjust to the limb length and height difference. She stumbled as she stepped back from a swipe of Florence's nails, the vampire immediately taking advantage by kicking her feet out from under her. Kee's back hit the hard floor and she was forced to roll to the side to avoid Florence's punch.

"I am disappointed," Florence sighed as she lifted her fist from the small crater she created in the floor. She stood from her crouched position and watched in boredom as the man climbed back to his feet. "I really expected more from you after that boisterous display earlier."

Kee cursed as Florence closed the distance between them in the span of a heartbeat. Before she could get Samson's body up to block it, a knee slammed into her gut, doubling her over and making her hack up a wad of phlegm. A bony elbow flew towards her temple, but she managed to jerk back enough so that it hit her cheek instead of her temple.

She wasn't dumb. She knew she wouldn't live if she got knocked out.

Florence tsk'ed. "At least you seem to have *some* intelligence."

"You *really* talk too much." Kee spat out another glob of spit, very conscious of the fact that her stomach was begging to empty its contents from the force of the hit. Curling her hands into fists again, she swung at Florence. Florence batted the hand away, but Kee anticipated the dodge and followed the movement up with a kick towards Florence's side.

"Child's play," Florence hissed as she caught the leg and used her strength to throw his body across the club.

Kee crashed into the barstools at the bar and gritted her teeth when she felt one of her ribs crack. When she tried to get to her feet, Florence was there, grabbing the front of her shirt and using it as leverage to lift and pin her back against the bar. Kee brought up her knee to try to put some distance between them, but Florence only released her long enough to grab her face instead.

"You will listen to me," Florence began, her voice becoming melodic despite its drop in octave. "You will obey what I have to say."

Kee had heard this tone before. It was when Lucas had compelled Giovanni after he took out her stitches. "No," she grunted as Florence tightened her hold.

"You will. You *want* to obey my commands. You *want* to please me," she cooed in the same deep, alluring tone.

Kee's knee-jerk reaction was to panic. If she fell victim to the vampire's spell, she could very well end up giving Florence everything she set out to gain. However, as Florence continued to talk, Kee realized she felt zero pull or desire to obey her. Her compulsion wasn't working and that was when realization dawned on her. It wasn't working because of her bond with Lucas. He had explained it to her when she first woke from her attack, but she had forgotten about that little bonus.

As if on cue, heat suddenly flared in her chest, and with it came a relief so strong her eyes stung with unshed tears.

Lucas was free from whatever Florence had done to him, and he was coming.

Kee met Florence's useless hypnotic gaze and made her own eyes go a little glossy. When a smirk of triumph appeared on the vampire's pained lips, she quickly brought up her fist, slamming it into the underside of Florence's jaw.

Florence let out a surprised shout as she staggered back. She rolled her tongue in her mouth and stuck her fingers between her lips to pull out a chipped piece of her fang. She dropped it to the floor with an ugly sneer and faced him once again. "You will pay for that. I am *done* playing!"

"So am I."

Florence's eyes widened in surprise as she whirled around to see her seething blood son. She blinked at him, taking in the gaping, bleeding hole above his heart and his sickly pallor. A little, sardonic smile curled up her lips. "My little Apollo, do you think you are really in any condition to fight me?"

Lucas' retort died on his lips when he glanced over her head to see Keira shifting. With a smug smirk, he met his maker's gaze. "Perhaps if there were two of me."

She lifted a mocking brow at him. "I doubt even then."

"Guess we'll find out, won't we?" Kee said in Lucas' accented baritone as she finished shifting into him. And she was, without a doubt, him exactly. She could feel the vein of heat within him and knew instinctively that it was his golden flame, ready to be ignited and wielded.

Despite how right it felt to be her lover, she knew something was wrong. As soon as she initiated the shift to become him, warning bells went off in her head. It started with a cold wave that had every hair standing up on edge, but even as it dissipated, a tingling numbness began to spread from her phalanges.

Florence's spine stiffened, but she didn't take her eyes off her blood son. "The shapeshifter," she stated. "I should have known."

"Indeed," Kee said, taking after Lucas' mannerisms. "I would never leave him at your mercy."

Florence turned so that both versions of Lucas were on either side of her. She flicked a pitying look at the copy. "But now you are both at my mercy." She licked her lips. "You have no idea what I have planned for you, shapeshifter."

Lucas growled at the threat to his woman. "You will never taste her. Not while I live."

Florence cackled. "Then it is good that you are technically dead, isn't it?"

While Florence's attention was on Lucas, Kee took the opportunity to act. She lurched towards the female vampire, perfectly adjusted for the speed that came with Lucas' body. She swung her fist at Florence's head, but the other woman hissed and leapt back.

Lucas was a step behind Keira, following up her punch with a kick at his maker's legs. A brief glimmer of pride swelled in him when Keira was there to tackle Florence as the other vampire jumped up to avoid his kick. As Keira hit the floor with Florence's head locked in a chokehold, he quickly brought his fist down towards his maker's chest. He had just briefly made contact with her skin before she rolled her lower body up and kicked him square in the chest where his stake wound was.

Kee flinched when Lucas clutched at his chest and staggered back with a pained groan. Her worry distracted her, earning her a sharp elbow to her already cracked ribs. With a grunt, her hold slackened, and Florence immediately freed herself. Wheezing with pain, Kee tried to get back on her feet, but Florence kicked her onto her back.

Florence sat down on the shapeshifter's stomach and grabbed her jaw, forcing the copy's head from side to side to inspect the image. "Truly a beautiful copy," she complimented before striking, lips pressing hard against the clone's so she could pierce it with a fang. She lapped at the blood and rolled her tongue over her teeth before letting out a dry laugh. "Oh, you stupid girl. Your blood even tastes like his. You truly are him, aren't you? You have no idea what you have done to yourself. What a waste."

Kee slid her hands up Florence's thighs and gripped the fabric of her dress tightly, holding the woman in place as Lucas rose up behind them. She saw his hands grab Florence's head, but as soon as his hands made contact, Florence's sharp nails dug into the tender flesh of her throat.

Kee saw Lucas freeze and growled, "Do it, Lucas!"

"You could," Florence cooed at her blood son, but her eyes stared down at the shapeshifter. She minutely wiggled her nails, causing them to dig in deeper to the shapeshifter's skin. "But you would lose her too."

Lucas' chest heaved with indecision. He could save himself, his blood son, friends, and coven. He could end all their torment at that moment, end the centuries of abuse. But at what cost? To potentially lose Keira forever? No. He couldn't. He was man enough to admit that he was irrevocably selfish when it came to his shapeshifter.

When his hands fell away, Florence ripped her hand from the copy's throat and was on her feet in the blink of an eye. Before he could react, she put her hand on her blood son's shoulder and held him in place as she punched his stake wound. "When did you become so bloody weak?" she hissed in fury. "I created a better son than this! You make me question if you are even worth keeping around anymore. You may be skilled in bed, but your weakness disgusts me."

Lucas spit out a wad of blood in her face. "I have been disgusted with you since you turned me."

Rage bled into her eyes, turning her irises red. She let go of his shoulder and kicked him hard in the stomach, sending him sailing across the bar until he crashed into the tables and chairs barricading the entrance to Byte. "You will pay, Apollo! Mark my words!" she screamed as she took a step towards him, but an unyielding hand landed on her shoulder and kept her in place.

When Florence turned towards her, Kee snapped her blood covered fingers together as she had seen Lucas do so many times. Obeying its call, his golden fire sprang to life in her hands. The flame was a comforting warmth in her palm, but she knew how hot it burned to anyone not Lucas.

Florence knew too; Kee could tell in how the red faded from her wide eyes.

"You don't—" Lucas' maker began, but Kee cut her off.

"*No.* No more talking from you," Kee growled and bared Lucas' fangs as her anger swelled. "You are done tormenting people. I'm going to kill you for hurting the ones I love." She choked on the grief that rose from the compartment she stuffed it in earlier. "For draining my great-grandmother." She pushed the sadness away and focused on her rage once again, letting it free from the chains she kept it locked down with. The golden flame flared with the fuel in response. "And I'm going to use your precious son's fire to do it. You earned it after everything you have done to him. For all of the pain and heartbreak you have caused him. He deserves better than you."

Without wasting any more time with words, she slapped the hand holding the flame to Florence's chest. The fire eagerly, almost hungrily, ate at the dress before spreading along the vampire's pale skin beneath it. Kee's eyes watered as the putrid scent of burning hair and sizzling flesh hit her nostrils. Still, she kept both hands in place as Florence screamed and thrashed against her hold, only pulling away when the stench became too much.

She took a step back from Florence as the flame greedily engulfed her from head to toe. She heard the clang of metal shifting, but she refused to tear her eyes away from the burning body as it crumpled to its knees, the screams becoming dry shrieks and undefinable wails for mercy. The flaming body started to become smaller and smaller with each passing second. Black specks of ash floated in the air from the heat of the fire before falling to the ground.

A final, broken cry for help escaped what was left of Florence's body before the flame took that from her too. The charred mass wasn't enough for the fire though, no. It worked at the remaining muscles then at the bones when only the skeleton remained. Finally, and gradually, the golden flame died out to leave a small pile of glittering black ash.

Kee scoffed at the plea, especially as Nana's dead body came to the forefront of her mind. The vampire bitch had died too quickly. Yes, she suffered the worst death a vampire could have, but it was too kind an ending for the woman that had caused so much pain.

She balled her hands into fists at the injustice but soon realized she couldn't feel them. Fearing she had burned her own hands, she looked down at Lucas' hands and found them perfectly intact and whole. She rubbed her fingers together, watched them make contact, but couldn't feel it. Placing one hand on the opposite wrist, she found she couldn't feel that either.

The warning bells from earlier went off again, and this time she heeded its call. With a deep breath in, she ignored the taste of ash in her mouth and closed her eyes. As she slowly let out the air in her lungs, she released Lucas' image and let her body shift back to her own. Her body settled back into its original form, but something was terribly, terribly wrong.

She couldn't draw in a breath. She tried to lift her hand to claw at her throat, but it didn't obey. Her body felt cold and numb and heavy. Her vision dimmed and she staggered. She wanted to cry out for Lucas, but that train of thought died as she did.

Eighteen

Something in him broke. It wasn't a clean break either, no. It was a shatter. Millions of tiny, jagged pieces seemed to cut through every part of him until there was nothing left.

Because beyond the agonizing pain, there was nothing.

Nothing.

Keira wasn't there. He couldn't feel her anymore. The bond was gone, taking her with it. She had been ripped out of the space that she occupied within him, leaving a desolate hole in its wake.

The force of the sudden emptiness brought him to his knees.

No, it wasn't just the emptiness. It was what the emptiness meant. What the pain radiating throughout his body meant. She wasn't just gone from him. She was gone. Gone.

Dead.

He squeezed his eyes shut as they burned and blurred. He had seen her body crumple to the floor, knew it still lay there. She didn't fall dramatically like in the movies, didn't clutch her chest and make a final, dying statement. He didn't get to make eye contact with her one final time to convey everything he felt in that split second that stretched on like minutes.

No, this wasn't a film.

He didn't get a final moment with his shapeshifter. His love. His—

"Keira," he croaked out, his voice hoarse from the excruciating pain of losing her physically, emotionally, and mentally.

He had to get to her, needed to hold her, but his body refused. He was frozen with pain, with shock. She couldn't be gone.

Look at her!

He forced his heavy head up and pried his eyes open. The pain doubled as he saw her lifeless form lying in a heap next to the ashes of his maker. His chest tightened and a strange sound ripped itself free of his lips. It was deep yet hallowed, like it came from the depths of his wounded soul.

Those same lips trembled as he called her name again, "Keira."

He needed to get to her. *Move, damn you, move!* He forced his arms down, his palms touching the icy floor. How long would it take for her to become as cold? How soon until her familiar, comforting warmth left her completely?

The thought that he may miss the last of her warmth terrified him. He forced his hands and knees to move quicker as he crawled towards her. The seconds it took him to get to her felt like hours. So much so that he feared he missed his chance.

He kneeled next to her and, with shaking hands, pushed her hair from her face. The wound inside him festered as he saw how pale she had become. He slid a hand to her uninjured cheek and cradled it with the softest touch he could muster. His thumb lightly ghosted over her cool, parted lips, begging them to draw in a breath.

"Keira?" *Answer me.*

His eyes blurred once again, but he barely noticed. As if afraid she would break, he carefully slid an arm under her shoulders and lifted her towards him. He punctured his wrist with a fang and waited until it welled up with blood before placing it over her mouth. The blood splattered her lips and dropped uselessly onto her tongue. His blood had saved her before. But then again, her heart had been beating the last time.

"Keira." *Please.*

He tightened his hold around her and gave a shake. She couldn't be gone. Not after all this. His other hand slid down to her chest. Searching for a heartbeat he knew wasn't there.

"Keira!" *Do not leave me.*

That retched sound came from his lips again. He felt nothing except the wet trails that slid down his cheeks. He gathered the rest of her limp body into his lap and cradled the back of her head, pressing it against his chest.

"Keira, Keira, Keira..." *No, no, no.*

He hunched over her, rocking back and forth, willing life to return to her once again. More foreign sounds came from him, but he didn't care. He needed them to come from *her*. He needed her to make any sound. He just... needed her.

"Kei—" He choked on her name, and it was then he understood that these noises were sobs.

Someone grabbed his shoulder, but they didn't matter. No one mattered but his shapeshifter in his arms. He clutched Keira tighter to him. It wasn't until another person tried prying him away from her that he reacted. He lifted his head and snarled at the person who would dare try to separate them.

Giovanni met his maker's wet, crimson glare and flinched. Dante had just popped his shoulder back into place, and he had no desire to break another collarbone. Hearing a commotion, he glanced towards the kitchen and saw Samson running towards them. He shot Kee's pack mate a warning look and held up his hand to caution him.

As if sensing the newcomers, Lucas' angry gaze held a lethality to it that made Gio go very still. "Lucas," he said as calmly as he could muster. "We only want to help."

Lucas heard nothing. Saw nothing but people who were trying to take Keira away from him. He wouldn't let them. He needed to hold on to her until the very last minute. Until her body went cold and stiff. And even then, he was not sure he would be able to let her go.

Gio glanced at Dante, who was holding Lucas' shoulder. "If I have any hope of resuscitating her, it needs to be soon, or it'll be too late. Plus, the chances of brain damage increase."

Dante shot Samson a warning look when the dragon snarled and tightened his hold on his lord's shoulder when he tensed. "You have to release her, Lucas," he said, trying to pull his friend away from Kee's body. "Gio may still be able to help."

Lucas' nostrils flared with rage as he felt people trying to tug him away from Keira. He ran his thumb over her bottom lip, smearing the blood while coating his own skin in it. Once the pad of his thumb was covered, he went to snap his fingers, but a third person grabbed his thumb even as the other two leapt away.

"Fuck that," Samson sneered. Lucas' thumb jerked in his hold, so he snapped it back, breaking it without a second thought.

Lucas felt his thumb pop, but it was nothing compared to the agonizing pain inside him. These people were trying to take Keira from him. Did they not realize that she was his light? That she was the closest he had come to the sun in hundreds of years? If he let her fleeting warmth go, he would be locked in an icy hell forever.

No, he would not be separated from her.

Samson snatched his hand back when Lucas' golden flame suddenly sprang to life. He glanced at Gio and Dante. "I thought he needed his blood as an accelerant?"

"He normally does," Gio mumbled, eyes wide as the flames formed a circle around the couple. "But I've never seen him like this."

"He's breaking," Dante commented solemnly. "It's costing him his control and sanity. We need to do something."

"Stay back," Samson said as he tugged off his shirt. He then kicked off his shoes and slid off of his jeans and boxers. With a dilation of his pupils into slits, he let his beast take over. His body stretched and grew, red and black scales sprouting from his skin. Webbed wings sprung from his back as a tail grew and lashed against the ground.

Gio and Dante stared at him, mouths slightly agape as they witnessed Samson's dragon form for the first time.

Be ready to grab her, Samson said to Dante as he snapped out his wings and angled them forward. He began to beat them, forcing gusts of wind at the circle of fire.

Dante waited until enough of the flames parted to lurch forward. He saw the death grip Lucas had on Kee and cursed. With a muttered apology, he slammed his fist into the side of Lucas' head. The flames flickered out and Dante saw Lucas' grip falter. The split second was all he needed to shove him back.

Samson slapped his tail at Lucas, forcing him back against the ground. He then pounced, pinning Lucas to the floor with his massive claws as Dante hauled Kee into his arms and ran to Gio. Samson tried to link with Lucas, to tell him they were trying to help, but the vampire's mind was a chaotic storm of dark, oppressive emotions. There was no getting through to him.

"Lay her on her back," Giovanni instructed. He kneeled next to Kee once Dante did as told and tilted her head back. He plugged her nose and covered her mouth with his, forcing a long breath into her lungs. He then folded his hands over Kee's chest, but before he could start compressions, a tormented wail made him falter. He tried to shake off his maker's pain and began pressing down on Kee's chest in quick, hard movements. "Help him, Dante!"

Dante was already running back to the duo. He saw Lucas grab Samson's foot, his hands snapping the toes caging him in. The dragon let out a roar and smacked Lucas with his snout, but he barely faltered before continuing on to the next toe. Dante dodged Samson's tail as it lashed out and moved to stand directly in front of them.

"Lucas, we are not your enemy. You know this. You need to snap out of it," Dante said, keeping his tone non-threatening as he crouched next to him. "Kee wouldn't want you to be like this."

The red of Lucas' irises darkened, the red seeping into the whites of his eyes to tinge them pink. He bared his elongated fangs and jerked under the massive weight on top of him. He had to get out. He had to get to Keira.

He's not coherent, Samson said telepathically to Dante. *Words won't work on him.*

I had to try. Dante shot back. He winced when Samson snarled again as Lucas broke the last claw holding him down.

Samson quickly removed his foot as Lucas tried to bite him. With those longer, sharper canines, he wouldn't be surprised if Lucas was capable of tearing a chunk out of his hide. Once the vampire was free, he leapt to his feet, but before he could attack, Samson slammed his tail into his side. Lucas took the impact and grabbed the tail before Samson could pull it back.

Seeing his friend about to tear into the dragon's tail, Dante quickly closed the distance between them. He came up behind Lucas and put him in a tight chokehold. He bent his body back, bringing Lucas with him to throw off his balance.

Samson drew his tail back as Lucas released him to grab at Dante's forearm instead. The dragon saw the moment Lucas decided to use his fire, saw that flicker of light in his crimson eyes.

Fire! Samson shouted.

Dante moved as fast as he could. He abruptly released Lucas and leapt back, but the fire was already flaring. It caught on his shirt, but he tore it off with a hard pull. He winced as the fire seared his hands and bit at his chest, but he remained whole and not a pile of ash.

Samson shifted back into his human form, scowling at Lucas as the vampire surrounded himself with his golden flame again. "Fucking idiot," his hissed. He quickly glanced at Dante when he approached him, but otherwise kept his attention on the crazed vampire lord in front of him. "You alright?"

"I will be," Dante answered but flinched back as Lucas' fire flared. "Hopefully."

Samson's sensitive hearing picked up the sound of a soft, muffled crack from behind him. He got into a defensive position as Lucas' head jerked towards the sound, baring his fangs. Samson was ready to tackle the flaming vampire until the beautiful sound of a sharp inhale filled the tense silence. Even the sputtering, hacking coughs was music to his ears.

His alpha was alive. He could feel her mental frequency once again.

Dante could hear Gio muttering to Kee but couldn't make out the words. His attention was still on Lucas. His friend was tense and unmoving, wild eyes wide and unblinking. Dante stepped aside, giving Lucas a clear view of Kee and Gio. "Look. Kee's alive. Everything is going to be okay. She is *okay*."

Lucas stared. Keira was being held upright by another. His need to tear the person apart was shoved aside by the simple realization that she was gasping in air. A new need consumed his entire being. He had to hold her again. Had to make sure her warmth remained. That she remained his sun.

Giovanni tensed when Lucas began to close the distance between them. Fire still licked at Lucas' person, flames remaining in his footsteps for a few seconds before flickering out. Gio would have scampered back, but he was still supporting Kee's body, and he wasn't sure just how coherent Lucas was.

When Lucas dropped to his knees next to Kee, Gio pulled her closer to him. When Lucas snarled, he snapped, "Would you hurt her with your fire then? Burn her as you did Dante?"

Lucas did not have to decipher the man's words. He felt a soft touch on his knee and his gaze snapped down to see Kee's shaking hand had reached out towards him, her fingertips grazing his leg. His fire immediately blinked out, and that strangled sound wretched its way out of his throat again.

As soon as the other person released her, he scooped up his shape-shifter and cradled her in his lap. He gently smoothed back her hair and just stared down at her. She slowly blinked open her bloodshot eyes, the grey speckled with his emerald green. His blood was still smeared around her lips, the red bright against her pale skin.

"Keira," he croaked out, his voice sounding rough even to his own ears.

A small, weak smile ghosted her lips. She lifted her hand, arm shaking from the effort, and touched his cheek. "Mm here," she breathed.

He took her hand in his and pressed her palm firmly against his cheek. "Keira," he repeated, his voice breaking on the second syllable. He pulled her hand back and placed a kiss to her palm, squeezing his eyes tightly shut as he did. When he opened them again, they were back to their natural green color and shining with unshed tears. "*Keira.*"

Kee's own tears stung her eyes as he bent over her, resting his forehead against hers. "Sorry," she mumbled. "I didn't—"

"I know," he whispered. "Do not apologize. Just—" He took a second to compose himself as his words wobbled with his lingering grief. "Do not *ever* do that again, Keira. I cannot lose you. Do you understand? I cannot lose you. I would not survive it."

Her bottom lip trembled. "I won't," she promised.

Lucas pulled back enough to look at her again. He wiped a tear from her cheek then pressed his lips lightly to hers, savoring and relishing in the way she kissed him back. He would never take a single kiss for granted ever again. He would cherish each and every one they had.

Giovanni approached Samson and Dante, giving the couple their space. He took note of the shining blisters along Dante's chest and hands before glancing at Samson's swollen, purple fingers. He ran his hand through his hair with a relieved sigh. "Well, it could have been worse."

"We could have all fried instead," Samson mused as he tried to straighten out his broken fingers.

"Don't," Gio chided the dragon as he took his hand in his. "Let me set them before they heal wrong. Where are the others?"

"Mira and Brent are knocked out in the kitchen," Samson said, wincing as the doctor prodded at his fingers. "Conrad and Tori are disposing the bodies of Aubrey and that other guy. I was helping them, but I felt Kee's wavelength disappear, so I rushed in here." *Terrified*, he refrained from adding. "And Lucy is home with Mia."

"What was the crack earlier?" Dante asked as he watched his friend begin to pop the dragon's fingers back in place.

Gio flushed with embarrassment but kept his gaze down on the broken fingers. "I was running out of time to keep her from brain damage. We had hit three minutes and I was panicking. I started to press harder, and I broke one of her ribs."

Samson winced and bit back a growl at the pain in his hand. "Well," he gritted out. "At least we came out of this mostly unscathed."

Giovanni let go of Samson's hand after setting the bones. "I mean, I have a broken collar bone."

Dante couldn't help it; he laughed. "Poor Giovanni, want me to kiss your owie?"

The Italian lifted his chin haughtily. "You can tend to your own blisters then," he said and crossed his arms over his chest as Dante and Samson cackled.

Samson cut his laugh short as Lucas came over to them, Kee held protectively in his arms. His eyes softened and his shoulders drooped as the gravity of what happened finally hit him. "Kee," he began, but the rest of his vocabulary vanished. He could find no words to say to her.

She had saved him from The Top and gave him a new family he wouldn't exchange for the world. And how had he repaid her? By endangering himself in some fighting pits. And for what? To make himself momentarily feel a bit better? What if he had been at a fight tonight and hadn't been there to help her? What if Gio hadn't been able to bring her back? He would once again have nothing.

"Sam," she croaked, drawing his attention back to her. "I'm okay."

He inhaled sharply through his nose. "I'm sorry."

Kee's brows scrunched together. "For?"

"For fucking up," he grunted. "I won't do it again."

She blinked drowsily at him before giving him a weak smile. "Okay."

Samson's smile slipped when her eyes fell shut. The only thing to stop him from panicking was the fact that he could still feel her mental presence.

Lucas, on the other hand, still couldn't feel her. She was physically with him but was still missing everywhere else. The empty holes within him remained. "Giovanni," Lucas stressed, his tone panicked as he looked at his blood son.

Gio's heart clenched at the helpless look his lord was giving him. He pressed his fingers to the side of Kee's throat and gave Lucas a reassuring nod when he felt her pulse. "She's alright," he said before looking over the bruises blooming on her face and the blood smeared around her throat. "She's been through a lot and will need time to recover. Let's get her to your room and I'll get an IV of fluids just in case."

Lucas clutched Keira tighter to him but nodded his agreement. "Alright."

Samson, Gio, and Dante watched him leave without another word.

Dante let out a soft sigh once his friend disappeared through the kitchen doors. "Well, I'm going to go tell the coven they can come down now. They'll need to feed, but afterwards they'll need to help clean up the place."

Samson looked down at his purple fingers. "I'll need to tell Conrad and Tori what happened. I didn't explain myself when I rushed in here but told them to stay and finish up the bodies." He blinked. "Oh, the dumpster is probably still on fire."

Gio shot him an incredulous look as the dragon hurried past him before rubbing his temples. "If I was still human, you all would have given me a heart attack already."

Dante laughed. "Good thing you're not," he said and gently set his hand on Gio's shoulder. "Don't forget to look after yourself too."

"I won't," he agreed. "But I'll try to patch up Lucas' wound once I get Kee hooked up to an IV. Then I'll go out and feed."

The two nodded at each other before both setting out to do their tasks.

Nineteen

Lucas squeezed the last drop of blood from the bag, swallowed, and tossed the crinkled, pink-tinged, plastic packet down on top of the others on the nightstand. These were a poor substitute for an actual meal after sustaining the wound he had, but he was too worried about Keira to leave her for a proper feeding.

His attention shifted so he was staring down at her again, willing her to wake with his gaze. She had been asleep for over twenty-four hours, and it was stressing him out. Her pack had spent the daytime hours with her, trying to get her to rise, but not even their pack bonds could rouse her.

Gio assured him that all her vitals were fine, but it did nothing to calm him. He needed to see her eyes, to talk to and hold her. He only briefly got any of that when she came back from death, but it wasn't nearly enough to sooth him.

Especially since he was still missing her essence within him.

Lucas found petty satisfaction that Cain was feeling the same loss he was. Conrad had told him that Cain came to Byte early in the morning, demanding to know what happened to Keira. Apparently, he had felt when she died and had panicked. The pack told him she was alive and explained what happened. He claimed he couldn't feel the mating bond between them anymore and wanted to see her, but the pack refused him.

Her broken mating bond reinforced Lucas' theory that her death had severed the blood bonds that connected her to both him and Cain.

It is still a bitter pill to swallow, he mused to himself as he reached down to brush a strand of hair off Keira's pale cheek. *But at least he does not have you either.*

Lucas grunted at the knock that came from the bedroom door and flicked his eyes to Dante as he ducked his head in, Gio lingering behind him. His spine straightened with apprehension at the stress radiating off his second. "What is it?"

Dante jerked his head over his shoulder towards the hall. "The Lord of California is here."

Lucas immediately stood from the bed, shock momentarily widening his eyes. "Abraham is here? *Now?*"

Gio nodded solemnly. "He's demanding to speak with you."

Lucas ran a hand through his mussed hair and looked down at his grey sweatpants and plain black t-shirt. "Tell him I need to change and shower." Because he most definitely had not showered since the New Year's party. He had been immobile with the stake, exhausted after Florence died, and too worried about Keira when he woke this evening and found she still had not risen.

"No, he said now," Dante retorted with a grimace. "He's not happy, Lucas."

Lucas let out a stream of curses in Greek. "Of all the timing," he murmured as he followed Dante and Gio out the door and closed it softly behind him. "Did he say why he is here?"

Dante shook his head as he followed Lucas down the hall. "No, but he did ask where Florence is. I think he knows."

Lucas very clearly remembered the warning Abraham gave him to tread carefully. He was sure that killing his maker went directly against that. It was true that he wasn't the one who did it, but he would be damned if he let Keira take the fall for it.

He turned to Dante and Gio stopping them before they all went up the stairs. "*I* killed Florence."

Giovanni blinked once in confusion before understanding hit him. "Kee—"

"Was hurt. That set me off after everything else Florence did to us. Do you understand? *I* am the one who did it," Lucas stressed.

Dante rubbed his hand over his bald head anxiously. "And if he compels us to tell the truth?"

Lucas' jaw clenched. "Then you tell him the truth. It was my fire that killed Florence. It is not a lie, is it?"

"Well, no, but—"

He cut Dante off. "There is no but. It was my fire, my curse." He squeezed Dante's shoulder. "I will not let Keira take the blame for what happened. She has been through too much these past months and dealing with the Lord of California is the last thing she needs. Besides, it was my temper that led to Florence's death."

Gio frowned at Lucas. "No, she had it coming. She purposefully came here to antagonize you."

"I know, and you can help correlate that to Abraham when he questions me, but I have to be the one to take the fall for her death." When Dante hesitated, he resorted to begging. "Please, Dante. I need you to do this for me. And for Keira."

Dante sighed but nodded his agreement. "I will. I'm just nervous with what will happen."

"That makes two of us." Lucas' hand dropped away as he turned to the stairs and climbed them. "But perhaps nothing will come of it since it was all in defense of my coven and bonded wolf."

"Hopefully," Gio murmured as he followed Lucas into the kitchen then through the doors leading into the club.

From the corner of his eye, Lucas saw Dante and Giovanni head to the bar, keeping a respectful distance away. Gathering his wits about him, he faced the unassuming male standing next to the Christmas tree, looking at the ornaments with fascination. The man was shorter than Lucas with pale skin and wavy reddish-brown hair.

"Abraham," Lucas greeted as he closed the distance between them. "My lord."

The Lord of California met Lucas' gaze. "Lucas Vranas, the Curse of Apollo." His dark brown eyes skated over Lucas' unkempt form before he clicked his tongue. "You must have quite the story to tell me."

Lucas steeled his spine and casually shoved his hands into the pockets of his sweats. "I do."

"That's quite unfortunate," Abraham sighed. He tilted his head to the side, eyeing Lucas curiously. "Tell me, where is your maker? I had a date with her this evening."

"Dead," Lucas answered calmly. "I believe her ash was gathered up by my blood son, but some of it is probably still on the floor. We're still in the middle of cleaning Byte up after her attack on my coven."

Abraham had his hand around Lucas' throat in the blink of an eye, an angry snarl curling up his lip to reveal elongated fangs. "I thought I had made myself clear when I told you to tread carefully, but perhaps you missed my intent." He squeezed Lucas' throat. "Killing your maker is going directly against my orders!"

Lucas didn't break eye contact with Abraham, nor did he react defensively. He felt Giovanni and Dante's tension, but they knew better than to intervene. "As I stated," he grunted out past the hold on his neck. "Florence attacked first."

Abraham narrowed his eyes as they shifted to a crimson red. "Are you honest in what you say? Repeat those words again if they are true."

He let the compulsion wash over him. It was a strange sensation, being the one compelled, but he knew better than to fight it. "Florence attacked me and what is mine first."

The Lord of California's cheek twitched in displeasure, but he released his hold so that he could get the full story. "Explain. Tell me truthfully what happened from start to finish."

"She arrived unannounced at my coven's home for our Christmas party," Lucas began. "Which was not an issue. She—"

"Stop," Abraham commanded as he held up a hand. "You lied there. Why was it an issue?"

Lucas sighed. "Lord Abraham, you do not know of my past with Florence."

"Then enlighten me," he demanded. "I need all details and facts before I make my judgement."

He ran a hand down his face. "Florence desired me from the moment she found me. Whether it was my curse she wanted to possess or my body, I am not sure, but she made sure she had both. After she turned me, she forced me to feed on humans and used those early days' lust against me." His jaw clenched, but he refused to look away from the gaze judging his words. "When I was acclimated to my new vampire nature and could control the lust that came from feedings, I realized how precarious my situation was."

Abraham's gaze narrowed slightly, but not with disbelief. "This is a serious crime and a breech of maker conduct. Why did you not say anything?"

"Florence was a gilded member in the vampire communities. Everyone held her in such high esteem that I did not try to reach out for assistance against her. Not when she killed the first woman I cared for in a fit of rage, nor the second. All I could do was act like she was my everything while putting physical distance between us." He balled his hands into fists and glanced over at Giovanni and Dante. "These two can corroborate what I say if you need further validation. They have been there for some of the interactions."

Abraham looked over at the two by the bar. When they nodded their heads, he let out a frustrated grunt. "I need *verbal* answers. Is this true?"

"Yes."

"Yes."

The Lord of California rubbed at his chin before turning back to Lucas. "Continue."

"To answer your question, that is why it was an issue. I detested and loathed everything about her. Her mere presence was enough to send me into a rage. However, the real issue in her being there is what it meant for my bonded wolf." His lips pressed together before he let out the next statement. He was wary of so many people knowing about his weakness, but he had to tell his lord the truth. Very softly he said, "I love my wolf, Lord Abraham, and I feared for her safety."

Abraham continued to hold his subordinate's eyes. "Given the history, I can see why you would be worried." His voice softened a fraction. "You do love your wolf. I can hear the truth in your words."

Lucas nodded. "Yes. I did not want her to face the same end the other two did. Together, Keira and I tried to disguise our relationship. We kept away from each other and when Florence demanded to meet her, we acted as if we were nothing more than wolf and vampire." His fingers flexed at his sides. "But I was unaware Florence already knew about us."

Abraham held up his hand to stop Lucas. "Only one of them is your blood son, correct?"

Lucas' brow furrowed at the random question. "Yes, Giovanni is my blood son. Dante is my second."

"Then I wish for Dante to tell me what happened next. I need someone not from your line to tell me their side of events." Abraham looked at Dante. "Were you there for what happened next?"

Dante startled when Abraham turned to him, the compulsion hitting him hard. "Y-yes, my lord." He swallowed when Abraham gestured for him to continue. "On New Year's Eve, Lucas went to his bonded wolf to console her when he felt her sudden grief. When he returned, he informed us that Kee's mother figure was murdered. We began speculating who could have done it and decided that Lady Florence was the best suspect. You see, she demanded we throw a party for the holiday but showed up late for it."

"People arrive late all the time," Abraham countered. "Why was that suspicious?"

Dante shook his head. "It was weird timing. But it turns out that we were right because Florence interrupted our meeting and admitted to it."

"Admitted to what?" the lord pressed.

Lucas' lips pressed together as his panic rose. Dante had to be very careful with how he worded what Florence said. He did not want Keira's identity as a shapeshifter to be outed to the Lord of California. He didn't know Abraham well enough to gage what he would do if he knew the truth.

Dante resisted the urge to anxiously rub his head. "Lady Florence said that she wouldn't let another woman have Lucas. When Lucas told her that he wasn't hers, she snapped. She admitted to killing Kee's great-grandma because she knew she couldn't kill Kee directly without causing political problems." At Abraham's questioning look, he explained, "She's mated to the Alpha of LA."

"Interesting," he murmured before waving his hand at Dante. "Go on."

"Lady Florence stated that she wanted to punish Lucas for his treachery. She said she wanted to feed from Kee with Lucas. And, well, my lord didn't respond well to that," Dante said, throwing a worried glance at Lucas. When Lucas nodded, he continued. "He attacked Florence, but she staked him in the chest before he could kill her. Giovanni was also attacked, but I managed to escape to get help."

Abraham turned back to Lucas, ignoring how Dante sagged in relief as the compulsion left. "She staked you?"

"Yes." Lucas pulled up his shirt to show the stitched wound on his chest. "It would have healed more if I fed, but I have been concerned about Keira."

He inspected the wound with mild interest, letting out a soft hum. His lifted his eyes back to Lucas'. "What happened to your wolf? Florence?"

Lucas lowered his shirt back down. "When she staked me, it left me immobile, and she used that time to take over my coven. She shut down Byte and locked my vampires in the upstairs rooms, making them rely on blood packets for sustenance.

"Keira and a few members of her pack came to Byte when Dante went to her. I did not witness what happened but was told that her pack members had to fight my blood daughter and killed her. But let it be known that I harbor no ill feelings towards them. Aubrey turned against me and assisted Florence in her scheme. I have no room for traitors in my coven."

Abraham rubbed the bridge of his nose. "The deaths of both your maker and your blood daughter does not look good, Lucas."

Lucas' hackles rose. "Was I supposed to let her keep control of my coven? Let her kill the woman I love? I would rather die, Abraham."

His lips pinched together. "Finish your tale."

"Dante snuck into my bedroom and helped free Giovanni from his silver restraints so he could then take the stake out of my chest. When Dante told me Keira was fighting Florence, I rushed to help her. Together we brought her down." He held Abraham's stare and sneered, "She burned with my flame."

Abraham narrowed his eyes at Lucas and rubbed at his bottom lip as he replayed the words given to him. "Tell me again how she died."

"By my flame," Lucas reiterated, trying to keep the panic at bay.

The Lord of California continued to rub at his bottom lip as his gaze skirted around the club. His eyes fell on the camera tucked up behind the bar. He jerked his head at it but looked at Giovanni. "If I watch this camera feed, who will I see killing Florence?"

Gio swayed, not expecting the sudden force of the compulsion that hit him. "L-Lord Lucas." It was the truth, after all. He would *technically* see Lucas killing her.

"Who would I see?" Abraham asked, now turning his power on Dante.

Dante flinched. "You would see Lucas killing Lady Florence."

Abraham sighed and dropped his compulsion, his irises turning back to brown. He regarded Lucas with a tired expression. "I have heard your account of what happened, as well as your second's," he announced. "Given what Florence did to you in the past, as well as her recent slights against you and yours, I agree her death was warranted."

The knot in Lucas' chest eased.

"But it is still a very serious crime to kill your maker, Lucas, and your recent track record is not helping you." Abraham smoothed down his cream-colored dress shirt. "If this had been an isolated incident, and you hadn't killed two high-ranking vampires before this, I could have slapped you on the wrist and called it a night."

Unease had that knot tightening back up, dread dripping down into his stomach to curdle the blood he consumed earlier.

"You agreed they were all justified the first time we spoke about it," Lucas pointed out, jaw clenching.

"I did," Abraham agreed. "And they were. *However*, you need to understand how this looks. You are directly under me as a lord of a county. I cannot let it seem that I am showing special treatment by letting you get away with killing this many high-ranking vampires."

Giovanni hurried towards them from the bar and stepped in, fear for his blood father rising. "My lord, technically Lord Lucas did demote one of them before killing them. And he only killed Alexander because he kidnapped and tortured me. He avenged and saved me."

Abraham gave him a pitting frown as the younger vampire shivered with his memories. "Yes, but then Lucas burned that coven down in retaliation. Thankfully no humans or other vampires were killed."

"I protect what is mine," Lucas declared. "As *any* vampire lord would. Are you telling me you would not have done the same if the roles were reversed?"

"Of course, I would have," Abraham said calmly. "But you need to understand how it looks from my end. You cannot go unpunished for all these deaths. If you do, it will set a bad example. I *cannot* allow anyone to think they can get away with this many deaths without repercussion."

"But—" Gio began but was cut off by Abraham.

"*Enough,*" the Lord of California snapped, immediately silencing him. "I have made my decision." He smoothed his hands down his shirt again and addressed Lucas. "Lucas Vranas, the Curse of Apollo, I sentence you to the grave on holy ground for exactly one year."

There was a buzzing in Lucas' ears, a roaring so loud he was sure he misheard. One year encased within holy ground. Was this a joke?

"That's unfair!" Gio shouted, throwing his hands up indignantly. "He was protecting everyone! I would be dead if it weren't for him! So would his wolf! Hell, the coven may have died too!"

"Giovanni," Lucas warned, but it came out as a hollow reprimand. He grabbed Gio's wrist to stop him from possibly getting in trouble with Abraham. "He has made his decision and we have to accept that." He shot his son a warning glance when he opened his mouth to protest and looked at Abraham again. "May I at least have the rest of the evening to get my affairs in order?"

"Granted. Tomorrow evening, as soon as the sun is down, I want you at St. Vincent de Paul's Catholic Church in Huntington Beach ready to go under. You will have a feeding tube that runs from your coffin to the outside so that you can be fed one packet of blood a night. Understood?" he asked.

"Yes, Lord Abraham. I will be there," Lucas replied, trying to keep his voice steady despite the turbulence of emotions welling up inside him.

Abraham's expression softened. "It is only a year, Lucas. I know you are strong enough to handle it. Everything will be cleared when you rise." He patted Lucas on the shoulder. "Well, I will see you tomorrow then."

The trio remained silent, waiting until the front door slammed shut behind Abraham before speaking.

"Lucas…" Dante started, but Lucas shook his head.

"Not now. I have to get things prepared for my year away," he said, voice void of emotion. "I will need you two to help keep things in order when I am away. I will write up a list of what I expect to be done in my absence and who will take over what."

"Of course," Gio mumbled. "But we should talk about this."

Lucas rolled his shoulders back and stood straighter. "There is nothing to talk about, Giovanni. I am going under for a year and need to prepare."

"What about Kee?" Dante asked, halting Lucas as he began to make his way to the stairs that led to his office.

He stiffened for a moment, hand tightening on the railing until it creaked. "I will speak with her if she wakes in time, but for now I need to make sure I do not lose anything else in the year I am away."

Gio and Dante exchanged a glance but didn't stop him.

Twenty

It was an hour until dawn when Lucas finally made it back down to his bedroom. With a heavy sigh, he closed the door and turned towards the bed, going eerily still when he saw it was empty. The panic he had been holding at bay flared with new vigor.

He had held his shit together when Abraham was questioning him, even refrained from snarling and fighting back when he was given his unjust sentence, but had started to lose a grip on the anxiousness when he was alone in his office. Different scenarios of what could happen with Keira kept circling in his head, none of them pleasant. However, he forcefully shoved them down so he could get everything ready for his reluctant absence.

But seeing his bed empty unleashed it all.

His one greatest fear about being locked up was losing his shapeshifter. They had been an official couple for such a short amount of time, and a year away could ruin it. She could so easily forget about him and find someone else. Especially now, when they were no longer bonded. There was no part of him in her, nothing that tied them together anymore. She was free from any influence, whether it was from him or Cain.

Cain, he seethed. *I should kill him before I go underground.*

Lucas had lost Keira to him twice. Once when he first refused to get involved in a relationship with an employee, then when she ran to him after their fight about Alexander. He could even say that he lost her a third time when Cain marked her as his mate, but Keira had remained by Lucas' side even after he had been a raging, jealous prick.

However, what would stop her now? With him gone and out of sight for twelve months? For fifty-two weeks? For three hundred and sixty-five days?

"Lucas?"

He jerked up his head and saw Keira leaning against the bathroom doorframe. His heart clenched with fondness at the sight of her wearing one of his plain black T-shirt's, the hem falling to her thighs. When she took a stumbling step towards him, he was at her side in the blink of an eye. He carefully swooped her up into his arms and carried her back to the bed.

"What are you doing up?" he chided softly, holding her just a little tighter before setting her down on the sheets.

"Had to pee," she croaked before gesturing at the borrowed shirt. "I stole this from you. The other clothes were gross from the fight."

A smile curved up his lips as he sat down on the edge of the bed. "There is no stealing. Whatever is mine, is yours."

Kee smiled back at him, but it was strained and tired. "I feel like death."

His smile slipped. "That is because you died."

She rubbed at her face. "I know," she grumbled. "I knew something was wrong as soon as I shifted, but I ignored it. I wanted to help kill Florence."

"There was no helping, Keira. You did kill her. You saved all of us," he said, taking her hand in his. "But you cannot tell *anyone* that you did. Do you understand? You will be in danger if you do."

She blinked at him, finally noticing the dark smudges under his eyes and the haunted look in them. She raised her free hand to cup his cool face, thumb rubbing over his cheekbone. "What happened?"

Lucas' eyes fluttered shut as he relished her touch. He nuzzled his nose into her palm before pulling it from his face so he could hold both her hands. "I have to tell you something."

Kee's brow furrowed. "Are you okay?"

He saw that emerald green still speckled in the grey of her irises as he held her stare and a not-so-small part of him was pleased that a piece of him was physically with her. An even larger, possessive part of him hoped it was permanent, that she would forever be marred by him.

"Lucas? Babe? You're worrying me."

Drawing himself from his thoughts, he ignored her concerned expression and took in the beauty of her face, committing it to memory. He would use this image of her to get him through the rough year ahead. He leaned forward and placed his lips against her forehead. "I love you, Keira."

She fisted his shirt in hand, holding him in place so he couldn't pull away. "And I love you, but you're really starting to scare me," she murmured. "What did I miss?"

He pressed his lips harder for a moment before pulling back as far as she would let him. He met her gaze and laced the fingers of their remaining joined hands together. "I have to go away for a while."

That was not at all what Kee was expecting.

"Go away?" she repeated. "Where? When? How long are you going to be gone?"

Lucas dropped his gaze to their hands and forced out the next words, no matter how much they pained him to speak. "A year."

Her mouth floundered. "A-a year?" she repeated, her anxiousness turning into that familiar cold panic. "What do you mean a fucking *year*, Lucas? Where are you going?"

His chest once again tightened as he saw the turmoil in her paling face. "I mean what I say. For twelve months I will be below ground," he stated solemnly. "It is my punishment for killing Florence."

She shook her head rapidly, not accepting it. "No, no, *I* killed Florence! You just said that—"

He pressed his lips to hers, stopping her from saying it again. "*No*," he stressed in a harsh whisper against her lips. "I did."

Her eyes searched his. "I don't understand," she whispered, barely hearing it over the pulse pounding in her neck and the rushing in her ears. He couldn't leave her.

He rested his forehead against hers once again, unable to look at the growing fear in her eyes. "I killed Alexander and Jada, burned down the Arcadia coven, and now burned Florence alive." When he heard her take in a breath to argue, he squeezed her hand. "I did all these things with proper reason. If I did not have just cause to do them, then my sentence would be much worse."

"But *I*—"

"Keira," he said sharply, jaw flexing. "We both know what really transpired, but I do not want the Lord of California to know what you are. There would be no other way to explain how my maker died without telling the whole truth. I told him she died by my flame and that is truth enough. I cannot let you fall into danger by exposing your heritage to someone neither one of us trusts. Especially if I am not around to protect you from them."

Kee quieted for a moment as she realized what he was saying. He was taking the blame for what she did because of what she was. He was getting punished because of her. "It's not fair," she finally murmured.

He exhaled in relief when she didn't fight him. "It is not," he agreed. "But it has been decided and I cannot go against it. He is the

Lord of California, and his word is final."

She removed her hand from his as tears burned her eyes. Closing the tiny remaining distance between, she crawled into his lap and wrapped her arms tightly around him. "It's not fair," she cried again as she buried her face in his neck. "It's bullshit!"

Lucas held her close and tight, one hand cradling the back of her head. "I know," he said softly, fully aware of the emotion threatening to seep into his words.

"I can't lose you," Kee whispered brokenly. "Not now. Not after this week apart, and I *just* lost Nana, and—"

A sob cut her sentence short, and he held her tighter as warm tears splashed against his skin. He fucking hated when she cried. "I *know*." This time his voice cracked. "I will not apologize for taking the blame because I will *always* protect you in any way I can, my sweet. I am, however, sorry for what it caused." His voice softened as his own eyes stung. "For what it will do to us."

"It'll be so hard without you," she mumbled in a watery voice.

Oh, it wouldn't just be hard. It would be excruciating.

"It will be," he murmured.

Her insecurities peeked out from their hiding. "I don't know if I can do it without you. You've been my rock since the attack, and I'm scared I'll fail at everything without you."

As much as her words warmed him, they also made him angry on her behalf. She dared doubt herself after everything she had been through? "You foolishly underestimate yourself, Keira. Look at everything you have accomplished. You do not need me to succeed at anything." His hold tightened. "You do not need me."

Kee shook her head and placed a tender kiss to his neck. "I will always need you."

His heart splintered. Both with joy and dread. "And I you," he whispered.

"We will make it work," she said determinedly, pulling back and sniffling as she rubbed the moisture from her nose. "It's going to be hard, yes, but we don't have to truly be apart. We can bond again and that way we'll still be with each other, right?"

Lucas avoided her gaze, instead looking at the bruising Florence inflicted around her neck.

A new burst of panic flared in her chest like an icy flame. "Lucas?" When he met her gaze again, she deepened her tone. "*Right?*"

His gaze dropped to her neck again, his hand lightly brushing against the soft skin there. He couldn't bond with her again, not while he was away. "No."

"No?" she repeated, back straightening with incredulity. "What do you mean *no?*" Those old insecurities crept out more with her spike in anxiety. "Is it me? D-did I do something wrong?"

He cursed at his tactless response, but his own heart felt crushed with his decision. "Of course not, Keira."

She shoved at his shoulders as that panic curbed into something that roused her dormant anger. "Then why the fuck not?!"

Lucas hardly moved from her push. "You just got your freedom and individuality back. You are free from the bonds that were forced on you and can finally be completely by yourself. Why would I take that away from you?"

She blinked before her brows furrowed. "You're not taking anything from me. I want to be bonded to you." Her expression softened into something tender as she cupped his face in her hands, frowning when he didn't look at her. "I love feeling connected to you. It brings me peace and warmth when I seek you out in my head. Your presence settles me, makes me feel safe and loved. Why wouldn't I want that back?"

Lucas sucked in a ragged breath. She was killing him with her words, and she didn't even know it. "I cannot."

Pain lanced through her as he still refused to meet her eyes. "Don't you feel the same way with me?"

Gods damn it. "Of course, I do."

She dropped her hands from his face, resting them on his shoulders again. "Then why? Why would you go away without establishing a connection between us first? Why isolate us from each other if we don't have to be?" Her frustration and pain caused her voice to rise. "Why would you willingly be alone?!"

A growl rumbled in his chest as he sharply looked up at her, meeting her distraught gaze with his own. "Because I could not stand it!" he answered vehemently. "If you were to become angry or sad, I would be tempted to break from my prison to comfort you. If you were in any sort of pain, every part of me would yearn to hunt down and destroy the reason you were hurting.

"Every time you felt overjoyed, I would wonder who it was making you feel that way in my stead. It would plague me, drive me to madness. Who was making you happy when I was not? Who was making you smile? Laugh? And *how*? What were you doing together? Did they make you happier than I did?

"And that leads to the worst of all scenarios, what if you did not wait for me? What if you moved on while I was stuck six feet under the ground? Without me near you to keep your attention, would you focus it elsewhere? Would you find pleasure with someone else since I was not there to please it? Would you fall for that person as you fell for me? As I fell for you?"

He was aware that his fingers had dug into her hips the more he spoke his fears aloud, but he refused to remove them or loosen his hold. He would hold tight to her for as long as he had her. "I could not stand it, Keira. I would rather die than feel you move on from me, feel your love for me dissipate."

Kee stared at him as if he had spouted some nonsense in a foreign language. So many emotions warred in her head and heart. "What?" she finally managed to ask. When he swallowed and went to speak again, she roughly slapped her hand over his mouth. And it *was* a slap, the sound and sting in her palm confirmed it.

"No, don't actually speak," she sneered, her anger at the wheel while disappointment and hurt sat in the backseat. "I'm so furious with you I could punch you. You literally just told me I underestimate myself, but how can I think otherwise if you-," she sucked in a shaky breath. "-if you think so little of me?"

Lucas saw tears well in her eyes again and tried to speak, but her fingers pressed harder into his cheek, tightening her hold.

"After all this stupid fucking *bullshit*, you think something as fickle as time will change what we've created?" Her voice once again rose with anger and cracked with her sorrow. "Will stop my love for you? Your physical presence doesn't keep my attention. I don't need you next to me to remind myself why I love you. That's what memories are for!" She eased her hold on his mouth and pressed her fingertips to his lips instead. "Every kiss, every hug, every intimate time I'll remember. Every single time you made me laugh or smile. Better yet, every time *you* laughed or smiled. Especially the times when your fangs show. That's how I know you're truly amused.

"Even the stupid fights we've had I'll remember fondly because even when I told myself I hated or wanted nothing to do with you, I did. I lied to myself knowing full well that you were the only thing I wanted." The tears rolled down her cheeks. "And making up was like coming home."

She blinked away her remaining tears and met his eyes, her heart clenching at the sheen of wetness there. "But as you once told me, *actions speak louder than words*, so I will prove myself to you. I'll accept this year alone, without you in my head, because I'll have you in my heart instead. And when you come back, it'll be the best homecoming yet."

Lucas grabbed her hand and pressed a kiss to her fingertips before releasing it. Cupping the nape of her neck, he brought their mouths together in a tender, loving caress. When she kissed him back with the same softness, he moved them so that they were lying flush along the bed, his body over hers.

"I love you," Kee breathed against his lips, the weight of his body on hers a comfort to her soul. She knew it would only hurt more when it was gone, but for now she would bask and revel in the calm it provided.

He brushed their lips together. "I love you," he repeated. When he felt her hands dropping to the waistband of his sweats, he didn't try to stop her and assisted in removing them completely. Even without their bond, he knew she needed this. Hell, *he* needed it before he left her. He would take this memory with him to the grave and use it to get him through the year.

He removed his shirt and tossed it to the ground. His hands skimmed up and along the soft skin of her legs as he settled between her thighs. His hand slid up to her hips, holding them as he slowly sank into her. He closed his eyes for a brief moment, committing the sound of her breathy moan to memory.

When she went to remove the shirt she wore, he stopped her so he could do it himself. Slowly, he peeled the shirt away from her body and tossed it to the floor. His breath caught in his throat at the sight of her naked beneath him. "I want to remember you just like this," he rasped, throat tight as he filled her to the hilt and made her cry out his name. "With you naked beneath me, full of my cock and crying my name." Her sprawled out on *his* bed, moaning *his* name, was an image he needed to hold on to.

Despite the short time they had left, he didn't rush making love to her. It wasn't the fact that they were both battered and weak, it was that he wanted to savor this last time with her. He bent over her body, elbows by her head so that his ear was near her lips. He listened to every different gasp, moan, and cry she made as he made long, slow strokes within her, the different pitches and tones creating a melody in his head. He would use it as a lullaby, replaying it each night in his coffin before the sun rose and dragged him to sleep.

When they finished, they lay cocooned in each other's arms, fingers deftly trialing over one another's bodies, trying to remember each line and contour. Each freckle and blemish. Each scar and brand.

"Can I be with you when you go under?" she whispered as she traced the dip in his collarbone.

He fought to keep his eyes open as he replied to her. "As much as I would love that, I do not think it is a good idea. The temptation to rebel would be too great." He brushed his lips over hers. "Besides, I want this night to be my last memory of you. It's perfect."

She hummed, not voicing her hurt. "Will you at least tell me where you're being buried?"

"No," he answered softly with regret. "I do not trust myself to not break free upon sensing you. And I do not want to make it any harder for us than it already is."

Kee frowned at him. "What about Gio and Dante? Will they know where you are? What do they think about all this?"

"They do not like it either. And yes, they will know, but I have instructed them not to tell you." He lightly pinched her hip when she scowled. "Do not make it harder on them by trying to wrangle it out of them, my sweet. They will already have a lot on their plate running things."

She sighed, temporarily letting go of her anger so it wouldn't ruin their last minutes together. "What about Byte? I'm assuming that's included."

His eyes fluttered, but he forced them open. "Giovanni will be in charge of the coven with Dante backing him up, but Dante is also still in charge of all of Byte's security measures. I had actually hoped you would agree to run Byte. You do not have to be here every night from open to close, but you know bars and how they are run. I know you are busy with your pack, so you can turn down the offer."

Her eyes softened. "Of course, I will help, Lucas. You don't have to ask."

"Thank you," he murmured.

They fell into a heavy silence, both knowing and dreading what was coming.

Still, as dawn officially hit, Lucas fought against the deep seeded urge to sleep. Because once he did, that was it, she would be gone. His eyes fell shut, but he snapped them back open, focusing on her now once glistening ones. "I love you," he breathed.

"I love you," she whispered, running the backs of her fingers down his cheek. A part of her continued to break as she watched him fight for consciousness, but she refused to let the last image he had of her to be filled with tears. She gave him a small smile but made sure it conveyed all her love for him. "It's okay, Lucas. You can sleep." When panic flittered across his vision, she gently shushed him. "It's okay," she repeated. "I *love* you, and I will see you in a year. I will be there when you get out, I promise."

Lucas' eyes closed without his permission, and the last thing he felt before the day claimed his consciousness was her lips pressing shakily against his.

Twenty-One

Kee dropped the bottle of concealer on the counter, giving up before she even tried to apply it. Fuck it, let the world see the dark circles under her eyes. Let them witness her grief. And honestly, why should she hide it? Why bother with makeup especially on a day like this? Why should she have to make herself look okay when she was far from it?

Yeah, fuck that.

"You okay in here?" Lucy asked, trying to keep her voice light as she stepped into the bathroom.

The pack was worried for their alpha. They knew Kee was struggling after being dealt two serious losses at the same time. Nana's death was hard enough for her to handle but losing Lucas three days ago had made it worse.

Lucy remembered going to check on Kee the day Lucas was supposed to go under. She found her alpha curled into his body as he slept, quietly begging him not to leave her. Smelling the tears and hearing the desperation, Lucy had hurried to Kee's side to console her. Cooing soft words, she had pet Kee's hair and rubbed her back, trying to calm her down while also trying to figure out what was happening.

When Kee had managed to regain her composure, she sat up and looked at Lucy with bloodshot, swollen eyes and told her everything that happened the night before.

"He's getting imprisoned for something I did," Kee sniffled. *"And he wouldn't bond with me because he thinks I'll forget about him. Which is so fucking stupid, but I know why he thinks that. He didn't say it, but it's because I ran to Cain when we got into a fight."* She rubbed angrily at her nose then pressed the heels of her palms into her eyes. *"All because I was so fucking stupid in my rage and wanted to get away from him! I didn't have anywhere else to go close by and so I chose my ex of all fucking people! I was so angry and blind that I made a mistake!"*

Lucy rubbed Kee's bare knee. "It was a mistake, Kee. You can't hold on to that."

"How can I not?" she cried. "When it clearly made him think so poorly of me?"

"He doesn't think poorly of you," Lucy said. "Otherwise, he wouldn't have asked you to marry him. He wouldn't have fought so hard to keep you, Kee."

Kee pulled her hands from her face and looked at the empty spot on her finger. "I had to take it off to shift. What if he also saw it wasn't there and thought I said no? That I would never be ready?"

"He's smarter than that," she scoffed and looked at the unconscious vampire. "Well, about some stuff anyways. His whole reaction to this is silly to me. We all know you won't get over or forget him, but he clearly has some insecurities."

"Yes, and I put them there." Kee scowled down at her hands. "He won't even tell me where he's being buried. He doesn't want to be tempted to break free."

Lucy lifted a brow. "No, I think he knows you're crazy enough to dig him out."

A startled laugh escaped Kee's lips. "Yeah, you're probably right."

Lucy drew her alpha into a hug. "I know this is going to be hard on you, but you have to remember that you're not alone. You have built an amazing pack, and we are here for you."

Kee sank into the fox's embrace with a heavy sigh. "Thank you."

"Fuck makeup."

Lucy blinked out the memory and gave Kee an enthusiastic nod. "Yes, it's truly torturous."

Kee looked at Lucy in the mirror. "I'm not wearing any today."

"Then don't." Lucy shrugged. "Today is about Nana, not anyone else. If they try to say shit to you, I'll probably dick punch them."

A reluctant smile pulled at her lips. "And if it's a girl?"

Lucy shrugged. "Same answer. Except I believe it's called a cunt punch."

Kee laughed, but it was brittle with her sorrow. "Thank you for that." Her face fell a bit as she turned and faced her pack mate. "I'm sorry I've been such a shit alpha these past couple days."

Lucy held up her hand. "Stop that right now," she scolded. "None of us think that. We know you're going through a tough time, and we're here to support you."

Kee nodded once, cherishing the warmth Lucy's words brought her. It wasn't enough to thaw the ice in her chest, but it helped. Turning back to the mirror, she ran her hands over the black dress she wore. It had sleeves to her elbows and hugged her torso before flaring out at her hips, the hem brushing the top of her feet while in flats.

"It feels wrong to get ready for Nana's wake at her house," she murmured. "Especially since she died here." Not that anyone could tell. Dan's pack cleaned the kitchen so thoroughly that the decades old grout looked brand new.

Lucy stepped into the bathroom and behind her alpha, gathering the long golden hair to fashion in a low fancy ponytail. "I think she would have liked it this way."

"I know." Kee closed her eyes as Lucy styled her hair, taking the comfort it provided.

At the soft knock along the door frame, they both looked up to see Tori. She tucked her freshly dyed blue bangs behind her ear and gestured at the outfit she borrowed from Lucy. "Is this okay?"

Kee took in the dark grey, silk blouse and black dress pants and smiled upon seeing the black converse. It was perfectly Tori. "It's perfect."

Tori smiled but frowned at Lucy as she stepped back from finishing Kee's hair. Her black dress was strapless and flowy, only cinching at her waist to accent her curves. To finish her look, she had a black shawl over her shoulders to give her a more elegant and modest appearance.

"Should I have worn a dress like the rest of you girls?" Tori asked. "You all look so pretty and girly and shit."

Kee couldn't stop her laugh. "No, don't change. Don't force yourself to be someone you're not, Tori," she said, remembering what Tori had told her about her past. She knew her newest pack mate only told her tale to distract Kee from her grief, but it made their bond just a little stronger.

"Thanks, Kee." Tori gave her a grateful smile and cleared her throat. "Anyways, I came to get you because people started arriving at the main house. It's only the Riverside pack right now and the boys are greeting them, but I figured I would come get you."

Kee's smile fell as she realized the wake was happening. She rubbed her face and reluctantly nodded. "Alright, let's go."

Tori and Lucy flanked their alpha as they stepped out of the guest house and made their way across the lawn to the main house. Kee spotted Samson first. He was standing next to Conrad at the base of the porch stairs, hands shoved in his front pockets as he listened to whatever Dan was saying. Her gaze then moved to Conrad, noticing the hand resting on Mia's shoulder as she clung to his side and refused to meet Dan's stare.

"Mia," Kee called, not liking how tense she was around another alpha.

"Auntie Kee!" Mia chimed, breaking away from her dad to run to Kee, holding up the hem of her long sleeve, black dress so she didn't trip. When she got to her alpha, she wrapped her arms around her waist and hugged her tightly. "You look so pretty."

Kee laughed, knowing damn well she didn't. "Thank you, so do you. Where did you get this cute dress?"

Mia shyly looked at Lucy. "Lucy took me shopping yesterday."

"Oh?" Kee asked with a small, genuine smile. "And did you have fun?"

"I did," she admitted almost grudgingly.

Kee smoothed her hand over Mia's blonde waves. "Good, I'm glad."

Tori stepped away from the girls when Samson walked towards them. She drank in his appearance, admiring the black jeans and the simple black tee he wore under an unbuttoned black suit jacket. With his nearly black eyes and hair, she could swoon. "Fuck, you're hot."

Samson blinked in surprise at the compliment before laughing. He cupped the back of her neck and pulled her towards him so he could bend and place a chaste kiss on her lips. "That's what I was going to say to you," he chided with a smirk.

She swatted at his chest, trying and failing to put distance between them. Her cheeks flamed red when he kissed her again. "Gods, *stop*, there are people around!"

Lucy let out a soft giggle at their exchange, smiling warmly up at Conrad as he came to her side. "Hello handsome," she greeted, smoothing a hand down his black dress shirt. "You clean up very nicely."

"Hello beautiful." Conrad brushed a strand of hair from her face and kissed her forehead. "You always look nice."

Kee admired her pack, even as her wounded heart twisted with jealousy. Feeling a hand slip into hers, she looked down and saw Mia looking up at her knowingly.

"The flowers he sent are really pretty," the youngest pack member stated.

Kee's brow furrowed. "Who? What flowers?"

"All the bouquets!" Mia said, tugging Kee towards the main house. "I helped set them up around Nana! Come see!"

Hesitation flitted through her as she reached the threshold of Nana's house, but Mia was having none of it. When she pulled her into the living room, Kee stopped and gawked at all the fancy, elaborate floral arrangements. There were several small bouquets with an array of different flowers ranging from white to pale pastels. Kee let her eyes fall on the urn standing alone on a small pedestal in the middle of the room then to the beautiful standing flower arrangement shaped into a heart.

Mechanically, she made her way to the standing bouquet and reached for the card folded next to a lilac rose. She got two words in before tears filled her eyes. She closed her eyes, took a deep breath, and continued reading.

My sweet,

*I wish you nothing but peace on this most difficult day. I am sorry
I cannot be there for you, but I know you are surrounded by your
loved ones, Nanette included.*

With all of my love,

L.V.

Kee clutched the card to her chest, letting the tears fall before wiping at her cheeks. Even though Lucas wasn't there physically, this thoughtful gift helped ease her yearning for him. It lessened the hurt just a fraction.

"Do you like them?" Mia whined, hugging her alpha and nuzzling into her side.

Sniffling, Kee wrapped an arm around Mia's shoulders and held her tight. "Yes, they're all beautiful, and you put them in such perfect spots."

Kee smiled softly when Mia beamed at the praise and looked up when she heard people shuffling into the living room.

"I am sorry for your loss," Dan said as he approached her, Gabriel and Christopher following closely behind.

"Thank you," Kee murmured, the words feeling hollow. "And thank you for coming, *and* for helping with everything."

Dan nodded. "You're welcome. Also, the men in your pack warned me about the situation with your fiancé." He cut a sharp look at Christopher, who pursed his lips and looked away. "And everyone will be on their best behavior."

Kee simply nodded, not having the energy to even look at Christopher. She did, however, open her arms to Gabriel when he stepped around Dan to approach her. She patted his back when he hugged her and couldn't help but inhale the cinnamon and clove scent of his warlock nature.

"I'm so sorry, Kee." He squeezed her tighter before pulling away to look down at the floor.

"It's okay." No, it wasn't. It would never be okay that Nana was dead, but what else was she supposed to say?

He sucked in shaky breath. "I keep thinking, if only grandpa and I had been there earlier."

Oh, *no*, she wouldn't allow that. "Shhh," she gently shushed him and put her fingers under his chin to tilt his head back up. She shook her head at the shining wetness in his eyes. "Don't do that to yourself, Gabe. Nothing that happened to Nana is your fault."

A sharp snap of anger hit the air, and she looked to see Christopher snarling at her with a ruddy face. "Of course, it's not our fault; it's yours!"

Dan whirled on his pack member with disbelief etched on his face. "Christopher!" he warned.

"What?! Everyone has heard the rumors! We all know why Vranas is in the ground!" he snarled angrily. "His maker killed Nanette! She never would have died if this fake alpha hadn't banged some—"

His words were abruptly cut off as his eyes rolled back into his head, his body falling forward to thud against the carpet. Standing behind him were Conrad and Samson, both looking deadly as they glared down at the wolf.

"Did you kill him?" Kee asked emotionlessly.

Samson cracked his knuckles. "Nah, I hit *just* hard enough to knock him out."

Conrad tilted his head. "But we can, if you want. The girls are outside greeting people, but they can easily turn them away while we deal with him."

Kee glanced at Gabriel, who was also scowling down at his grandfather. "I think Gabriel needs a guardian until he's eighteen. Let him live until then."

Dan was flushed with embarrassment as he looked at Kee again. "I'm sorry. I really thought we had an understanding, but apparently, I underestimated his anger and stupidity. I'll remove him from the premises."

She didn't bother replying as he hoisted his pack mate over his shoulder and carried him out the house. When he cleared the doorway, she saw her little brother pop in with a bemused expression.

Zach jerked a thumb over his shoulder as he approached the pack. "What was that about?"

"Rude, disrespectful people," Conrad answered as he clapped Zach on the shoulder in greeting.

Zach rolled his eyes as he hugged Mia then approached his sister. "Asshats," he scoffed. When Kee gave a weak, one shoulder shrug, he gave her a tight hug. "I'm sorry for your loss."

"Thanks," she mumbled into his shoulder, the word still not sitting quite right. "Thank you for coming." As they parted, she noticed his attention fall on Gabe, his eyes widening a fraction as his nostrils inhaled the warlock's scent. "Zach, this is my cousin Gabriel," she introduced. "Gabe, this is my brother."

"Um, hi?" Gabriel squeaked, his tan cheeks blushing as her brother stared at him.

Kee elbowed her brother in the ribs when he continued to gawk at Gabriel. "Stop staring him down, creep."

Zach's cheeks warmed in embarrassment. "Sorry. Um, hi, I'm Zach."

Kee looked between the two as they tentatively shook hands and stole glances at the other. Just in case she was sensing what she thought she was, she felt the need to clarify. "Well, technically Gabe and I aren't blood related, but it's a lot to get into. Anyways, I'll let you two talk; I have to go do something else," she announced and stepped away from them, clutching Lucas' card to her chest.

—

After a few hours, Kee sat at the dining room table, staring at the platters of food people had brought. Neighbors, friends, and most members of Dan's pack had each brought something for the wake and something extra specifically for her. Dealing with people she didn't know was one of the hardest parts of the day. All of them had come up to her to pay their respects. Some cried, some air kissed her cheeks in well wishes, and others gave her one-sided hugs. Which she only allowed because of Nana.

It was bizarre to see the different people Nana had influenced or left an impression on. Like her pack, it was a wide variety of people. Humans, wereanimals, and magic users were just the most prominent.

When the sorrow and buzz of people got too loud, Kee had stepped out onto the back porch for some fresh air and found flowers, berries, and mushrooms stacked artfully on the bottom step. As she stepped down the stairs to take a closer look, she heard a rustle and saw a shadow of small creature ducking out of sight. Samson had come out to smoke and saw the offering; he told her that it had probably been a pixie or brownie paying their respects. He told her not to touch it because a gift from any creature of fae could come with stipulations. She knew nothing of the forest folk, so she followed his advice and left it alone.

Then night hit and two vampires came to the wake, quietly paying respect to Nana by stroking her urn then bowing to Kee before leaving. Speaking of vampires, Giovanni and Dante also stopped by to lend her support and encouragement, making her love them all the more.

"I think everyone is just about leaving," Lucy said as she sat down next to Kee, letting out a soft, tired sigh. "Overall, I think it went well, hm?"

"I guess," Kee murmured. "As well as a wake can go."

Tori picked at a lid covering a glass baking dish and scrunched her nose at the scent of baked tuna. "What the fuck are we supposed to do with all this food?"

"Eat it?" Lucy suggested with a laugh.

Tori made a face at the tuna casserole. "But some of these we can toss, right? This smells gross."

"Maybe apple cake will smell a little better?"

Kee stiffened at the voice. It was one she hadn't heard since her mom died. She snapped her head to the doorway and saw her grandma standing awkwardly with a covered plate in her hands. Her hair was the same color as Nana's was, a rich reddish brown with natural waves. She was a little taller than Kee with sun kissed skin and similar freckles to Nana's. The only stark difference was that Sasha had hazel eyes.

Tori and Lucy bristled at the tension that leaked from their alpha and quickly filled the room. Lucy scooted closer to Kee as Tori moved to stand in front of her. Tori's eyes flitted to slits as the woman cautiously stepped forward and set the plate down on the edge of the table.

"It's my mom's recipe," she whispered, clasping her hands in front of her as she straightened. When no one made a move or spoke, she cleared her throat and addressed the two she didn't know. "Hello, I'm Sasha, Kiki's grandma."

Lucy snorted. "No, *Kee's* real grandma just passed, in case you weren't aware."

Sasha prickled. "Yes, I suppose I deserved that."

Kee put a hand on Lucy's knee to stop her. "Did you need something, Sasha?" she asked, finally looking at the grandma who had abandoned her all those years ago. The familiar face looking back at her only made Kee miss Nana more.

"I was hoping we could talk." She gestured at the two other women. "Alone?"

"There's nothing you can say to me that can't be said in front of my pack," she stated, tone still empty.

Sasha pursed her lips together for a moment before speaking. "Well, I wanted to first apologize." When Kee scoffed, she scowled a little. "I did, Kiki. I never should have abandoned you back then."

Kee made a show of looking at an invisible watch on her wrist. She looked at her grandma again with a deadpanned expression. "It's been seventeen years, Sasha."

She winced. "I know," she stressed. "But I thought I had time."

Kee tapped the non-existent watch. "Seventeen. Years."

Sasha made a frustrated sound. "*I know*," she repeated. "But we're basically ageless, Kiki. Every time I thought about reaching out to you, I would remember my daughter, get angry, and tell myself to wait. That it wasn't the right time. I wanted to be able to face you without any remorse. Without anger or judgement. I wanted to be your grandma like I used to. It's also why I waited so long to come today. I was nervous."

She shook her head. "If you think the sting of my mother getting murdered is ever going to go away, you're dumb as fuck."

Sasha inhaled sharply in shock. "*Kiki—*!"

Kee slapped her hand on the table and stood abruptly. She felt more than saw Lucy and Tori flinch slightly back from her but kept her fury focused on her grandma. "No," she snapped. "You do *not* get to scold me. You gave up all rights of telling me to do *anything* when you left me."

Sasha swallowed, taking a step back from the raging energy. "I'm sorry."

"You should be." Kee's hands balled into fists. "You're not the only one who lost someone. You lost your daughter, but I lost my mom. My *mom*! And I was only seven! Not just that, but that same night I lost my dad *and* my grandparents, but you didn't think of that, did you?" Before Sasha could reply, Kee stopped her by continuing. "Rhetorical question. No, you didn't. But I suppose that I should technically, in some twisted fucked up way, thank you." Tears stung her swollen eyes again, the feeling almost gritty at this point from the overuse. "Because I gained Nana, and she was both a parent and a grandparent. She was everything you guys were supposed to be."

Sasha's eyes watered, her bottom lip quivering. "I *also* just lost my mother, Kiki."

"It's *Kee*," she corrected. "And yeah, my condolences on you losing the mother you hadn't talked to since *my* mom died, but again, you had all this time to make amends."

Sasha flinched again. "I thought I had more time."

"Well, you didn't, did you?" Kee felt a hand on her shoulder and took a small breath to try to quell her anger. She plopped back down and rubbed at her forehead, suddenly more exhausted than she had been since Lucas left. "What do you want from me?"

"A relationship," she stated but seemed unsure. "Your grandfather and I both want to reconnect with you. He's here, too. He's saying goodbye to Mom while I talk to you."

She was silent for a while, mulling over the idea of reconnecting with more family, but honestly it seemed exhausting. "I don't know, Sasha. He saved me and I'll be forever grateful, but I don't need you two in my life."

"But...we're family."

Kee's hand slid from her face to gesture at the girls next to her. "I have a new one."

"One that won't abandon her," Lucy chimed in, bumping shoulders with Kee.

"Or try to take advantage of her during a very emotional time. Real classy, babe," Tori snorted, crossing her arms over her chest.

"I wasn't—"

Tori jerked her chin at the door. "You should go, really."

"*Really*," Lucy echoed with a sugary sweet fake smile.

When Sasha looked at Kee, the alpha merely shrugged her shoulders. "You heard them."

She blanched and dropped her chin, eyes looking off to the side. "Fine. Sorry to bother you. But we'll see each other again soon at the will hearing."

Tori made a shooing motion with her hand, not stopping until Sasha left the dining room. "Stupid cow," she mumbled before turning to face her worn out alpha. "Alright you're done. Let's get the fuck out of here. Let any stragglers figure it out for themselves."

"Agreed." Lucy stood and held her hand out to Kee. "Let's go."

Kee felt her shoulders drop in relief. She didn't realize how much she needed someone's reassurance to leave until her pack gave it to her. She took Lucy's hand, and Tori's when it was offered, and let them pull her to her feet. A warmth settled in her chest when they kept hold of her hands while escorting her back to the guest house, scaring off anyone who tried to stop them.

It was going to be a very long year without Lucas, but with her pack at her side, the ache wouldn't be quite as bad.

Twenty-Two

February

"I'm sorry I'm abandoning our plans," Tori said for the third time that night. She pulled nervously at the sleeves of her sweater, tugging the hem down over her palms. "I was looking forward to Galentines, I swear."

Kee waved her hand from her spot on the couch with a knowing smile. "Sam's back after being in Muir Woods for a while. I don't expect you to abandon your boyfriend on Valentine's Day."

The basilisk gnawed on her bottom lip. "But I told you I would. Especially since Lucy and Conrad are out on a romantic getaway for the weekend." She hesitated briefly before stating her worry. "I don't want you to be alone."

Kee's eyes softened. Conrad and Lucy had also called her earlier to express the same concern. "I appreciate that, Tori, but I'll be okay. I'm a big girl and I have Mia. Plus, what kind of alpha would I be if I told my pack they can't spend time with their loved ones on a day all about love?"

Before Tori could reply, Samson strode into the living room with Mia clinging to his back like a monkey. She watched him carefully take her arms and swing her off his back, gently dropping her onto the couch next to Kee. Mia landed with a soft bounce in a fit of giggles.

Samson straightened his shirt and flashed a grin at Tori as he closed the distance between them. He kissed her hard, making up for the time missed between them. "Ready?"

She sucked in a shaky breath and turned back to Kee. "You sure? I can stay, really."

Kee rolled her eyes. "Yes, get out of the house. Go. *Shoo*. And don't come home tonight either."

Samson's grin turned devilish. "Oh, we won't. We're ending our night at Byte so I can ravage her thoroughly."

"Samson!" Tori hissed, cheeks bright red.

"What does *ravage* mean?" Mia asked.

Kee and Samson laughed while Tori shook her head.

"Nothing!" Tori insisted and grabbed Samson's hand, pulling him along as she stomped towards the front door. When she swung the door open, she paused briefly to look back at Kee. "Call us if you need anything, okay?"

"I won't," Kee replied with a smile. "Enjoy your night, love birds."

Samson waited for Tori to walk out before looking at his alpha again. "No, but seriously, at least text us if it gets to be too much."

Kee gave him a small smile. "I *won't*," she repeated. "Go take care of your girl. You owe her after being gone for so long."

"Fine." Exasperated by her stubborn refusal, he gave her a two fingered salute and shut the door behind him.

Forcing her smile a little wider, she turned to Mia as the little girl sat up with a hopeful expression on her face. "Ready to make Nana's brownies?"

Mia let out an excited squeal, leapt off the couch, and bee-lined it for the kitchen. "Brownies!"

Kee laughed at Mia's banshee scream as she stood and walked over to the bookcase, carefully pulling out Nana's recipe book and taking it with her to the kitchen.

The will reading happened a week or so after Nana's wake and was almost as brutal. Sasha and her mate had been there, along with Dan, Gabriel, and Christopher. Almost everything had been left to Kee, and anything she didn't want was left up to her to do with as she seemed fit. It was a heavy burden.

Luckily, when it came to money, Nana had specified that it be put into a college fund for Gabriel. She stated she didn't want him to have to pay for anything in the four years he was there. Even then, some money was put aside for him to live comfortably until he had a stable job.

As much as she hated that Christopher got anything, she understood why Nana left him all her mate's remaining items in the house. It was only fair since John was his father. Still, she would have loved to snicker at him for not getting a single thing after all the drama he caused.

Sasha received a few small heirlooms from their homeland, but otherwise was told verbatim that she could have whatever Kee did not want. That Kee did snicker at.

Still, Kee didn't want much. The possessions all around Nana's house that she had grown up with *weren't* Nana. They weren't going to bring her back, and she didn't need them to remember fond times. Maybe she would regret it later on, but she let Sasha have most of what she wanted. The two things she absolutely refused to give up were the pendant around her neck and Nana's cookbooks.

The final part of the will was where Nana wanted to have her ashes scattered, and Kee was surprised to find out she wanted them to be scattered along a field by a very specific small town in Ireland. When

Kee asked Christopher about it, he grudgingly admitted that it was probably where her and John met since that was where his dad was scattered too.

So, she started looking into travel arrangements but couldn't find the will to lock any in yet.

"Can I lick the batter off the spoon?"

Kee blinked and looked at Mia as she tied a pink, frilly apron around her waist. "Obviously, that's the best part."

When Mia grinned at her in response, she opened Nana's cookbook and skimmed through until she found the brownie recipe.

—

After putting a sugar-crashed Mia to bed, Kee pulled the covers up to her chin and kissed the top of her head before quietly sneaking out of her room. She tiptoed down the hallway towards her bedroom but went predatorily still when she heard the front door click shut. Flashbacks of her attack surfaced immediately, but she wasn't a victim anymore and would rather die than anything happen to Mia.

Backpedaling, she went to the living room, squinting in the dark for an intruder. When she saw the outline of a figure in the darkness, she lunged without a second thought.

"Wait! It's me!" Dante said, holding up his hands as she swung at him like a savage animal.

"Dante?" Kee exclaimed in a harsh, hushed whisper so she didn't wake Mia. She shoved him in the chest with a growl. "What the fuck? I was going to kill you."

He sniffed. "Hey, don't insult me. I'm the one who trained you."

She released a slow breath, forcing her muscles to uncoil and relax. "What are you doing here? How did you get in?"

He held up Lucas' key ring, the metal gleaming in the dark. "I used Lucas' key. I thought you were coming to Byte tonight, but Samson and Tori told me you were babysitting so I had to move all your stuff here."

Her brows knit in confusion. "Stuff? What stuff? What the hell are you talking about?"

He made a frustrated noise in the back of his throat and pulled an envelope out of his back pocket. He pushed it into her hands then pointed towards the hall behind her. "Just…go look in your room. It's not as pretty as he wanted, but I was rushing to finish before you noticed I was here." When she shot him an incredulous look, he rubbed the back of his head. "Read the card. I'll see you at Byte tomorrow."

Kee watched him go, mouth slightly open in bewilderment. With a furrowed brow, she locked the door behind Dante and made her way to her room, looking down at the plain envelope in her hand. As she neared her door, the scent of roses filled her nose. Understanding hit her, causing her eyes to sting. She quickly threw open her door and turned on the lights, revealing several vases of her favorite peach-colored roses on both nightstands and the dresser.

She softly closed the door behind her and made her way to the bed, heading straight towards the wrapped bouquet of red roses on her pillow. Sitting down on the bed, she gingerly picked up the bouquet and inhaled the sweet scent. Cradling the bundle to her chest, she opened the card and read Lucas' note.

My sweet,

I do not need this day to express my love for you, but I will use it to remind you of it.

I love you, Keira.

Always,

L.V.

A little sob escaped her lips, and she covered her mouth to muffle it so she didn't wake Mia. Holding the roses and card to her chest, she laid down on the bed and curled into a small ball to silently cry into her pillow.

Twenty-Three

March

"It's crowded as shit right now. You mind if I drop you here?"

The thick Irish accent of the driver roused Kee from her light sleep, making her sit up straighter in her uncomfortable, springy seat. After rubbing the wariness out of her eyes, she blinked a few times to adjust to the dim lighting of the bus. She looked up when someone cleared their throat and saw the driver looking at her expectantly.

"Sorry," she mumbled as she finally noticed they were stopped. Through the windows on one side of the bus, all she could see was the black of night broken up by the glow of streetlamps. On the other side was a small bustling sidewalk illuminated by shop signs. "I take it we're here?"

"Aye, lass," he responded and flicked a switch on the dashboard, causing the doors to slowly creak open.

Forcing herself up on stiff, sore legs, she gingerly lifted her backpack and carefully slung it onto her shoulders. She wasn't sure why she bothered being gentle, it wasn't as if Nana could feel the jostling.

When she heard the older driver grunt his way down the three steps of the bus, she followed after him. She watched the human unlock the latch for the luggage compartment and struggled to lift the heavy door.

"I got it," she offered, helping him lift the door. Before he could protest, she bent down and grabbed her suitcase, pulling it from the metal confines under the bus.

"Enjoy your young age while you have it." He laughed and locked the latch again once she slammed it shut.

Kee tried to give him a small smile but knew it looked tired and forced. "I'll try."

When he nodded and hobbled back up the stairs, she lifted her suitcase and turned to the darkness in front of her but squinted at the harbor in confusion. Whirling back to the bus, she peered around it to see a bar called Murphy's across the street but not her hotel.

"Wait!" she called, but the doors had already slid shut, the bus pulling away from the curb. With a grumbled *fuck*, she looked at Murphy's and made her way across the street.

After asking for guidance, and getting a few wrong, drunk directions, she finally ended up on the cobblestone sidewalk outside the blue-grey building of the Benners Hotel. When she opened the door, she immediately was met with a warm, comforting lobby that reminded her of a small lounge. Spotting the front desk, she rolled her suitcase across the plaid carpet toward it. A wide mirror along the wall behind the desk reflected her tired, almost haggard image.

"Gods damn," she cursed as she set her suitcase down and tugged at the messy bun on her head, trying to put some sort of semblance of order to it. It mocked her by flopping back to the side, a strand falling and stabbing into her eye. "Bitch."

"Pardon?"

Kee blinked away from her reflection to the woman coming out from behind the wall. "I was talking to my hair." They paused in awkward silence at the absurdness of the sentence until Kee forced herself to continue. "I'm sorry. I've been traveling for damn near a whole twenty-four hours and I'm exhausted."

The clerk nodded as she went to her computer. "Checking in?" she asked.

Kee refrained from a snarky retort. "Yes."

The woman stared at her expectantly after another bout of silence. "And your name?"

Kee rubbed at her face, frustrated at herself. "Keira Quinn." As she pulled her hand away, she saw a brief flicker of surprise from the clerk before it disappeared.

"I have you down for three nights, correct?" When Kee nodded, the women began typing on her computer again. "Okay, perfect. If you could sign here for me."

Kee signed her name on the printout that was slid to her, not bothering to check the rates. She was too exhausted to care.

The clerk took the paper back and gave Kee an appraising once over. "So, what brings you to Dingle?"

Kee's brow furrowed, her backpack feeling a little heavier. "Business, I suppose."

The clerk gave her a scrutinizing look before handing over the key to the room. "Right, well, you're in 304. A complimentary breakfast is served from 7:30 to 10."

"Thanks," she murmured as she took the key and rolled her suitcase back the way she came. Not immediately seeing an elevator, and not wanting to make a further ass of herself, she decided to bite the bullet and haul the suitcase up the stairs.

When she found her room, she pushed the suitcase into a corner. As it banged loudly against the wall, she made a mental note to apologize to her neighbor should she see them. After setting her backpack down very carefully on the desk, she flopped onto the bed with a loud groan. Her eyes fluttered shut and she wanted nothing more than to pass out, but she had a promise to uphold to her pack. Mia demanded that her alpha call them as soon as she settled in, and Samson followed up the threat by saying he would fly to Ireland if she didn't.

With a tired smile at the memory, she rolled over and pulled out her phone to check the time. It was a little past three in the morning in Dingle and only about seven in the evening back in LA. After grabbing a pillow and shoving it under her head, she started a video call to Conrad's phone. She only had to wait a few moments before Mia's face filled the screen.

"*Auntie Kee!*" she all but screeched.

"Hi, little queen," she said, fondly using Lucas' nickname for her youngest pack mate. "How was your day at school?"

"*Good!*" she beamed. "*Today we went more into pack dynamics and high archery.*"

Kee laughed. "Hierarchy?"

"*That's what I said!*" Mia made a face before continuing. "*So, based on what I learned today does that mean that Dad is the second strongest in our pack? Since he's beta? If that's the case, then why does Sammy's aura feel stronger? What does that make Uncle Luke? What if—*"

"*Emilia, baby, give your alpha a break. She's probably exhausted. She can answer all your questions when she's back.*" There was a blur of movement on the screen before it focused on Conrad's face as he took the phone. "*Hey, everything go alright?*"

She shrugged. "As well as it can, I suppose. I had two flight delays and missed my first bus here. Luckily there was one running this late."

"*That's good,*" he commented before softening his voice. "*I wish you would have let at least one of us go with you. None of us are happy you're alone out there.*"

Kee sighed. "I know," she murmured. "But I really think this is something I needed to do alone, you know? Every step of the way after her death I've had one of you with me, but this I need to do by myself."

Conrad nodded in understanding, but she could tell he didn't like it. "*Did Sasha keep blowing up your phone?*"

She rolled her eyes. "Sure did. I think I had ten missed calls from her by the time I landed."

"*You think she'll just show up?*" her beta asked.

"It's possible," she mused. "But I don't care. Nana specifically stated in her will that she wanted me alone to scatter her ashes. She even specified where I needed to stay." She paused, brows scrunching. "That's weird, right?"

Conrad hummed in agreement. "*Knowing Nana, she had her reasons.*"

"I know," Kee mumbled before shaking her head. "Anyways, where are you all right now?"

"*Byte,*" Conrad replied. "*And I'm actually walking to Gio right now. He told me to get him when you called. So, here he is.*"

Kee waited until the camera settled on Giovanni. "Hey," she said with no small amount of awkwardness.

"*Hello,*" he began and ran his hand through his hair. "*Are you still angry with me?*"

Kee sighed as she remembered their argument before they left. Gio had changed and washed Lucas' bed sheets when she was away, rinsing them of his scent. To say she hadn't responded kindly to it was an understatement. She had almost attacked him physically but let her words do the work instead. In turn, he berated her, telling her it wasn't healthy to wallow in Lucas' bed all the time.

"No. I know why you did it," she paused. "And why you said what you did." But that didn't stop her from stashing away a shirt or two of Lucas' before she left.

He dropped his hand from his hair to rub at his jawline. *"I'm sorry about what happened, Kee, but I don't take back what I said. I am worried for you. I think you are depressed."*

Kee looked away from her screen and huffed. "It's not easy, Gio."

"It's not for us either," he fired back. *"Granted, we did not lose our grandparent, but we lost Lucas. He was our lord and, in my case, a parent. You are not alone in this."*

She sighed and turned back to her screen. "I'm not trying to be selfish, Gio."

"I'm not saying you are, but as your doctor, as well as your friend, I am worried for you." Giovanni scratched at the back of his neck. *"At least consider talking to someone, okay? That's all I ask."*

"I will," she promised him and meant it. "And I know you're not the only one worried for me."

Gio shot her a relieved look before handing the phone off to one her pack mates.

After a few more greetings and check-in's she finally hung up and set her phone on the nightstand next to the bed. She toed off her sneakers, slipped off her bra, and promptly passed out.

—

Kee was *over* it.

She had woken up after only five hours of sleep to a stomach pang. When she groggily did the mental math, she realized all she had eaten in the last day was an old croissant from an airport Starbucks. With a groan, she changed into new clothes, but that was the extent of getting ready. She didn't even brush her hair out before throwing it back up into a messy bun.

After eating enough for two wolves in the small dining area down-stairs, she trudged back up to her room to get started on her task. She shoved her passport, wallet, and phone into Nana's backpack and set off.

All day she walked up and down the streets of Dingle, stopped at the harbor, and stared at the rolling hills, but nothing stood out to her. Quite a few people gawked at her as she made her rounds around the village. Some looks were concerned, some suspicious, but she tuned them out the best she could. Looking as haggard as she did, she didn't blame them.

Still, she wasted a day and was no closer to finding a spot to scatter Nana. So, she made her way back to Benners, grabbed a local map from the check-in desk, and went straight to the hotel bar. She wasn't sure how long she had been there, but she was two drinks in before she felt someone approach.

"What brings you to Dingle, lass?"

Kee looked up dispassionately as a man pulled out a chair next to her, the stool screeching in protest. She lifted a brow at the tall man as he straddled the chair and crossed his arms along the back of it. She made it a point to flash the ring on her wedding finger as she replied, "Business."

He grinned at her short retort. "Aye? What kind?"

"I don't believe that's any of your concern," she responded coldly as she folded up the map in front of her. She scowled when he set his hand on it, stopping her from putting it away. "Excuse you?"

"I heard you're a Quinn," he mused, eyes twinkling with mirth. "And you've been quite the talk around town."

She scowled at him as he scooted closer to her, distrust instantly rising her hackles. "And?"

He grinned at her. "And I know why you're really here."

Kee narrowed her eyes at him, already fed up with this game. She leaned back and crossed her arms over her chest. "Aye?" she mocked in his Irish accent. When he laughed, her lip lifted in a snarl. "What's your problem? What is it that you want from me?"

He palmed his chin and continued to give her a saucy grin. "I like a feisty-," he began before leaning towards her, lips by her ear. "-shapeshifter."

Kee tried to keep her face neutral, but when he waggled his eyebrows at her knowingly, she knew he wasn't fooled. Glancing over her shoulder to make sure no one was listening, she hissed, "Who the fuck are you?"

"Ah, there's the right question," he said. He signaled at the bartender before looking at her. "This is goin' to be quite the talk and we'll need a round. What are you drinkin'?"

Kee hesitated at his relaxed demeanor. He didn't seem even a bit fazed by the subject. She wasn't sure where this was going or his intentions, but she was tense with unasked questions. How did he know what she was? Was this a trap?

When he tapped the side of her empty glass with an audible *tink tink*, she glanced at her empty drink then at him again. "I don't know want you from me, but I don't need you to buy me drinks. I'm engaged."

"Good for you." He lifted his hand, showing off an intricate black knot tattooed on his ring finger. "I'm mated myself. Been together almost ninety years."

Kee's reservation ebbed a bit at his declaration. "I'm trying local stuff," she finally admitted. "But I'm not much of an ale girl."

"You like the sweet shit? Maybe to counteract your bitter attitude?" When she fumbled for words, he laughed again. "Oh, I'm just playing. That's what my mate says. She says she likes the sweet stuff because she's so bitter." Without waiting for Kee to respond, he nodded at the bartender when he came over. "Get her a Magners, aye? I'll take a shot of the house whiskey."

Kee scowled at him as the bartender walked away, distrust rising up in her again. "Don't order for me. I don't even know you."

"Don't get your knickers in a twist. It's a cider," he explained. "And I'm Patrick Quinn. You? I'd offer my hand, but I don't want to add to your mental collection."

Kee stared at him with a surprised expression, brow furrowed and eyes slightly wide. If he knew about the skin collections, maybe he really did know her kind. "How do you know that?" she whispered.

His grin relaxed into a warm smile. "My aunt is a shapeshifter," he said, voice low. He then tapped right under his left eye. "Here in Dingle, the grey eyes give you away."

Kee turned away from him and stared down at the bar top, her fingertips running lightly over the worn, polished wood. She couldn't believe she was talking so freely to a complete stranger about her kind. "You said you are also a Quinn?" She glanced at him from the corner of her eye. "But you're not…one of us?"

Patrick shook his head. "Doesn't run in my bloodline, but the wolves of Dingle hide your kind among them."

Her chest felt tight as a breath settled heavily in the middle of it. To think there were shapeshifters hiding out in the country that originally eradicated them was insane. Did Nana know? Was that why she sent Kee there? "How many?"

"Hard to say," he said as their drinks came. He lifted his glass and inhaled the scent of his whiskey. "A few we know for sure, but there are more who haven't revealed themselves. Two hundred years isn't long for those of us who are ageless."

She pursed her lips to the side so she could chew at her cheek. "My whole life I wanted to know that there were more people like me and my great-grandma, but now that I do, I don't know what to do with the information."

Patrick scooted her drink towards her. "Well, cheers to heritage."

She numbly clanked her glass against his small one and took a tentative sip of the cider as he shot back his whiskey. "Can I meet your aunt?" she asked tentatively.

"Maybe once you go back home," he laughed. "She lives in the states. I haven't seen her in a long time."

Kee sat up straighter. "Where in the states?"

"California, I believe."

The blood drained from her face. What were the fucking odds? "Quinn," she repeated. "Any chance your aunt was mated to an alpha named John?"

He blinked at her and slowly set down his shot glass. "Aye. John was my uncle by blood; Nanette is my aunt by mating."

She swayed on her stool as she sucked in a startled breath. When he placed a hand on her shoulder to steady her, she squeezed her eyes shut. "This is why Nana told me to come here specifically." She opened her eyes and leveled him a glare. "Did you know who I was before this?"

"No." He squeezed her shoulder. "But Evie, the girl who checked you in, told me about you. She described you and said I should feel you out for why you were really here."

Kee's brow furrowed once again. "Why do you guys think I'm here?"

He tilted his head to the side in a very werewolf manner. "To find your kind, aren't you?"

Her expression softened. "No, Patrick." She gestured at the back-pack sitting on the stool to her left. "Nana died. I'm here to scatter her where John was."

Patrick's face fell, his skin pale against his freckles. "Oh," he breathed, slumping in his chair. "I had no idea. When did she pass?"

Kee looked down at the gold cider. "New Years. It took a bit to get through the will." She hunched her shoulders. "And then the courage to actually get over here," she admitted in a shamed whisper.

He nodded. "It's never easy to say goodbye."

"It's not," she agreed and took a deep drink.

"I hope I'm not oversteppin'," he began as he faced her again. "But I can take you to where she scattered John. The land changed a bit, but I know it well. Many of us do. It's where my uncle and the pack originally lived before the genocide."

Kee turned in her barstool and gave him a grateful smile. "I'd really appreciate that."

—

Kee pushed back a snarl of wind-whipped hair from her face and tucked it behind her ear. Despite braiding it tightly, the icy wind pulled a few strands free as she and Patrick trekked along the green hills of Dingle. They started in a car, driving a few miles down the road that ran along the ocean before pulling off to the side to finish the journey on foot.

Patrick was patient with her as she stumbled and slipped her way after him through the slick grass and rocks. It didn't take a rocket scientist to realize she wasn't an outdoorsy person, and she was thankful he took mercy on her. He went as far as to babble about Dingle and the history of the wolves that lived there, even gave her some information about the shapeshifters hiding there.

"Here we are," he announced, bringing them to a small clearing.

Kee, slightly panting, put her hands on her backpack straps as she looked around the area. There wasn't anything physical to signify that a town or village once dwelled here two centuries ago, but it felt... heavy. There was an invisible force she couldn't explain settling on her shoulders, a thickness to the air that made her exhale through her lips.

"This is where my ancestors were murdered?" she whispered.

"A few," he agreed. "This is where my uncle's pack lived when the murderin' spree began. I wasn't born yet when it happened, but the stories get passed down through the generations. Some shapeshifters fled here to hide, but the ones who were already out weren't spared."

"I don't understand," she said as she spun in a small circle to take in everything around her. "Werewolves helped wiped us out."

He growled low in his throat, making Kee turn sharply towards him to defend herself. "Not all of them," he rumbled. "The Dingle wolves were against it. Uncle John was our alpha, and he loved Nanette. She was the alpha female of the pack, and they respected her. When rumors of the hunt began, John had a pack meetin' to discuss it. Story says that he gave them an option to leave the pack if they agreed with the hunters' ideals. I think one or two left, but John killed them as soon as they were exiled."

"Killed them?" Kee echoed with a furrowed brow.

Patrick ran his hand through his dark red hair, bits of silver shifting in the strands with the movement. "Aye. He wouldn't risk them tellin' the hunters about his mate or the other few shapeshifters. The pack seemed to support his decision, too."

"How do you know?" she pressed, shifting her backpack when it started to feel heavier.

"Because Nanette's mother was killed for being a shapeshifter. The hunter knew who she was because she never hid it. I mean, she never had a reason to. When someone told the hunters that her daughter was mated to the Dingle's alpha, they all but ran here." He gestured around the clearing. "John and Nanette denied the claims, the rest of the pack too. Sasha, their daughter, had also already turned into a pup so they left it be."

"That's my grandma," she commented quietly. She wondered if Sasha remembered any of that time. Maybe she would ask when she got back home. Probably not. "But you said others still died here."

He sighed. "The Dingle wolves couldn't protect everyone. They tried, even managed to save a few, but I think the hunters started to get suspicious. John was nervous for Nanette, so he let them find shelter if they came lookin' for it but didn't actively hide them. And if the hunters were already on the chase, well, he didn't stop them."

Tears welled in Kee's eyes, but she quickly brushed them away. It seemed silly to mourn people she never knew, but she couldn't deny the ache in her heart. The loss of innocent lives due to a groups' fear was incomprehensible.

"Sorry to upset you." Patrick stepped closer to her. "You alright?"

"I haven't been alright since New Years," she admitted in a wobbly whisper. "I lost Nana, and then I lost my fiancé."

He sucked in a breath. "He passed as well?"

She shook her head. "No. He's locked up for protecting me." She rubbed hard at her face, her frustration and sorrow mounting. "It's only a year. That's what I keep trying to tell myself. And I know it's what others are thinking, but it's a *year*! It's been so hard to heal from losing Nana because if I'm not thinking of her, I'm thinking of Lucas. And if it's not Lucas, it's Nana! And it's just a sick cycle of grief that I can't get out of!"

Kee felt Patrick's assessing gaze on her, and her cheeks heated with shame at the outburst. "I'm sorry."

"You shouldn't apologize for how you feel," he began nonchalantly. "And there is no time limit on grief. I think havin' to deal with both those makes it harder, and it explains more of why it took you a tick to get out here. You'll have to let her go today, and that's not easy either. But this, at least, is in your control. You decided when to release her ashes, and there's some security to find in that."

Kee mulled over his words, hands tightening on the straps of her backpack. She *did* decide when to do it. She put it off, claimed the dates and airlines and hotels didn't lineup, but finally put it in action when she was ready. *Ready* being the key word.

What happened to Nana and Lucas had been out of her control.

And she, admittedly, had become a sort of control freak since her attack. But *this* she could control.

"You're right," she said as she slid her backpack off her shoulders. "I'm ready."

Kneeling down on the wet grass, she unzipped her backpack and took out the plastic bag of Nana's ashes. Cradling the bag in one arm, she stood and opened it. The air felt taut and charged around her, as if holding its breath in anticipation. Nodding to herself, she put a shaking hand into the bag withdrew a handful of the cold ashes. As she held Nana tight in her fist, tears gathered in her eyes again.

This was it.

With a thick swallow and a final silent goodbye, she opened her hand and let the wind take that piece of Nana away from her. The energy around her shifted, almost impatient, and so she gave it what it wanted. As soon as she dumped the bag upside down, a huge gust of wind swept in, taking the rest of Nana with it.

She watched it go, her shoulders feeling lighter than they had since New Years.

Patrick stepped up to her side and dropped an arm around her shoulders. When she gave him a questioning look, he gave her a reassuring grin. "Come, I think there are some people you need to meet."

Twenty-Four

May

"You sure, you're okay?" Samson asked, black gaze falling on his woman as she anxiously bit at her fingernail.

Tori jolted at his deep baritone. Realizing what she was doing, she pulled her hand from her mouth and spit out the remnants of a nail. She lifted her middle finger at the prim and proper wereanimal sitting across from them when she huffed in disgust.

"Excuse you?" the woman growled, offended by the vulgar gesture. "You apologize this instant!"

"Fuck off, Karen," Tori hissed. Her pupils dilated into slits when the woman leapt to her feet in challenge. She eagerly jumped up, ready for a fight to distract her from the inevitable. "You want to go?! You want to fucking *try me* right now?!"

"Sit down." Kee's voice seemed to boom in the waiting room without her having to raise her voice, her aura bouncing off the calming-colored walls.

Both women immediately complied.

Tori raked her hands through her blue bangs, pushing them back as she exhaled loudly. "I'm sorry."

Kee put a hand on her knee and gave it a comforting squeeze. "That was more for her than you," she explained. "But the last thing we need is to make this situation more tense for you."

Samson dropped his arm along the back of Tori's chair. "I mean it, Tor; we can go back."

She leaned into him or tried to, at least, with the arm of the chair in her way. "No, no. If you both can have the balls to talk to someone, then I can also face my own issues."

"You don't have to," Samson pressed. "Kee and I came to an agreement about talking to a therapist after Conrad and I got into a fight. Yes, you set this up to get a referral, but that doesn't mean you have to do anything else."

Kee nodded her agreement. "Don't do anything you're not ready to do."

Tori placed her hand on Kee's and gave it firm squeeze while she nuzzled her face into Samson's warm neck. "I have you two here with me," she murmured. "I won't be more ready than this."

They fell into a comfortable silence, the three of them all lost in their own thoughts. The television was a quiet rumble in the background, the receptionists' and other patients' muffled chatter louder than the actual show.

The door leading to the back squeaked open. "Quinn?"

Kee looked up and saw a petite Asian human standing there with a small smile. She wore chocolate brown slacks and a cream silk blouse. Her black hair was cut into a sleek bob, and a pair of glasses hung around her neck on a thin gold chain.

"Here," Kee said as she stood up. She glanced down at her pack mate, concerned for her reaction.

The therapist's smile grew as she saw her, but it abruptly dropped when she spotted the woman sitting down next to her. She dropped her clipboard and clutched her hands to her chest. "B-Bai Suzhen?"

Samson's eyes narrowed as Tori sucked in a pained breath. He followed her suit when she stood and stayed protectively close to her side as she approached her mother.

"Bai Suzhen! You're back!" Tears filled the therapist's eyes as she bowed at the waist. "I didn't think I would see you! I'm so honored!"

"Mom," Tori whispered in mortification, glancing at the people who openly gawked at them in the waiting room. "Please stop. Um, can we talk in your office?"

Mrs. Zheng straightened, tears rolling down her cheeks. "Of course!" She wiped at her cheeks and stepped aside with a sweeping arm gesture. "After you!"

Cheeks burning, Tori ducked her head and led her boyfriend and alpha towards her mom's office. No one said anything as they walked into the large, welcoming office, but she could feel Sam's anger radiating off of him. Certain parts of her tingled at the thought of him being angry and protective on her behalf.

When Tori's mom shut the door behind them, she turned to her daughter with wonder in her eyes. "Oh, Bai—"

Samson didn't let her finish, his control snapping. "It's Tori!" he snarled as he stepped in front of the stiff basilisk. "Her name is fucking Tori. Vittoria! Ring any bells? It should since you're the one who named her!"

"Sam," Tori whispered, putting her hands on his forearm. "It's okay."

"It's not," Kee chimed in as she put a hand on Tori's shoulder. "Let him do this."

Samson gestured at the two women behind him. "You hear that? It's not okay. She's your daughter, not some god for you to worship!"

Mrs. Zheng startled at being yelled at. She hunched her shoulders and looked away from the imposing male shouting at her. "Of course, she's my daughter," she began in a small voice. "And she has been blessed by the spirit of Bai Suzhen. She is practically a god."

"Do you hear yourself?!" Samson growled, his eyes transitioning to the amber of his dragon, pupils contracting into slits.

Tori's mother gasped at the sight of his eyes. She took in the way her daughter held on to him and his protective stance. "Are you the lover from the legend?"

Samson stared at her with a flabbergasted expression. Was she serious? "And you are supposed to help people with their issues? Lady, you've got some of your own to deal with. Maybe you should solve yours before trying to help others."

Kee snorted out a laugh but cut it off when Tori came to her mom's defense. "She's an expert at what she does," she started.

Samson exhaled a plume of smoke from his nostrils, making the therapist take step back. "I'm a fucking dragon," he bit out as if Tori hadn't spoken. "And your daughter is a fucking snake. We were unfortunate enough to get turned into what we are, but that's it. The sooner you understand that, the sooner you can have a relationship with your daughter."

Tori's mom furrowed her brow. "T-that's not for you to decide."

"No, but it's for me to decide," Tori spoke up tentatively. She laced her fingers with Samson's and found solace and strength in his hold. "And he's right, Mom. It's why I left. I'm only here because my alpha and boyfriend needed help. I reached out for them, not for me."

"Alpha?" her mom echoed, looking at Kee.

Kee gave her a mock salute. "That'd be me."

"I have a new family, Mom," Tori stated confidently. "As much as I'd like to have a normal relationship with you and Dad, I don't need it."

"You need to choose today," Samson snipped out. "She deserves that much from you."

Mrs. Zheng swallowed roughly. "I want a relationship with my daughter," she stated in a soft whisper. "I always have, but we wanted to please the spirit of Bai Suzhen." She twisted her fingers together much like Tori did when she was nervous. "But perhaps I have just succeeded in making them both unhappy." She shot her daughter an apologetic look. "It will take time for me to adjust, but I will try to be better Ba-*Tori*, if you give me a chance."

Tori shuffled her feet but gave a small nod. "I would like that."

Mrs. Zheng let out a relieved breath and gave her daughter a tentative smile when they looked at each other. She cleared her throat and pushed her shoulders back as she got into her professional mode and headed to her desk. "So, let's get to why you are all here. *Tori* said on the phone you needed referrals for therapists? I know a few others who treat the preternatural and each have their own specialties. May I ask what you wish to discuss? I don't need details, but a clue would help me steer you to the right doctor."

Kee felt Samson tense again and decided to speak up first. "I lost two loved ones and past trauma."

Mrs. Zheng nodded and jotted something down on paper before cautiously looking at the dragon. "And you?"

Samson felt Tori's hand slide into his and squeeze. He let out a tiny sigh. "I also have past trauma? I don't know. I thought I came to terms with everything in Muir when I went in January and that it solved my issues, but I lashed out at my pack mate a few weeks ago."

"Coming to terms with something doesn't mean you fully heal from it. There are often underlining things that need to be addressed." She grabbed a new piece of paper and began scribbling. "I specialize in trauma, but because of your relationship with Bai—*my daughter* it would be unethical for me to treat you. Fortunately, I know someone who's *almost* as good as me," she said with a light tease before handing them each a paper. "These are who I would recommend for each of you. And both offer online video calls."

"Thank you," Kee said, taking her paper as Samson silently took his.

"You're welcome," Mrs. Zheng replied and walked to her door, opening it for them. "I hope everything works out for you two." She watched Kee walk out, followed by Samson, but hesitantly stopped her daughter. "Um, would you be willing to have lunch with me some-time this week? Or next? I want to try to be the mom you needed."

Tori gave her mom a small smile. "I'd like that, Mom."

Twenty-Five

July

"No! Don't come in here!" Mia shouted with panic.

Kee stopped before she could round the corner to the kitchen. The smell of baked sweets filled her nose, but there was just the faintest whiff of something burnt.

"Oh, it's going everywhere!" Mia wailed, a whimper following her words.

"I told you it was still too warm," Lucy chided gently. "It's okay, we can still make it work."

A corner of her mouth quirked up as Kee turned away, leaving Lucy to monitor what their youngest pack mate was doing. As she stepped back into the living room, Tori and Samson came up to her with a colorful gift bag, green tissue paper covering the top.

"Happy birthday!" Tori beamed, thrusting the gift at her.

Kee took the bag from her with a small smile. "You guys didn't have to get me anything," she said as she sat down on the couch with the present. "Can I open it now?"

"Yes! Open it!" Tori grinned excitedly while Samson nodded in agreement.

Pulling out the tissue, she stuck her hand in the bag and pulled out a square bundle wrapped in more tissue. After ripping apart the paper, she unfolded the black fabric and laughed at what she found. It was a zip up jacket with 'Alpha Bitch' scrawled across the back shoulders.

"I love it," Kee said with another laugh. She stood back up and hugged Tori. "Thank you so much. You guys really didn't have to."

Samson patted her head when she hugged him next. "Of course, we did," he scoffed. "It's your birthday."

"Yeah, but I don't expect anything." She pulled away and smiled up at him. "But thank you, really."

"You're welcome," he said and nodded at Tori. "But it was Tor's idea."

"Thank you," Kee repeated when Tori grinned with self-satisfaction.

"You're welcome! But that's only my part of the present," she rubbed her hands together almost manically. "Samson is paying for your second part!"

"Second part?" Kee asked with a shake of her head. "Guys, really, I don't need anything else."

Samson crossed his arms over his chest. "Too bad because tonight we're getting tattoos."

Kee blinked at him. "You want to take that risk?"

They all discussed getting tattoos from time to time, but none of them followed through with it. With their rapid healing, it was tricky to do tattoos on wereanimals without their body basically absorbing and breaking down the ink. She had no idea what her own body would do with it but was willing to try.

"Yep. Met an artist at Byte last night when I was behind the bar.

He's a weretiger and specializes in tattoos. Says he uses a silver needle so that it takes longer for our bodies to heal." He grinned when she winced. "Yeah, it's going to be a pain in the ass, but you better start thinking of what you want now."

"I have a few ideas," she murmured thoughtfully.

"Okay, look, this is the best it's going to get," Conrad declared as he walked into the living room with a lump of pink wrapping paper. He handed the bundled wad of paper to Kee and glared when one of the ten pieces of tape popped off.

Kee laughed at the atrociously wrapped present. It was a small rectangle, but Conrad had used enough paper for an object three times its size. "It's the thought that counts?" She started to peel off the remaining pieces of tape and laughed when she realized what the paper was. "Is this the princess wrapping paper we used for Mia's birthday presents?"

Conrad held his hands up in defense. "It was all we had! And it was short notice to wrap! It's not even our present to you!" He ran his hand down his face, trying to wipe away his embarrassment before fixing a knowing look at her. "It's from Lucas."

Kee's humor dissolved, that keen longing rising up in her again. She looked down at the present in her hands and slowly unwrapped it, dragging it out so she felt like she had a bit more time with him. It was silly, but her therapist explained that grief had no set rules. When she was met with a small black box, she lifted the lid to see a small pair of sun-shaped, gold earrings, the center of each one housing a diamond. When she went to tuck the lid of the box under the bottom, she saw something written on the inside.

My sweet,

Now more than ever, you are my sun. The light to my dark.

Happy birthday, my queen. I love you.

-L.V.

"Fucking fuck," Kee cursed as a tear rolled down her cheek. She brushed it away with an angry swipe of her fingers. "Just when I think I'm done crying about this."

Conrad, Samson, and Tori exchanged a look.

"Kee, it's okay to cry about this," Tori said softly. "I don't know him, but I can't imagine what you're feeling. Hell, if Samson went away for that long, I'd be crushed."

Samson placed his hand on her head, bringing it closer to him so he could press a kiss to her hair. "I'm not going anywhere," he told her then looked at Kee. "But she's right, Kee. None of us think less of you for it."

When Kee remained quiet, her eyes glued to the note, Conrad wrapped his arms around her, pulling her into a tight, comforting hug. "The last note you got from him was on Valentine's, right?"

She nodded bleakly against his chest, arms wrapping around his waist. "I know Dante and Gio explained that he was short on time and did what he could, but they almost make it harder. Especially when I don't know when or if I'll get another one."

"They may make it harder, but I'm glad he did it. It's his way of reminding you that he's still here, even if he's not physically here with you." Conrad squeezed her tighter when her breath stuttered. "He loves you, Kee."

"I love him, too," she said before pulling away from him with a sniffle. She rubbed at her nose and looked down at the earrings again before reading the note for the fifth time. An idea for her tattoo formed in her mind, but before she could voice it, the lights dimmed.

Looking up, she saw Mia and Lucy walking towards her with a cake. The white frosting all but dripping down the sides, causing the lit candles to teeter. Lucy was quick to pick up each one that fell before stabbing them deeper into the cake, trying to make them sturdier. When they stopped in front of Kee, her whole pack started singing happy birthday, all of them off-key.

She couldn't help but laugh, the grief easing its claws out of her heart as the love for her pack sank in. She blew out her candles when they were done singing, wishing the next five months would pass in a hurry.

—

Kee locked the door behind her as she entered the pack house. She gingerly slid off her new jacket, wincing a bit as her new tattoos pulled with the movement. Setting her keys down in the bowl by the door, she made her way to the kitchen aiming for the left-over pizza they had for her birthday.

Lucy rushed into the kitchen, stopping short when she saw her friend. "Kee?"

Kee closed the refrigerator door at the tone. Worry prickled her shoulders when Conrad came into the kitchen a few seconds later, face pale. "What is it?" she asked softly. "What happened? Is Mia okay?"

"Yes, she's fine," Conrad began. He anxiously looked at Lucy, who flashed a strained smile at him in return. "But we need to tell you something. Something we just found out."

Kee's eyes narrowed slightly at the tension that radiated off her beta. Her gaze returned to Lucy, taking in the slight tremble in her bottom lip. "What is it?"

Lucy hesitated before reaching for Conrad's hand. When his fingers slid through hers, she swallowed thickly. "I-I'm pregnant?"

The alpha blinked, not at all expecting those two words. "Okay," she started slowly. "Is this a good or bad thing?"

Lucy shrugged, her gaze falling to her flat stomach. "I don't know."

"If you don't want a baby, Lucy, that's something you need to find out sooner rather than later." Kee's gaze slide to Conrad and his ramrod straight back.

"No, no, you misunderstand!" Lucy said before a smile twisted up her lips. "I want this baby! I'm actually really excited to be pregnant; I'm just nervous."

Dawning hit Kee. "You mean, you're not sure if you can resist shifting."

"That's why I don't know if it's good or bad. I mean to me it's good! I'm so excited to have a kit or pup with Con." She released Conrad's hand so she could rub at her flat stomach. "I want to believe I'm strong enough to resist the moon's call, but I can't do it alone." She sniffled as her eyes watered, but a smile was on her lips as she met her alpha's gaze again. "Will you help me?"

Kee pulled her friend into a hug. "You are strong, Luce. And of course, I will be with you every step of the way. You know the moon doesn't have the same sway over me, so I can be with you each night as your alpha."

"And I'll be there," Conrad said, nuzzling his nose into her hair. "As your mate."

Lucy pulled out of Kee's arms to whirl towards him, eyes wide. "Mate? You want to mate me?"

He gave her a loving smile. "I have since I first met you at the bar, Lucy. I didn't want to rush you into anything, but if you'll have me, I'd mate you in a heartbeat."

She shoved weakly at his chest. "You idiot! This is the worse proposal ever," she chastised before flinging her arms around him. "Of course, I'll be your mate!"

Kee crossed her arms over her chest and gave them a knowing look as they shared a tender kiss. "So, which news will you break to Mia first?"

Conrad cursed under his breath as Lucy flinched. "You guys have been getting along so well," he sighed as he looked at his intended mate. "I hope this won't set you guys back."

Lucy gave him a hesitant smile. "It might," she agreed. "But I hope it'll be okay down the road. We should start with the mating since she seems to have accepted us dating. Then we can tell her about possibly having a sibling."

Conrad tensed at her word choice but nodded. "I understand. We'll wait until after the full moon."

The werefox pressed a light kiss to his cheek. "I love you, Conrad."

His eyes softened as she pulled back from him. "I love you, too."

"I'm going to call Tori and Sam to tell them the news!" Lucy beamed with happiness before practically skipping out of the kitchen.

Kee waited until her friend was far enough away in the house before speaking. "Out with it, Con. I can practically taste your fear."

He ran both hands through his hair before grabbing the back of his neck. His face crumpled, amber eyes glistening. "I'm terrified, Kee."

She closed the distance between them, hugging him tightly as his façade broke. "Talk to me."

"All I can think about is Michelle," he whispered as his arms wrapped around her. "I know it doesn't make sense because Luce will be my mate, but fuck I'm still scared of losing her."

She rubbed his back, trying to soothe him. "It doesn't make sense," she agreed. "You would never hurt Lucy, and you know that's your pup."

"I know." He released her to rub his palms against his eyes. "But then I have all these other fears. What if she can't resist the change? Or, what if she can for only a few months? And then loses it? It will crush Lucy. Fuck, it'll crush me too. It won't be like how it was with Mia. I'll be attached from the beginning."

Kee brushed her knuckles across his cheek, wiping away a tear. "It might happen, Conrad." His eyes squeezed shut at her statement. "But that is the risk that comes with wereanimals getting pregnant. None of us want either of you to go through that, so you can bet your ass that we will all do what we can to make sure it doesn't happen."

"How?" he murmured, his eyes opening once again to look at her almost desperately.

She let out of soft sigh. "I don't know," she admitted. "I'll exert all the power I have on the full moons. And we'll partner with Gio. I'm sure he wouldn't mind being her doctor for this. He can look into it; maybe there was something he studied long ago that can help."

His head dipped once in a nod. "I guess that's the most I can hope for."

"Just don't *lose* hope, Con." She gently rubbed the top of his head. "You need to be strong for Lucy."

He accepted the warmth and comfort his alpha's touch brought, let it sooth his riled beast. "I'll try."

Twenty-Six

September

Hearing a groan, Kee tore her gaze away from Lucas' computer to turn it on her youngest pack mate. Mia was sitting across from her, homework spread out on the desk. When the little wolf crossed her arms over her papers and rested her forehead against them, Kee reached out to smooth her hair back.

"Still don't feel well?" Kee asked.

Mia shook her head minutely. "No. I feel gross."

Kee frowned with concern and glanced at the clock on the desktop. "Gio should be up in about an hour; do you want him to give you a checkup?"

She shook her head. "No, I know he's busy helping Lucy. I don't want to bug him."

Kee had been right about Gio wanting to help with Lucy's pregnancy. What she hadn't expected was for him to dive headfirst into studying. To say he was excited was an understatement. In the basement, he had converted Aubrey's old room into a mini exam room.

He had bought an ultrasound machine and all the necessary gadgets needed for future exams, stirrups included.

"He won't mind looking you over, Mia. Conrad and I can handle Lucy's change until he's done. We have Dante, too," she explained.

On the last full moon, Kee had an idea to assist Lucy in preventing her from shifting. As her alpha, she was using her aura to demand Lucy not to shift. To *compel* her to resist the change. But what would happen if a vampire actually compelled her with their power?

Dante had been humbled when Kee, Conrad, and Lucy had approached him for his help. He easily agreed, and they were going to try it that night.

Mia shook her head and slowly raised it to look at Kee with sleepy eyes. "I'm okay. I want him to worry about my little brother or sister."

Kee continued to lightly pet her hair as the little wolf groaned again. "Can you explain more of how you're feeling?"

Mia shrugged. "I feel heavy," she mumbled. "And hot."

Kee slid her hand down to rest the back of her hand against Mia's forehead. "You do feel a little warm." *But werewolves don't get sick*, she refrained from adding. "How long have you felt this way?"

"A few days, but it's worse today." The little wolf sighed, a small whine echoing in the back of her throat. "And my skin itches." She backed the statement by scratching at the back of her neck.

The alpha blinked then uselessly looked at the clock on her computer again. She didn't know why she bothered, she already knew it was almost nighttime and that it was the night of a full moon.

"Oh shit," she muttered, quickly grabbing her phone next to the keyboard. She found the pack group message and sent a text demanding an emergency meeting in Lucas' office ASAP. Setting her phone back down, she stood up and made her way to Mia's side. Kneeling down, she rubbed the wolf's back and waited for her pack to arrive.

She didn't have to wait long. A few minutes later, the four of them walked in with tense anticipation.

Conrad immediately became worried when he took in Kee comforting his daughter. He closed the distance between them and squatted down on the other side of Mia. As soon as he touched her head, she slipped off her chair and burrowed into his chest. He held her to him, easily supporting her weight as she sagged against him. "Baby? What's wrong?" he asked as he stroked her hair.

"I don't feel good," she murmured into his shoulder. "My whole body hurts."

"Con, I think she's going to shift tonight," Kee pointed out softly.

Conrad perked up with excitement. He had been waiting for this, for the moment he could run alongside his daughter in their wolf forms. He couldn't wait to teach her about her instincts and how to hunt. How to listen to her wolf and trust it. He couldn't wait to have her join him and Lucy on a run. Well, once Lucy was able to.

His face fell. *Lucy.*

Lucy and his pup needed him tonight. But so did Emilia. This was her first shift, and no one else in the pack was a wolf.

"She needs you tonight, Con," Lucy said firmly when she felt his panic in their mating bond. When he looked at her with a torn expression, she shook her head. "No. Don't fight me on this. If Mia's really going to shift, she needs you with her tonight. Shifting for the first time as an adult is terrifying, I can't imagine how it may be for a child."

"Luce," Conrad began but stopped when a shudder ripped through his daughter, her small body jolting into his arms. "Damn it. She's definitely shifting tonight."

"I'm scared," Mia whined, grabbing a fistful of her dad's shirt.

Conrad stroked her hair. "I know, baby, but it'll be okay. You're going to love being in your wolf form, I promise you."

Kee stood and noticed both Sam and Tori standing closer to Lucy, lending her support with their proximity. She turned back to Conrad with firm resolution. "You will be with Mia tonight. We have Dante and Gio helping us with Lucy and the pup."

"Tori and I will stay as close as we can to her after shifting so she can feel our pack bonds. It's a little tricky with my wings, but I'll make sure I can still touch her mind if I need to." Samson ruffled Lucy's white-blonde hair when she shot him a smile.

Tori nodded. "I can stay coiled in the corner of the room too. We'll all be there for her, Con."

Lucy's smile widened despite the worry she felt. "See? I'm in good hands, babe."

Conrad tightened his hold on Mia when she thrashed in his arms again. "I'm sorry," he whispered, eyes on his mate. "I don't like that I won't be there for the experiment with the compulsion, but I can't let Mia do this alone."

Her pale green eyes softened as she joined them on the floor. She pressed a kiss to his temple. "I know, don't apologize." She leaned down and gently nuzzled Mia's hair. "You are going to be perfectly okay, Mia. It's a little scary at first but is so much fun once it's done. I know you are strong and brave on your own, but your dad will be with you the whole time to guide you."

Mia pulled away from her dad to turn to Lucy, leaning into her. When Lucy wrapped her in a hug, she let out another whine. "I'm sorry, Lucy."

Lucy hugged her tighter. "No, no apologies. This is a very big night for you, and you have nothing to be sorry for." When Conrad's arms came around both of them, she continued, "I love both of you, and all four of us will be just fine."

Kee could only hope she was right.

—

Kee flopped down on Lucas' bed and released a long, exhausted groan. The sun had just started rising, painting the sky in soft hues of orange and pink. The full moon fled upon the sun's presence, taking its influence with it. It had been a long, draining night but worth it once the threat to shift left. Lucy pulled through, giving her pup at least another month of life.

The vampire compulsion worked, thankfully, but Kee saw the drain it had on Gio and Dante. The three of them rotated their time with Lucy, but each time one of the vampires stopped, they had to feed from a blood bag. Gio was also forced to multitask. Between feedings and compelling, he was monitoring Lucy's vitals, making sure her blood pressure didn't stay high, or at least rise any farther.

Conrad and Mia had ended up coming into the exam room around two in the morning, both still in their wolf forms. Mia had curled up next to the coiled snake in the corner and promptly passed out, but Conrad stayed neared his mate, rubbing his wet nose along her cheek and neck when she struggled.

It was a lot of work for the pack, vampires included. It would be completely and utterly worth it if the pup made it to term, but that wasn't for certain. Maybe it would be more assured if they had another, stronger vampire to help them.

Kee rolled onto her side and looked at Lucas' empty side of the bed. She reached out and ran her hand over his pillow, wishing for the millionth time that he was there. But this time it wasn't just for her own selfish gains, it was because he was stronger than Gio and Dante. His compulsion would go a lot further than theirs did. Then again, if everything worked out, he could still be there to help her with the final push.

She rolled onto her back and grabbed her phone from the nightstand to pull up the calendar. Gio guessed that Lucy was about three months pregnant. She scrolled through the months, counting as she went until she reached January. Lucy would be around seven when Lucas came out.

Wondering at how long she would have with him before she had to share him with others, she brought up the internet on her phone and googled what day the full moon for January landed on. She stared at the date, shock making her go almost numb. Her hand clenched around her phone as she closed her eyes tightly, silently cursing the gods who continued to punish her.

Of course the full moon would be on January third.

Twenty-Seven

December

With a twitch in her cheek, Kee pressed the microphone button on her headset. "Does someone want to explain to me why I just caught an underage girl with a red blood donor wristband?" Silence echoed in her ear. "I swear to the gods, Brent, I will shatter your nose again. I am not getting Byte closed down because you don't care enough to check if an ID is real or not."

"*It seemed legit to me.*" His voice was just a little too smug for her liking. "*And who am I to deny a willing bleeder?*"

She resisted the urge to rub her temples as she moved through the crowded dance floor towards the bar. "I'm sure the fact that her tits were spilling out of her dress had a lot to do with your decision," she hissed before taking a calming breath to address the rest of the staff. "It's a busy night, people; we need to make sure we're extra vigilant. Only a couple more hours until we're free. We can do it. And please, will someone get that bitch off the table before she breaks her neck?" She only had to wait a minute before the girl was no longer standing above the rest of the crowd. "Thank you."

Releasing the small button, she finally made her way to the bar and jerked her chin at Lucy questioningly as their eyes met. When she gave her a thumbs up that everything was fine, Kee tapped the bar top before heading towards the kitchen to make sure they weren't behind. As she pushed open the swinging doors, her back pocket buzzed rapidly with an incoming phone call. Seeing that it was from Zach, she pulled out her earpiece and stepped out the back entrance to Byte so she could hear better.

"Hey, little bro," she greeted, her breath fogging in front of her with the winter chill. "What's up?"

"*I need your help,*" Zach panted. "*Please, Kee.*"

Her brow furrowed at the sound of muffled shouting in the background. "What happened?"

Zach whispered something away from the phone but came back a second later. "*Dad found out about Gabriel and me.*"

"Ah, fuck." Kee rubbed at the bridge of her nose. "How?"

"*I wanted to celebrate Christmas with Gabe. We're both busy with family stuff tomorrow and on Christmas, so I brought him to my mom's house for dinner tonight,*" he rushed out. "*Dad was supposed to be gone for an alpha trip to San Bernardino. He was supposed to be there until tomorrow evening! How was I supposed to know he'd try to surprise my mom by coming back early? He never cares about holiday shit with her! They don't even live together!*"

Kee gently shushed him as his panicked rambling made his voice rise. "Take a breather. Is Gabriel with you right now?"

"*Yes,*" he sighed, taking a few deep breaths. "*We're locked in my room. Gabe put a warding spell on the door to stop dad from breaking it down, but he said it won't last all night.*"

Good boy, Gabe, she thought. "Where's Liam now?"

"*Arguing with Mom downstairs.*"

"I take it he's mad she didn't tell him about your boyfriend," Kee drawled.

Their father was raised by someone who grew up in the nineteenth century and had been taught old, bigoted ways. At least Zach's mom seemed to be more understanding. Still, many werewolf packs had closed-minded ideals and rules. It stemmed from the way of living from earlier times. It was why most of them believed women couldn't be alphas and men couldn't be gay. Women could only be interested in other women if it *benefited* their husbands or mates.

It was honestly disgusting. There was no reason *not* to change in order to adapt to the current times.

"*She didn't because she was protecting me,*" Zach whined. "*I should have taken you up on your offer months ago. I should have let you petition him for me, but Dad and I were getting along so well, and he changed since last year.*"

"Someone like Liam won't ever change," she spat out. "He's had too much bad grooming to change."

"*But he did, Kee,*" Zach stressed. "*He even started talking about you, told me a few stories and—*"

"I don't care, kid." She most definitely didn't want to hear about her sperm donor reminiscing on her childhood. "So, what do you need me to do?"

"*Take us away from here. He might have changed, but it's very clear he doesn't accept me being gay. I don't know what he's going to do to me, but I need to at least get Gabe out of here.*"

Kee agreed but had to remind him what her interference would mean. "If I come to you, Liam and I may end up fighting. You know that, right? This will be a fight to, in shit terms, own you. Whether I win or lose, it'll only worsen your relationship with him."

He was quiet for a moment. "*I know, but I'm willing to take that chance so Gabe and I can be together safely.*"

Fuck, fighting Liam the day before Christmas Eve had not been on her agenda, but she couldn't abandon her brother. "Alright, I'll head out right now. I'll try to get there as fast as I can, but plan on a half hour, okay?"

"*Thank you.*" His relief was almost palpable through the phone. "*We'll be here.*"

"Stay safe," she said before hanging up.

She stepped back into Byte long enough to grab the car keys hanging next to the door and hurried over to the Jeep. After climbing in and firing up the engine, she waited for her phone to connect to the car's system before dialing a number that was nearly foreign to her now.

It wasn't until she was buckled in and pulling out of the parking lot did Cain answer, voice a bit breathless, "*Hello?*"

She couldn't blame him for sounding hesitant and unsure. After their mating bond broke, they had exactly one conversation and Kee had basically told him she was starting over and wanted to distance herself from everything that reminded her of what happened. He had taken it better than she thought, but a part of her wondered if that was because his wolf technically got what it wanted and now that it was gone, it was free to lust after someone else.

Also, she had sneaking suspicion that he didn't just have Katie to keep his bed warm.

"Hey, sorry to call like this, but I have a quick question. You busy?"

"*Yes, he's fucking busy!*" Kee was fairly certain that was Alyssa's voice. Ha, suspicion confirmed.

"*Cain,*" Katie whined. "*Come back to bed with us.*"

Well damn, okay Cain. Good for you, Kee mused, genuinely happy for him. "Tell your ladies it'll only take a second."

"Yes, you guys can wait out a minute by playing with each other." He let out a soft chuckle before directing his next words at Kee. *"What's your question?"*

"So, say I want to take a wolf from a different pack, how exactly is the best way to do that?" Her fingers drummed on the steering wheel with anticipation as she made her way onto the 10 freeway.

Cain made a soft noise of disbelief. *"Well, you'd have to challenge that alpha for the right to take the wolf."*

"I figured as much," she drawled. "But can you go over specifics? What happens after?"

"It depends on who wins, Kee," he said, suddenly serious. *"If you win, then good for you; you get the wolf. And if you kill him, you can claim his pack. But if you lose, your life can be forfeit. You went into another alpha's territory and tried to take one of his wolves. That's a whole lot of disrespect that won't go unpunished."*

"So, win or die is what you're telling me." She figured that was what it would be. And honestly, when it came to Liam, she always knew it would come down to a fight to the death.

"Yes," he stressed. *"So, make sure this wolf is really worth taking."*

"No one more worthy than my brother, I'd say," she scoffed. "Anyways, thank you for the information. I just needed to know what I was getting myself into."

"You're welcome," he said softly. *"Good luck."*

"Thanks." She disconnected the call and took a deep breath. She let it out and took in another before texting her pack and letting them know what she was doing. Immediately offers to come and back her up came through, but she denied them. Facing her father was something she had to do alone. If she were to fail, well, she'd hope Zach and Gabe would at least tell her pack so they could come get her body.

Her fingers wrapped around the steering wheel tightly at the idea of losing and never seeing her pack again. Never seeing *Lucas* again.

Both thoughts caused an ache to swell in her chest. No, she couldn't think like that. She had to be confident in herself because she *wouldn't* back down. So, she took another breath and used the rest of the trip to steel and fortify her nerves.

—

Kee parked outside Zach's mom's house, a nice sized two-story house in Claremont. It wasn't too far away from where her own childhood home had been, and it made her wonder if Liam still owned it. Probably not if he now lived in Christian's pack house.

As soon as she got to the front door, it swung open, revealing a very disheveled Gabriel. "Gabe?"

He flung himself at her, holding her tightly as his body trembled. "I couldn't hold the spell longer," he rasped through tears.

She rubbed his back before gently prying him off her so she could get a better look at him. His face was red from crying, but other than that it didn't seem like he was hurt. "You did what you could," she reminded him gently. She glanced over his shoulder and didn't see anyone in sight. "Where are they?"

"Out back," he said as he rubbed at his eyes, but his expression remained crestfallen. "Liam dragged Zach downstairs by his neck after hitting him." His eyes welled up again. "He hit him so *hard*, Kee. I thought he broke his face. I was so scared, especially when Liam told me to get out of his sight before he made me, but I knew you were coming so I stayed. Carla quietly told me to wait by the door, so I did."

Carla was too good a woman for Liam.

Kee handed him the keys to her Jeep. "Go get in the car and wait there."

He took them with a shaking hand. "Okay."

She put her hand on his shoulder. "If I don't come back then you need to leave. Call my pack and they'll come find you."

Gabe's eyes widened in horror. "Don't say that," he cried. "You have to be okay!"

She gave him a gentle push towards her car instead of replying. Flexing her hands at her side, she turned back to the house and made her way towards the backdoor. It wasn't hard to find, not when it was wide open and letting in a cold breeze tinged with the scent of blood.

Pushing down the wave of anxiousness that threatened to climb up her throat, she stepped out onto the patio. With more difficulty than she would have liked to admit, she disregarded Liam and his warning growl and made her way directly to her brother. He was sitting down on a chair next to his obedient mother, shoulders slumped with defeat and pain. She gingerly cupped his jaw and raised his face so he would look at her.

Anger surged through her at the sight of him, almost eclipsing her anxiety.

Only one pool of ice blue was visible, the other eye swollen shut. Both his nostrils bled freely and had been smeared onto one puffy cheek.

"He's seventeen, Liam," Kee spoke with a cold calmness. "But it seems age doesn't play a factor to you, does it? Seven, seventeen, both ages get beat."

Liam snarled low in his throat. "This has nothing to do with you, Kiki. Get out of here before I truly show you a beating."

"We'll see who will do the beating." She carefully released her brother's face and nodded at the hopeful gleam in his one good eye. When she turned to face her father, he was already standing, aura flaring wildly. "I'm here to challenge you for Zachary."

Surprise flitted across Liam's features before he let out a loud laugh. "You? Challenge *me*? You still think you're an alpha, little girl?"

Unphased, Kee unzipped her jacket and handed it to Zach to hold.

"Yes, and my pack backs my claim." She rolled up her sleeves and met Liam's eyes once again. "How do you want to do this?"

His face scrunched with amused disbelief. "You really want to challenge me? You think you can win a fight against me?"

She shrugged her stiff shoulders. "I'm going to try in order to save my brother from you."

He scoffed. "And what do I get if I win? Why would I even bother if there's nothing in it for me?"

Kee kept her gaze leveled with his. "You finally get to kill me if you win."

Some emotion flickered in his expression, but it was gone as quickly as it appeared. "Finally eradicating my mistake, hm? Fine, I agree." He looked to Carla. "You will bear witness to these results."

"Yes, Liam," she answered softly as she rubbed her son's back.

He turned back to his first child. "I'll make it even easier on you. No wolf shifting, how's that?"

She cocked her head at him with a haughty look. "I think we both know I don't have a wolf to call on."

He sneered at the reminder of what she was. "No animal shifting then."

"Deal," Kee agreed after pretending to think about it. She slid into a defensive position, one that she had learned from Dante, and quirked a brow at her father. "Shall we?"

Liam narrowed his eyes, the blue a frigid hue, and assumed a similar position. They stared at each other, taking in one another's posture and the way their shoulders lifted and chest expanded as they breathed. He knew he was stronger than Keira, of that he had no doubt. But a nagging at the back of his mind reminded him that she had killed three of his wolves.

The cold wind chose that moment to pick up, the force making Kee blink her eyes shut. It was all the opportunity Liam needed. He rushed at her, his preternatural speed having him in front of her by the time she reopened her eyes. She raised her arms in time to parry the attack of his right fist, but his left one connected with her ribs. She wheezed out a breath, but it didn't stop her from throwing her knee at his gut.

Liam caught her knee with his right hand and yanked it towards him, trying to throw her off balance. She caught his shirt in her hands and used the momentum of his pull to add force behind her headbutt. Her forehead slammed into his, and he let out a snarl as he staggered back, dropping her leg in the process.

Trying to use the advantage, Kee shoved his chest as he wobbled, her newly released leg hooking behind his ankle. Instead of falling like she hoped, he pivoted his weight onto his other foot, did a spin, and kicked her hard in the chest. She flew back and gasped in pain as she landed hard on her back.

Liam immediately leapt at her with a fist drawn back, but she managed to get her bearings enough to roll away at the last second. He punched the concrete hard, cracking it and a knuckle or two from the force. He turned towards her again with a savage snarl twisting his lips, but she kicked him hard in the side, sending him off balance once again. She then tackled him with all her weight, rolling them over so his back was on the ground.

Kee hurried to take lead once again, silently thanking Dante for all of her training. She quickly straddled Liam's torso and reigned down a flurry of punches, trying to hit whatever spots were open. Managing to land a good one to his collar bone with satisfying *snap*, she tried to hit it again, but in her eagerness, she got tunnel vision. The side of his fist slammed into her temple, making her see black spots.

When she swayed, he knew he had won. He quickly lurched up into a sitting position and grabbed her throat when she tried to get away. Using his hold, he shoved her to the side and moved so that he reversed their positions. Tightening his grip, he pulled her neck off the ground so he could slam her head back down into the concrete with a *crack*. Her hands feebly came up to attack him, but he easily swatted them away.

"See, Kiki? I am a *real* alpha," he goaded. "There's no place in the world for shapeshifters, let alone in a werewolf pack. And most definitely not as an alpha."

"Fuck you," she spat as she swung at him again. "You don't know shit."

His fingers tightened around her neck. "I know that you may be able to change your animal, but you can't change who *you* are and that will be your downfall."

Oh, but I can, she thought before she let the skin file she'd been holding on to click into place.

"Liam," she choked. She felt her own eyes water at the familiar sound of the voice she used.

Liam froze, his hackles rising as he stared down at his mate. Trinity's wavy, reddish-brown hair was fanned out around her, eyes glistening up at him. His eyes fell to her plump lips when she licked them then shot to the tear that rolled down from the corner of her eye.

"Trin," he whispered, eyes wide with wonder and awe.

"You're hurting me," Kee whispered, trying to recreate her mother's cooing, soothing voice. It pained her to hear it, tugged at her heart, but this was her best shot at beating her father.

Her long, slender fingers wrapped around his wrists, squeezing lightly as her beautiful cheeks turned a deeper shade of red. Panicking, Liam quickly eased his hold but didn't release her. He couldn't, not when he finally had her back again. His bottom lip trembled slightly as her hands came up to his face and stroked his cheeks before dropping to the sides of his neck. "*Trinity,*" he breathed.

Kee almost felt guilty at the regret and pure unadulterated longing in his eyes.

Almost. But then she remembered her brother's beaten face.

As quick and hard as she could, she shoved both her thumbs into his neck, right below his Adam's apple. When he hacked, she removed one of her hands and slammed her fist into the same spot, making his head snap back. His grip fell away, and she shoved him off her. She jumped to her feet, wobbled, then kicked him hard in the stomach while he was on all fours.

Spit and blood spewed from Liam's mouth, but he didn't bother to wipe it away as he looked up at his mate again. No, not his mate. His *daughter*. He watched with no small amount of dismay as Keira shifted back into her own form, the image of his mate disappearing once again. He tried to say her name, but his throat was crushed, and he had to focus on breathing more than anything else.

"I win," Kee declared, ignoring the blood oozing down the back of her head and the pain in her ribs as she breathed heavily.

He shook his head and scowled at her. He gestured at her form then at himself before mouthing the word 'cheat' at her.

She scoffed. "Cheat? No. You said no animal shifting, so I didn't. I simply used what makes me a *real* alpha." She threw his words back at him with satisfaction. "Not all power looks the same, Liam."

He tried to growl at her, but as soon as the vibration hit his throat, he hacked and coughed and spit up more blood. He made a singular cutting motion across his neck, his eyes mocking her with question.

Kee flexed her hands at her sides as she searched for the rage that had been her constant companion, but it didn't so much as rear its head in interest. Weird. Maybe seeing the torment on her father's face when seeing his mate had softened her.

Or maybe the therapy really did work.

"I should kill you," she told him honestly. "I've waited so fucking long to pay you back for what you did to me and Mom. Seeing you a year ago only drove that need further."

She thought back to what Cain said about taking over his pack. With Lucas coming out soon, and her own pack slowly growing, she couldn't fathom taking over a wolf pack. Besides, they were a *wolf* pack and she had had enough of those.

"But now? Now I find you're just not worth it anymore. Your old school, bigoted pack definitely isn't worth it either. And really, I think I like the idea of you having to live with the fact that your so-called biggest mistake *beat* you. The spawn you deemed unworthy bested you in a fight." She laughed. "Yeah, I like that much more. Shove the metaphorical knife in a little deeper, I say. Throw in some salt as I take your only son too."

Turning her back to him, she went to her brother who was looking at her in awe. "Come on, little bro. Your new pack awaits." She held out her hand to him, and he took it, letting her help him to his feet.

"Thank you," Carla said, rising to her feet as well with tears in her eyes. "My baby deserves so much better than this."

"He does," Kee agreed, giving her a once over. "And so do you."

Her cheeks flamed. "He's never touched me."

"No, but he beat both his kids and killed his mate, so there's that." She looked at Zach and squeezed his hand. "Come on."

"Wait," Zach gave his mom a pleading look. "Please don't tell anyone about Kee's shifting. You know how the pack is."

Admittedly, Kee hadn't thought of Carla's response to her being a shapeshifter. She looked at her, curious for her answer.

Carla gave them both a reassuring smile. "I'll keep your secret. It'll be my payment for you taking my son somewhere safe."

"You don't owe me anything, but I appreciate it," Kee responded earnestly.

"Thank you." Zach gave his mom a one-armed hug and kissed the side of her head. "Be careful."

She hugged him back. "Be happy," she countered. "Gabriel is a wonderful boy."

"He is," he agreed with reddened cheeks. "I'll be in touch, Mom. Love you."

"Love you, too," she said before ushering them away. "Go. I'll need to tend to the alpha."

"Let him bask in his pain," Kee muttered under her breath as she pulled her brother back through the house and towards the Jeep. When they were close enough, Gabriel hurled open the car door and ran towards Zach. She let her brother's hand go as the two boys collided in a tight hug.

"I'm okay," Zach murmured, petting Gabe's hair affectionately as he cried into his shoulder.

"I'm sorry I wasn't stronger," Gabe cried. "I'm sorry I couldn't protect you!"

Zach held his boyfriend tighter to him. "Shh, stop. I don't expect you to protect me, and neither one of us would have stood a chance against my dad, okay? No one is blaming you, especially not me. I'm just glad he didn't hurt you."

Gabriel pulled back so he could take in Zach's battered face, fingers lightly resting on his swollen cheek. "He hurt me by hurting you," he whispered. "That's worse."

Zach kissed his palm. "I'd rather me take the physical pain than you."

Kee clapped her hands loudly. "Okay, love birds, pause the cute shit," she said and leaned against the Jeep. "Who has a driver license? Because this bitch has a concussion and is seeing double of every-thing."

Gabriel's tanned cheeks darkened with his blush, but he pulled away from Zach to jingle the Jeep keys. "I do. I can drive us to Byte."

—

The pounding in Kee's head woke her up early Christmas Eve morning. When she got back to Byte, Giovanni had looked her over. Along with cracked ribs, she had a bruised temple, a laceration on her forehead, and a gash at the back of her head. He said most of it would be fine on its own, but as a precaution, she couldn't sleep for a few hours. Once he gave her the go-ahead, she promptly passed out in Lucas' bed.

Remembering Gio left her some pain relievers, she rolled over towards her nightstand. She turned on the lamp and winced at the stab of pain the light brought. She blinked a couple times to let her eyes adjust and that's when she noticed the card stock leaning against the bottle of pills. Happiness surged through her as she picked it up, hoping it was what she thought it was. Sure enough, it was another note from Lucas. This one didn't come with a present, but she never needed one to begin with. The words themselves were enough to make her smile, her heart swelling with joy.

My sweet,

Ten more days.

-L.V.

Twenty-Eight

January

For the three hundred and sixty-fifth day in a row, Lucas opened his eyes as he felt the sun sink from the sky. Or perhaps his count was off. Was he a day off? A week? Maybe he was off even more and only a month or two had passed. He was not sure he could accept that if that was the truth.

The concept of time had tried to allude him many times. He lifted his hand and began to count the gouges in the wood of the lid. Abraham had been kind enough to give him a wider and taller than normal coffin so he could shift around a bit, but it was still a small wooden box. He had diligently carved a line in the wood with his nail each time he woke at night, but there had been times where the thirst had put him in a mindless craze.

He paused his counting to scowl in the black void above him. There was nothing more demeaning than being treated like a rodent trapped in a cage, suckling at a plastic tube like a babe on a tit when his handler decided to feed him. And when they did feed him, which varied different times in the evening, he was only given one bag of blood. It was just enough to barely stave off the haze that came with thirst but kept him on the edge of madness.

The madness brought along thoughts that threatened to break him. He had held on tightly to all his good memories. Of his blood son, his coven, and of course his sweet. But it was especially the thoughts of Keira that tried to undo him. As he vowed to himself, he replayed the sounds of her pleasure and laugh when he became unbearably lonely, picturing her beautifully laid out under him. But then the insanity would twist his memory, instead playing for him the scene of some other male on top of her, drawing the sounds out of her instead. When he pictured her cuddled up to him, fast asleep and snoring softly on his chest, it warped until it was someone else.

Those bitter images sent him into a spiral of questions and doubts. Where was Keira that moment? Who was she with? Was she getting all of his gifts and cards? Did she happily accept them, or has she tossed them aside rejecting him in the process? Was the wait as unbearable to her as it was to him? Did she give up waiting for him?

Worst of all, did she give up on him?

Shaking his head of the madness, Lucas resumed his counting, grown-out nails tracing over each groove. If he had miscounted yesterday and was indeed off on his tally, he may very well weep. And he was not ashamed to admit that during his year in captivity he cried many a time. Tears of longing and loneliness. Tears of desperation and frustration.

Tears of madness.

When he got to two hundred and fifty-three, he paused at the sound of scuffling above him. Hope swelled almost painfully in his chest. He raised his thinned torso up high enough to put his ear to the worn wood. It was only a second, but it felt like hours until he heard a metallic clang followed by a scraping sound. There was no mistaking the sound of a shovel, but a part of him wondered if he was dreaming a cruel nightmare of freedom.

He waited, body tense with anticipation as the sounds came again and more frequently, slowly get louder as they got closer. A flinch twitched his features as the metal came down hard on the lid above him and created a loud thud. He could feel his chest heave in a heavy breath as he heard muffled voices.

Lucas still did not believe it was happening, not until the lid was removed and he was out of that damn forsaken box.

His arms shot out to either side of him, not that they had far to go, to brace himself as his coffin shifted and lifted. There was a brief weightless period until he felt his coffin connect with the ground again. He closed his eyes and counted, begging to whatever god would listen that they hadn't left him at the bottom of the hole. That this was not some cruel joke Abraham or his caretakers had played on him.

"Lucas?"

His eyes shot open at the familiar sound of his blood son. There, bending over the casket to look at him was Giovanni, Dante bent over the opposite with a wide grin. He stared at them both, eyes shifting back and forth as he took in their appearances. Neither one had changed from the memories he had of them, but they looked so… happy.

He tried to say Giovanni's name, but it came out as a rasp.

"Easy there," Dante said and held out a bag of blood to his lord. "Drink this first."

Lucas felt his eyes flash red at the sight of the blood. He shot into a sitting position and eagerly snatched it out of Dante's hand. Sinking his fangs through the plastic, he practically inhaled the liquid and relished the feel of his hunger subsiding. When he was done, he held onto the bag with slightly shaking hands, the haze of insanity receding once again.

With newfound clarity he looked at Dante and Giovanni again, finally accepting that they were really there, and his imprisonment was over. He was out; his year was up. With a hint of desperation, he looked around his vampires, looking for the one person who had been both his salvation and his torment during his incarceration.

But Keira was nowhere to be seen.

The disappointment was crushing. Because it wasn't just disappointment, no. It was rejection and heartbreak. It was all his nightmares and doubt made true. She had promised to be there when he came out, but her absence screamed her decision to let him go. She didn't wait for him, didn't choose him in the end.

He bent over his legs as his lungs seemed to fill with tar. He didn't need to breathe but found he couldn't draw in a breath when he tried. He felt he was suffocating, his heartbreak causing his lungs and chest to fill with blood and drown him from the inside. A part of him wanted his vampires to put the lid on and toss him back into the hole. He'd almost prefer the madness to this living nightmare.

"Here." Gio shoved another packet of blood at his maker, willing him to take it. "You need to drink more."

Dante frowned as his lord numbly took the bag and bit into it, draining its contents in robotic gulps. He waited until he finished the second bag before asking, "How are you feeling?"

Lucas met his eyes then couldn't help but glance around again. "B-better," he said, voice hoarse. He had talked to himself during his imprisonment so his vocal cords didn't deteriorate or fatigue from lack of use. He wanted to make sure he could talk to his vampires. To Keira.

Gio saw the disappointment in his maker's face as he looked away and had a very strong suspicion of who he was looking for. "Lucas, Kee—"

"No," Lucas said sharply, the blood finally healing the dryness in his throat. "I do not want to know."

Gio blanched at the quiet pain in his voice. "I think you misunderstand. She—"

"Please." Lucas turned to his blood son with desperation. "I just want to go home."

When Giovanni looked at Dante, imploring him to help, the head of security gave a pointed, knowing look. "He said he wants to go home," Dante said before offering his lord a hand. "Come, Lucas. Let's get you back to Byte."

Lucas accepted the help, letting Dante pull him to his feet. He carefully stepped out and scowled down at his box once he was finally free. Pricking his thumb with a fang, he snapped the bead of blood between his fingers and dropped the resulting flame inside the coffin. Dante and Giovanni stood on either side of him, giving him silent support as he burned his cage.

"We have a bleeder in the car," Gio commented a few minutes later as he and Dante led Lucas across the church grounds to the Jeep parked alongside the curb. "He's AB-, the rarest blood and your favorite!"

Lucas gave him a small, forced smile and refrained from correcting him that Keira's blood was his favorite. "Thank you." When Giovanni beamed at him, he turned towards his blood son and pulled him into a hug. He tightened his hold, appreciative that someone didn't give up on him and was happy that he was back. "*Thank you.*"

Gio hugged his maker back, a little surprised at the affection. "You don't need to thank me," he murmured. "We all missed you, Lucas. We're so glad you're out."

Lucas pulled away, only for Dante to then sling an arm around his shoulders and pull him into a hug. "Thank you as well, Dante," Lucas said, patting the arm affectionately. "Both of you mean too much to describe."

Dante released his friend and rubbed at his nose. "You better stop, or you'll get me emotional."

Giovanni was already emotional, eyes glassy with unshed tears. "Agreed," he mumbled, wiping at his eyes. He opened the door to the backseat and nodded at Lucas "Now, get in the car and get to feasting. We have a party planned for you tonight."

Lucas slid into the backseat, giving the human male waiting for him a weak smile before looking at Dante and Giovanni as they got into the front. "I do not want a party," he argued. "I want to feed, shower, and get caught up on everything."

Dante snorted as he put the car in drive and headed towards Byte. "Your coven is waiting for your arrival at Byte. They are very excited to see you."

Gio nodded. "Your people want to pay respects their lord. You can spare them an hour."

Lucas, drained from both his ordeal and the recent emotional wound, didn't argue. Instead, he sank his fangs into the human's wrist and drank his fill.

—

Lucas had humored his coven, allowing them to shake his hand or press air kisses to the sides of his face once he arrived. He could not understand how they could want to be around him in his disheveled, unwashed state, but none of them had seemed remotely phased by it. He almost felt guilty for leaving them early, especially when they were all so happy to see him, but he needed to be alone.

He knew Giovanni and Dante meant well, but all he could think of during that party was that Keira was not here. A rather large part of him had hoped that she would have surprised him at Byte, her and the pack mixed in with his vampires to welcome him home, but he had been disappointed once again. More disappointment had hit him when Giovanni and Dante both disappeared from the party soon after they arrived.

Freshly out of the shower with a towel around his waist, he approached his bathroom mirror and wiped away the steam. He grimaced at his reflection. His hair had grown out to his chin, adding about six inches of length to his usual style. He'd have to ask Mirabella to cut it, but that was for a different night.

Leaning closer to the mirror, he saw faint traces of bruising under his eyes and noticed his cheeks were still a tad hollow despite all the blood he consumed since his freedom. He then looked at the light, coarse stubble lining his jaw and sighed. He usually didn't have to worry about shaving but apparently his body decided to grow everything while in prison. He cut all his nails before the shower and took care of manscaping while *in* the shower but couldn't delve up the extra energy to shave his face.

Rubbing tiredly at his face, he turned from the mirror and made his way to his bedroom. Or rather, he tried to, but his body locked into a frozen position when he gazed into his bedroom. There, sitting on the edge of the bed facing him, was the sight of his dreams. And it *had* to be a dream. His mind was conjuring this image to haunt him. To taunt and torture him. But still, no matter how many times he blinked, the image remained.

Dressed in nothing but his plain black t-shirt was Keira.

Kee kept her eyes on Lucas, a watery smile on her lips. "H-hi," she breathed as she slowly got to her feet. Those two letters were so simple and utterly lame in retrospect, but all other words seemed to disappear upon finally seeing her man for the first time in a year.

He didn't move for the longest time, instead drinking in the sight of her like she was fresh blood and he a vampire starved. When she spoke, his body jolted, surprised by her voice. Not that it had changed, because it hadn't, but because it had been one of the only things his mind played for him during captivity.

She fidgeted nervously as he just continued to stare at her. She licked her lips and looked down at his shirt. "You said-" she paused to swallow down her nerves. Why was she nervous? This was Lucas. *Her* Lucas! It was ridiculous. "-that this was exactly how you wanted to remember me and—" She gasped when he was suddenly in front of her, emerald eyes blazing as he stared down at her. Still, she didn't back down; she met his gaze and held it, her hands shaking with the need to touch him.

"Speak again," Lucas begged softly, his eyes watching as she moistened her lips.

Her eyes stung with tears at his pleading tone. "Lucas," she whispered.

His knees threatened to give out, but he locked them in place. At an almost glacial speed, he lifted his trembling hands and reached for her face. He paused, his nightmares causing him to hesitate, but she closed the distance for him, leaning her cheek into his palm.

"I missed you," she cried, a tear falling. "I missed you *so much*."

"Missed me?" Lucas echoed, the ocean in his chest draining so he could finally take a breath. "You did?"

Kee scrunched her brow. "Of course, I did. Every single *fucking* day, Lucas." His thumb swept over her cheek, taking her tear with it, but he didn't release her face or make any other movement. "And it was so hard. You're everything to me, and I can admit that I struggled a lot without you here."

His fingers ever so slightly tightened their hold on her face when he saw that the grey of her eyes was still speckled with his green. He had to make sure this was real but was also scared of dissipating the image of her if it wasn't. "You were not there."

His accusation cut her, causing more tears to fall. "I know," she mumbled sadly. "And I am so, *so* sorry I broke that promise to you. It gutted me to think that you would assume you were right. Because obviously you were wrong."

"Was I?" Lucas questioned.

Kee scowled at him, hands lifting to grab onto the ones on her face and hold them tightly. "Yes, you asshole! You were wrong. I'm here and I waited for you because I love you!"

He sucked in a sharp breath that was full of her scent. There was no doubt now that this was his spitfire. His sweet, delectable, slightly unhinged shapeshifter. The woman who conquered him so thoroughly when he hadn't been looking. The sun to his moon. His Keira.

"Say it again," he demanded breathlessly.

Again, that begging tone would be her undoing. "I love you, Luc—."

He swallowed his own name as he kissed her. When he broke away from her lips, she followed him, rushing to connect their mouths together again. They bumped noses in her clumsy haste but found each other's lips once again. Her arms wound around his neck, and he dropped his hands from her face so he could wrap his arms around her, holding her tightly to him.

He groaned into her mouth, the feel of her body against his almost an overstimulation after a year of yearning for her. Still, he wanted more. He needed her, needed everything about her. His hands slid down to her ass, cupping her bare cheeks to haul her more firmly against him. She couldn't be close enough.

"I love you," Lucas whispered against her lips as she regained her breath.

Kee's hands dropped to his towel, quickly untucking so it fell to the floor and left him naked. She cupped the back of his neck and stepped backwards until she was falling against the bed, taking him with her. She scooted up the bed until she was lying down on the pillows, Lucas trailing after her. She bent her knees when he situated himself between her thighs, eagerly accepting his kiss when his lips found hers once again. Her fingers trailed over his shoulders, and she hated how thin they felt. She hated Abraham, and Florence, and everyone else who had put them on the path that separated them for a year.

Lucas slid his hands out from under her and took the hem of the shirt in his hands so he could remove it. Once it was no longer obstructing his view of her, he marveled down at his woman. Lowering his head to her chest, he found one of the scars that ran diagonally across her torso and gently flicked his tongue over it, tracing the familiar silvery skin. When he got to the part that ran next to her nipple, he gave it a gentle bite before soothing his tongue over it.

"Lucas," Kee pleaded, pulling on his shoulders. "I need you. It's been too long."

His stomach flipped as if he were a schoolboy talking to his first crush. She still wanted him, needed him even. He bumped against her core, feeling her slickness in response. Even her body wanted him.

"It *has* been too long," Lucas agreed as he grabbed his cock and rubbed his head against her slick entrance, coating the head in her arousal. "I will not last long, but I need to be inside you, Keira."

She nodded fervently, spreading her legs wider as he began to press into her. She hissed in a breath as he eased himself in by inch before bottoming out. "Fuck," she cried as he gave a shallow thrust, letting her adjust to him again. While she had experimented with toys during her forced year of celibacy, it was nothing like having Lucas back.

He rocked his hips, staring down at her as she squirmed in response. When he pulled out to the tip and pushed back in, his heart swelled as she made her familiar little mewls of pleasure. The same little moans in his dreams. He bent his body over hers, one of his arms dropping above her head so he could bury his face in her neck. For a few lazy thrusts, he simply drank in her sounds and the way her fingers dug into his shoulders. The way her back arched and how she breathed his name.

This was exactly what had gotten him through the year. Yes, sometimes it haunted him when the madness took over the scene, but mostly it was what had grounded him and kept him alive. Kept him fighting.

He was free.

He was home.

She was home.

Tears stung his eyes, and he buried his face in her neck. He stopped moving and just settled his weight against her, pressing their bodies flush together.

Kee felt something hot and wet on her neck and immediately her own eyes welled with tears in response. She slid her hands up his shoulders, one hand cupping his neck while the other slid into his hair. "It's okay," she whispered, holding him tightly. "It's okay. You're here now."

He nodded once, emotion clogging his throat so words couldn't come.

She kissed his head and stroked his hair. "You're back, my love, and you're not allowed to leave ever again."

"I will not," he promised once he managed to compose himself. He drew back to look down at her, their noses nearly touching. "Thank you for waiting for me."

Kee tightened her hold on his long hair and brought him down so she could kiss him hard. So hard, she purposefully nipped his bottom lip, causing it to bleed. Before he could pull back, she sucked on the wound, drawing his blood into her mouth and swallowing it. When he looked down at her with confusion, she gave him a teary eyed, wide smile. "I will *always* wait for my fiancé. My future husband."

Lucas blinked twice as she brought her left hand between them, showing him her ring. And indeed, his engagement ring was nestled on her left ring finger. His gaze shot back to hers, hope and excitement in his eyes. "Fiancé?"

"Yes, Lucas. I accepted your proposal a year ago, but I never got to tell you. Everything happened at once and I had left the ring at the pack house before fighting Florence. It was one of my regrets when you left." She pressed a soft kiss to his lips. "*One* of them."

Despite the joy he felt at her accepting the proposal, he cocked a mocking brow at her. "And you had to maul me to tell me that?" He ran his tongue over the wound on his lip. "A bit dramatic."

Kee laughed a bit, glad to hear him sounding more like himself. "I had to start the bonding somehow, didn't it?"

His face fell serious again. "Bonding? You want to be blood bonded again?" When she nodded, his brow furrowed. "Keira, the bonds that were forced upon you were finally cut free. Why tie yourself again?"

She shot him a look as if the answer was obvious. "Because it's *you*, Lucas."

His whole body warmed. "You want to tie yourself to me?"

"Always and forever," she responded without hesitation. She then waggled her ring at him. "I want the ring *and* the bond."

He kissed her again, letting the love he felt for her seep into it. How did he ever doubt her? Still, he pulled back and looked at her with reservation. "You know what your blood does to me, my sweet. I do not want to hurt you."

She cradled his face in her hand, stroking his cheek bone. "Why do you think Dante and Gio were shoving blood at you all night?"

Again, he was surprised. "They know about this?"

She nodded. "Yes." She shifted so she could pull her hair away from her shoulder. "But we can talk about that later. Right now, I need you to bite me. I don't give a fuck about your previous promise to not do it. I'm *telling* you to do it."

Lucas hesitated before lowering his face to her neck. He ran his tongue over her skin, tasting his own tears. "Stop me if I hurt you."

"I trust you," Kee said firmly. "Now bite me."

"Yes, my sweet." Lucas licked her neck once more as he slid a hand into her hair to hold her in place. With a baring of teeth, he sank his fangs into her neck. Her blood spurted into his mouth, the overwhelming taste immediately exploding on his tongue. He swallowed and groaned, his body eagerly accepting the power boost that came with her blood. His hand fisted in her hair as he swallowed another mouthful. Another, new wave of need shot through him, and he pulled his hips back to thrust hard into her.

Kee moaned, the feeling of him pulling blood from her neck while pumping into her was a weird but exhilarating sensation. She gripped his hair again, rocking her hips to meet his thrusts as he began to pound into her with hard, powerful movements. By the fifth pull of his mouth, she felt her lips tingle. Despite the pleasure his bite was bringing her, she knew he would never forgive himself if he crossed the line again. She yanked at his hair, nails scraping against his scalp.

Lucas felt her pulling at him and unlatched from her neck without difficulty, licking at the traces of blood left behind. Being fully fed helped greatly, but he also felt the bond begin to settle. He kissed her hard, tongue dipping into her mouth so she could taster her own blood. As she kissed him back, he felt the bond fully click into place and immediately felt everything she did.

He felt her love for him first and foremost, but beyond that he felt her relief and happiness, and those mattered just as much to him.

The bond snapped into place and Kee could have wept with joy.

She felt complete again, like the piece that had been missing the past year finally returned. She had her anchor back physically and mentally, and she couldn't be happier. She searched through the bond and found him, her stomach fluttering when she felt his feelings reflected her own.

They came together again in a clash of lips and teeth, feeding off each other's love and desire and happiness. Their tongues touched and danced, both of them sharing a moan. He broke away from her as he felt a tingle start in the base of his spine and slid his hand between their bodies. His thumb found her clit and began rubbing it in firm circles, determined to get her to finish before him. There was no way he would come first their first time back together.

Kee didn't need much encouraging. The feeding, coupled with the bond locking into place and his hard thrusts, already had her teetering at the edge. As soon as he began playing with her sensitive bundle of nerves, she fell. Her back bowed as she came, and she cried out as his thrusts became jerky and erratic with his incoming release. She felt him thrust a final time, a shudder running through his body as he stilled and came.

Lucas eased himself out of her, grunting softly as he left her warm body. He collapsed next to her on the pillows and was pleased when she immediately cuddled up to him, head on his chest. He wrapped an arm around her shoulders, fingers lazily trailing over her skin. When she slid her hand up his chest, his eyes fell onto his ring once again.

"I am sorry I doubted you," he said softly.

Kee hummed. "You should be," she responded, but it lacked any bite. "But I understand your reasoning, Lucas. It was a hard pill to swallow, but I know it was my own fault."

"Still, I should have known." He briefly closed his eyes. "However, I think it was best that you hadn't been bonded with me while I was imprisoned. I often fell into a very dark place."

She traced invisible circles on his chest. "I did too," she admitted quietly. "So maybe it *was* for the best." She tilted her head up to look at him. "But at least I had my pack; it hurts me that you were isolated during those times. I'm sorry you had to endure it alone."

A tentative smile curled up his lips. "I would rather endure it alone than have you suffer with me." His fingers traced over her shoulder again. "But it was worth it now that I know you waited for me."

She was going to repeat what she said about always waiting for him, but his touch reminded her of the tattoos she got on her birthday. "Can I show you something? Something that will prove that I will always wait for you?"

His eyes softened. "You do not have to prove it to me, Keira. You already did."

"Yeah, but I want there to be zero confusion in the future." She held up a finger to him when he opened his mouth to protest again. "Shush. Just, look at it, okay?"

Lucas gave her an amused looked as she sat up, but it disappeared when she turned her back to him, showing her tattoos. He sat up and moved closer to get a better view. On her right shoulder was a crescent moon, but on her left one was a sun. Not just any sun, his branded sun. It didn't have any of the puffy scar tissue that his did, obviously, but the shape and size was the same.

"Keira," he breathed as he traced it with his fingertips. "Why?"

She turned back to him with a shy expression. "Because you always say I am your sun, and I wanted proof of that."

He leaned forward and pressed a chaste kiss on her lips. "And the moon?"

She smiled against his lips. "For my pack."

Lucas kissed her again, unable to help himself. "And how are they?"

Kee pushed him back against the mattress so she could curl up against his side once again. "Good. You've missed a lot, you know."

"Have I?" Lucas mused, sliding his hand into her hair and watching the dark gold silk run through his fingers. "Why don't you catch me up?"

And so Kee got comfortable in her most favorite place in the world and began to tell him about her year, starting with why exactly she hadn't been there when he got out.

Epilogue

"What do you mean 'there's a delay'?" Kee barked into the phone, pacing the small room she had gotten ready in. "The Den project is supposed to be finished by the end of the year."

"*I know,*" the lead contractor said nervously. "*And the buildings are nearly finished, but some of the other alphas paying for the project are saying they don't like certain aspects of the units.*"

Kee rubbed the bridge of her nose as she stopped pacing, the heavy taffeta fabric settling at her feet once she went still. "*Now* they voice their concerns? It's a little too fucking late for that. We have lone shifters already signed up and ready to move in once the final touches are complete." She looked up when the door cracked open, her brother stepping in and shooting her a disbelieving look. She held up her finger to him. "What exactly are they bitching about?"

She could hear papers being shuffled around. "*The paint color and certain appliance choices.*"

She snorted at the ridiculousness of it. "They can take their childish antics and shove them up their—hey! Zach!" she exclaimed as he snatched the phone out of her hand and ended the call. "That was a business call about the Den! You know how big that project is to me."

He muted her phone and slid it into the inner pocket of his tux before giving her a pointed look. "You know what else is big to you?" He paused for dramatic effect. "You're fucking *wedding*! Which is about to start, might I add."

Kee blushed and turned sheepishly away from him, looking at herself in the full-length mirror. She lightly ran her hand over the off-white material of her dress, both admiring and fretting about the fit. It was beautiful, hugging her frame down to her hips before flaring out around her feet and trailing behind her a few feet. However, it was a sweetheart neckline, showcasing the scars that started at her collarbones and disappeared under the fabric. At first, she wanted to hide them with a lace design, but instead decided to embrace her scars.

However, a small part of her still cringed at the ugly sight of them.

"Are you having second thoughts?" Zach asked softly, seeing the concern flash over her features.

Her gaze immediately found his in the mirror. "About marrying Lucas? Never. My dress choice is another story."

Zach approached his sister, putting a hand on her shoulder. "You look beautiful, Kee. Lucas is going to lose his shit when he sees you."

Kee almost bit her lip but refrained so she wouldn't smudge her lipstick. "I know. The girls went with me to go dress shopping, and as soon as I stepped out in this, they all lost their shit. Even Mia." She smiled at the memory. "But I can't just turn off my self-esteem issues either."

He nodded in understanding. "I get that, but let's be honest, Lucas' opinion is the only one that matters. Fuck what anyone else thinks."

She let out a surprised laugh. "When did you get so wise?"

"When I joined the most ridiculous pack ever," he laughed. "So, I've been wise for a about a year."

She playfully shoved his shoulder. "You love us."

He flashed her a grin. "I do, even the new guy."

Her face softened. "How *is* Jasper? Is he doing okay with the crowd down there? I know he startles easily."

Zach waved off her concerns. "He's fine. He's sitting with Gabe, Samson and Tori. They're letting him hold Ezra. I think it calms him down to focus on the one-year-old instead of what's going on around him."

She sighed with relief. "He'll get better."

"He'll adapt," Zach agreed. He then tilted his head when he heard the chime of a piano key being struck. "You hear that? It's time to hand you off, sis."

Kee's stomach pitched with nerves, but she nodded. As they made their way out the bridal suite, she grabbed her bouquet of dark purple flowers from the table sitting by the door. They walked side-by-side until they reached the curtained off area that led to the ceremony setup. Immediately the wedding coordinators fussed with her dress, flaring the train out behind her and fixing the long veil that fell from her fancy bun.

She and Lucas had tried to keep the wedding relatively small for intimate purposes but underestimated just how many people they had met and considered friends. Kee's list was much smaller than Lucas', but that was to be expected with his age as well as the coven he led. Still, her list had been a bit bigger than she anticipated. They agreed on fifty guests, cutting out people that were on the 'eh' list, but that still felt like a lot to her.

"Ready?" Zach asked, holding out his elbow to her when the piano hit a different pitch.

She grabbed his elbow, giving him an anxious smile. "I feel nervous," she admitted softly. "Which is dumb, right? Like, I'm marrying Lucas. I shouldn't be nervous."

He patted her hand reassuringly. "I'm also nervous. Walking my big sister down the aisle and giving her away? It's a big responsibility.

What if I trip? Oh Gods, what if I take you down with me?"

Kee laughed and squeezed his elbow reassuringly. "I'll tell you what, you make sure I don't trip in these heels, and I'll make sure you don't eat shit."

Zach smoothed back his blonde hair. "Okay, deal." He straightened when the coordinators moved to the sides of the curtain. "Here we go."

Kee swallowed her nerves. "Here we go," she echoed.

The curtains parted, revealing a white aisle that was littered with purple petals. Mia, their flower girl, had scattered them as she went down the aisle right before Kee. The white chairs lining the sides of the aisle were decorated with purple linen, the gazebo behind the alter covered in purple and white flowers.

As the guests stood upon her entrance, her eyes immediately went to Lucas, standing at the alter with Gio and Dante at his side. Even from down the aisle, she could see his face light up as their eyes met. He was absolutely breathtaking in his black tux. Everything about his tux was black with the exception of a dark purple tie and the matching boutonniere.

She gave him a wobbly smile then looked at the audience as Samson and Tori hooted for her. She laughed when the other guests shot them incredulous looks, but she didn't care. Her eyes then fell to Jasper and the child he held. Lucy and Conrad's son was the perfect blend of his parents, ice blonde hair with honey-gold eyes.

Speaking of, she looked forward again as they neared the alter and gave Lucy and Conrad a smile as they stood on her side of the podium. Conrad was her man-of-honor, Lucy her bridesmaid. She hadn't wanted it to seem like she was playing favorites in her pack, but Samson and Tori assured her that they understood and wouldn't have expected it any other way. Jasper, being so new to the pack, hadn't taken even the slightest offense.

"You got this," Zach whispered to his sister as they stopped in front of Lucas and the officiant. He took her hand in his, kissed her cheek, then offered her to Lucas.

Kee's smile turned watery as Lucas' hand slid under hers, his fingers wrapping around hers. With her free hand, she turned to Conrad, handing him her bouquet. He took it silently but was grinning at her, his eyes a little misty. His mate, on the other hand, was full on crying behind him. Kee blew Lucy a kiss and turned back to her fiancé, placing her remaining hand in his.

"Keira," Lucas began in a soft tone but had to stop and swallow to collect himself. "You are so devastatingly beautiful." His green eyes gleamed in wonder. "How did I get so lucky?"

Her eyes stung with tears. "We're both lucky," she whispered as she squeezed his hands. "And we are owed this luck after all the shit we've been through."

He pressed his forehead against hers, a light, teasing smile on his lips. "Careful, my sweet, you tempt the gods with that declaration."

"Well, whatever they try to throw at us next, we'll get through it together." Kee brushed her lips over his. "Right?"

He chased her lips with his, placing a soft kiss against them. "Always, Keira. There is nothing that will separate us."

The officiant cleared her throat in mock scolding. "I do believe you are supposed to kiss *after* the nuptials."

Kee and Lucas pulled apart as the crowd laughed, letting the rest of the world come back into focus once again. Kee gave him a loving smile and tilted her head a bit towards the officiant. "Shall we get married then?"

He smiled at her, the tips of his fangs showing. "We shall."

<u>Author's Note:</u>

Hello! Thank you so much for joining me on this journey with Kee, Lucas, and the pack! The love and support I have received is way more than I could have ever asked for or dreamed of.

I shamelessly fell in love with this world I created and simply cannot let it go. With that said, if you also enjoyed it, please check out my other work. Everything is set in the same universe, just with different flawed (as hell) characters. And hey, you may just find a few *Skin* Easter eggs waiting for you.

(psssst, check out the deleted chapter after this message)

Howdy (again), this deleted chapter was originally going to be the prologue for this book, but it just didn't sit right and felt disjointed from the flow of the story. However, I feel like what happens in this chapter provides a little more insight to the events that occur in Sever so I decided to include it afterwards.

Enjoy!

Ireland, 1797

"Do you hear anything?" Abagail whispered as she clutched her husband's sleeve, trembling fingers digging into his stiff forearm.

They hid behind one of the large Sitka Spruce trees outside their village, staying low to the ground. Releasing his sleeve, she shifted to her knees and bent towards the dirt, barely feeling the sharp needles stab into the flesh of her palms as she braced herself. She tried to listen for anything following them but her hammering heartbeat drowned everything else out. At times like this, she wished she had the heightened senses of a true wereanimal.

"Shh," came the hushed reply. He tilted his head towards their ransacked village, listening for the hunters. He tilted his head back and inhaled deeply through his nose. He tried to catch the scent of the murders chasing them, but only the thick, putrid smell of smoke and burning flesh filled his nostrils. It was too overwhelming to smell anything else. "I cannot tell."

"Perhaps they moved on then?" she asked hopefully, her hand going to the star pendant at her throat as she thought of their daughter. "D-do you think they will go after Nanette and her mate?"

He rubbed the coarse hair decorating his chin before letting out a heavy sigh. "I do not know, Abagail. She should be safe with the wolves' alpha, but there is no way to be sure. They are slaughterin' people left and right. Burnin' down all of your kins' houses."

"Why have they turned on us? Why now? We all agreed to live in secret from the humans. I thought we were a united front. We didn't hurt anyone, did we?" she pressed, grey eyes glistening with unshed tears.

"I do not know, Abs," he said in a sharp tone, his fear for his mate manifesting. When he saw her bottom lip tremble, he cursed. Gently, he framed her pale face in his rough hands and pressed a soft kiss to her forehead. "Of course you did nothin' wrong. I do not know about others, but no one deserves this." He pulled her into his arms and stroked her hair. Looking over her head, he took in the orange glow in the sky as their village and friends burned. He squeezed her tighter. "They will not be gettin' their hands on you, I swear it. You are my mate, and I will protect you."

She closed her eyes tightly, trying to calm her racing heart as she clung to her mate for strength. "What do we do? Where do we go, James?"

"Away," he stated gruffly and forced himself to release her so he could start stripping off his clothes. "I am goin' to shift into my wolf form. I want you to shift into somethin' else. Somethin' small and quick in case they catch up to us."

"A rabbit? Squirrel?" She began undoing the buttons at her throat and down the front of her dress. "A fox?"

"Fox," he agreed. "There's a clan of them a few miles north of here. I know their beta, he'll help us."

Abagail nodded once as she stripped off the rest of her clothes. She hesitated a moment, her fingers hovering at the clasp of the pendant around her neck and swallowed thickly. "Do you think we will come back here? Back to our home?"

He stepped closer and placed his hands on her shoulders. "Love, elves, warlocks, vampires, and whole packs are *huntin'* your kind," he reminded her with a firm shake. "Not animal shifters, *shape*shifters. I do not know why, but they have decreed your race dangerous. They will not stop until you are all dead."

Tears welled in her eyes. "James—"

"I said I will not let them have you," he growled, her tears making him feel useless. His mate wasn't a fighter, had never had a reason to be. "Trust me."

"Such pretty words." A velvety smooth, feminine voice cooed.

James pushed his mate behind him, a snarl curling up his lip as he faced the female standing before them. Her dark red hair was pulled back in a series of articulate braids that showed off the perfect, sharp bone structure of her face. She was dressed in a typical English hunting outfit, the jacket formfitting and skirts narrow. A harrowing grin spread across her face as she removed her gloves, blood-stained fangs gleaming in the dim moonlight.

A vampire. James sneered, cursing his nose for not picking her up. "What do you want?"

"That pretty little shapeshifter behind you, of course," she responded, taking a step towards them.

"I am a wolf, and she is my mate," he protested. "Why would you think she is anythin' else?"

"Oh, little pup, I heard your conversation," she laughed, the sound sending chills down their spines. "My fellow hunters have moved on to the next village, but I knew one of her kind was still hiding here."

Abagail grimaced. "What did we do for you to hunt us?"

The vampire titled her head slightly, her eyes taking on a gleam of mock innocence. "Why, you are just too dangerous. Some of you have decided to shift into...*unfavorable* things. We do not like the possibilities of where this could go."

"So, you decide to eliminate us all? Just like that?" the shapeshifter shouted in disbelief.

"Yes," the vampire answered simply and then looked on curiously as the male shifted into his wolf form. "Now, now, do not make this more difficult than it has to be."

"James!" Abagail cried as her mate launched himself at the vampire. She watched in horror as James tackled his opponent to the ground, his jaws trying to chomp at her neck. Abagail let out a cry when he was suddenly flung off the vampire, his back slamming into one of the thick trees next to her. She heard a crack as he made impact and prayed it was the wood and not his spine. She tried to run to him, but only made it a few steps before she was yanked off her feet.

"Shh, it will all be over soon," the vampire purred as she fisted the woman's curly dark brown hair and yanked it to the side. She held tight as the shapeshifter struggled against her, pleading over and over again to let her go to James, but not once begging for her own life. "You will join him quickly enough."

"Please," she asked one more time before she let out a yelp as the vampire sank her fangs into the exposed skin of her neck. Still, her eyes never left her mate, even as her blood began to drain from her body. "*James*," she breathed, her strength slowly dissipating the longer the vampire fed on her.

After a few minutes, the vampire pulled her fangs out of Abagail's neck, carelessly tearing the flesh as she did. She let out a throaty moan, her pupils dilating with euphoria and power. Already full from her previous feasts that night, she physically could not stomach draining the shapeshifter dry. She already knew she would not be allowed to keep the shapeshifter as a blood bank. The other preternaturals had strictly forbade it. Was it possible they knew the power rush it gave vampires?

"What a waste," the vampire murmured as she pulled out a small skinning knife and pressed it to the shapeshifter's neck.

James' body twitched with pain, a shudder running through him as he came back to consciousness. He tried to rise up on his paws, but a spasm of agony had him lying flat on the dirt again. His back was broken and would take a while to heal. He tried to focus his green eyes on his mate, but his vision swam with dark spots. His beast, the primal part of every wereanimal, howled inside him with the need to protect his mate.

He suddenly felt a wave of panic and his inner wolf snarled in warning. He forced his eyes back open just in time to see a steel blade slice across his mate's throat, cutting her from ear to ear. His heart stuttered in grief even as his brain tried to comprehend what he was seeing.

No, there was no way this was happening.

Abagail's blood was *not* flowing from her body like a waterfall. No. It just could not be. He had spent six decades with his mate, spent sixty years with his soul entwined with hers.

James watched helplessly as the vampire released Abagail, her body dropping to the floor unceremoniously. The vampire disappeared, but he didn't care in that moment. All his attention was on his mate. He tried to make his body shift into his human form, but pain consumed him as soon as he tried. Stuck in his wolf form, he weakly crawled over to her, front legs dragging the rest of his useless body over to her convulsing form. As he got to her, he realized he could not call her name, could not tell her he loved her as she started to fade away.

Abagail, he cried mentally. *Do not go!*

She choked on her blood as her mouth floundered, trying to say something. "Nan," she coughed, blood splattering onto his fur as he nuzzled her cheek.

He gave a high-pitched whine at the mention of their daughter. *Nanette will be safe; her mate will protect her,* he wanted to assure her, wanted her to be at peace even if he could not.

"—ove oo."

I love you! he screamed in his mind with a desperation for her to hear him even though he knew she would not. He felt the tie that bonded them together rip apart as the gleam of life left her grey eyes, her lids sliding shut as her heart gave out.

Abagail! He pressed his snout against her face and let out a mournful whimper. *Abs, do not leave me, please.* He begged his mate, oblivious to his own heart rate slowing and stammering out. As his eyes grew heavy, he closed them with a final thought of their daughter. *I am sorry, Nana.*

www.ingramcontent.com/pod-product-compliance
Lightning Source LLC
Chambersburg PA
CBHW051133190726
48290CB00006B/1823